PETER MARABELL

A MICHAEL RUSSO MYSTERY

Kendall Sheepman Company, Cheboygan, MI
ISBN: 978-0-9903104-5-7
Cover photo: Marta Olson (Mintaka Design, mintakadesign.com)
Printed in the United States of America

Carole M. Eberly, 1943-2017

Mother, grandmother, journalist.
Carole was a respected political journalist in the most honorable sense of the profession. She worked hard, dug deep and found the details. She stuck a well-deserved pin into pomposity and arrogance wherever she found it, especially in academia and the halls of state government. She will be missed by those of us who loved her. But she will be missed most by people who never knew her. Her diligent work to hold the powerful accountable made their lives — our lives — better.

"What Kind of Day Has It Been?"

— Aaron Sorkin

1

I'd finished Frank Bruni's op-ed in the *New York Times* while a heavy April wind churned water on Little Traverse Bay. I thought about moving on to the latest *Runner's World*, when Sandy appeared at the door. Sandra Jefferies kept the office at Michael Russo Investigations running smoothly.

"Your 10:30 appointment is here, boss. Mrs. Camille North."

"Show her in," I said, and came around the desk.

Mrs. North was five-seven, about one-thirty-five, with an oval face and oval green eyes. Her hair was an easy mix of dark brown and gray. I guessed she was in her mid-sixties. She wore tailored linen slacks and a burgundy blazer.

She shook my hand with a firm grip.

"Please sit down," I said, pointing to one of the client chairs in front of my desk.

"Thank you."

"Can I get you anything, Mrs. North?" Sandy said. "Coffee or water?"

"No, thank you," she said. Mrs. North smoothed her slacks slowly and looked up. I thought she was about to say something. I was wrong. She simply stared at a place over my left shoulder and behind me, so I waited.

After a while, I said, "What brings you here this morning, Mrs. North?"

"Mr. Russo, mind if I ask you a question first?"

"Not at all."

"You have a long history on Mackinac Island. Isn't that right?"

"I've never been a voting resident, if that's what you mean." I smiled. "But I have history. Lived there one winter. I go across year-round. I have clients, business associates, life-long friends. Mackinac's an important part of my life, and has been since I was a kid."

Mrs. North nodded. "Me, too, Mr. Russo. Me, too." She crossed her legs and adjusted her blazer.

"I asked around," she said. "That's how I found you. People speak well of you."

"That's nice to hear." Most of the time, anyway.

"I wanted someone who appreciated Mackinac. Someone who doesn't just think it's a fun place, someone who really understands how the island gets into your blood."

I nodded and smiled. She hesitated, but I waited her out this time. It didn't take long.

"My family name is Sanderson," she said. "My husband's name is North. But I'm a Sanderson. I'm the fourth generation on the island." Moisture appeared in the corners of her eyes. She hesitated again, but only for a moment. "Mackinac is my life, Mr. Russo."

"Please, call me Michael."

She smiled. "I would prefer Camille, if you're comfortable with that?"

I nodded. "Then Camille it is. Sorry to interrupt."

"That's all right," she said. "Mackinac is my life. I'm happiest when I'm there. Content, at peace. I've spent more time in that house than anyplace else. It's my home. Mackinac is my home."

"You're on the East Bluff?"

She nodded. "Right in the middle," she said. "The gray clapboard two-story, with a small turret on the front." She made a circular gesture with her hand, like a turret, I guess.

"Isn't Carmine DeMio your neighbor?"

"Yes, indeed," she said, and smiled. "When the cottagers gather for a cocktail party, which is often, Mr. DeMio is everyone's favorite guest.

They tell the folks back home. Their friends are quite jealous that a Mafia Don lives in our neighborhood. And comes to our parties."

"I can only imagine."

"Anyway, Michael," she said. "I'm divorcing my husband, and . . ."

"I no longer handle divorces."

"I know that, Michael," Camille said. "Ruth Avila is my attorney. From Jagger-Stovall here in town?"

"I know Ruth. You're well-represented."

"I think so, too," she said. "Ruth convinced me. About you, I mean. When she said you could be trusted and knew your way around Mackinac . . ." Her voice trailed off.

I nodded and said, "What can I do for you, Camille?"

Tears came this time. Camille pulled out a tissue from her jacket pocket and dabbed her cheek.

"He's taking the house," she said. "My husband's taking my home." Despite the tears, anger and resentment crept into her voice. "My husband is Conrad North. Conrad Nordschleife."

She said it, and stopped. Like the name meant something important. Not to me it didn't.

"His family in Chicago changed the name to Hoffmann during the First World War. It was not a good time to be German. Not even if you'd lived in the Midwest for two generations, and were successful industrialists." She shook her head. "But Conrad, well, Conrad lives his life as Nordschleife whenever he can."

"Meaning what?" I said.

"He was born one war too late, Michael. He's aristocratic, distant, aloof. He wishes the Nordschleife family had worked for the Nazi war machine instead of the Kaiser's."

"Seriously?"

Camille laughed. "Only in Conrad's fantasy world, I assure you."

"So he wants your house?" I said, preferring to return to the 21st Century.

"He's taken the house," she said. Her face tightened, and the words had a hard edge.

"Did you agree to give it to him in the divorce settlement?"

"It's not done yet, Michael. The divorce. Are you familiar with how Mackinac property is leased?"

"A little," I said. "You own the house on the East Bluff, but you have to lease the land from the State Park. The state of Michigan actually owns the land."

Camille nodded. "That's close enough," she said. "The lease has always had the Sanderson name on it, Michael. Four generations of Sandersons. My name was the only name on the lease when I met Conrad. My name was the only name on the lease even after we were married forty-two years ago."

"What went wrong?"

"My name's not on the lease anymore," she said. The tears came back. "My husband's attorney filed the papers. Only his name appears on the lease now."

"Not yours?"

Camille shook her head. "My name's gone." The tears flowed freely now. She wiped her cheeks as best she could. I took a box of tissues from a desk drawer and put it in front of her.

"I want you to find out what happened with the lease. Find out what happened to my name, Michael. Will you do that?"

"Yes."

"How much do your services cost?"

I told her. She wrote out a check and gave it to me.

"Thank you."

"Here's my cell number," she said, and handed me a card.

I took it and said, "What can you tell me about the divorce?"

"When can you start?" Camille said. Her voice was steady and clear, but she ducked my question.

"I'll call Ruth Avila this afternoon," I said.

"Ask Ruth about the divorce. Whatever you want. I don't feel . . . I just don't want to talk about it right now."

"All right," I said, and handed her one of my cards.

Camille North reached for her purse, then looked at me.

"I want my home back, Michael. Get my home back."

2

"The husband's a Nazi?" Sandy said. She put down a mug of coffee for me and one for herself, settling into the same chair recently vacated by Camille Sanderson North.

"That's not exactly what she said."

"Close enough for me," Sandy said, and drank some coffee.

"Maybe you should stop eavesdropping on our clients."

"It's the only fun I have in my otherwise-dreary life." She tried to say it with a straight face, but it didn't work.

"You need to get out more," I said.

"Maybe I'll try the bar scene again. Find a hunky law school grad looking for a good time."

"Only thing a law school grad looks for is a job," I said. "Besides, the last time you tried that all you got was two middle-aged deans from Bannister College."

Sandy laughed. "And one of them's dead, the other's in prison."

"Don't remind me," I said. "You want to get to work now?"

Sandy drank some more coffee. "Whatever you say, boss."

"You know where Henri is?" Henri LaCroix was a close friend and former Army Ranger. Henri was back-up when things got ugly. He was as smart as he was lethal. Born and raised on Mackinac Island, Henri knew a lot of people.

"I'm not sure where he is, but I'll find him. Think he knows our Nazi husband?"

"Wouldn't be surprised," I said. "Mackinac's a pretty small place. While you're at it, find Lenny Stern." Stern was a wily veteran reporter for the *Petoskey Post Dispatch*. He spent his professional life digging up news the old-fashioned way, with hard work and trust. If there was gossip in the air anywhere in northern Michigan, Lenny knew about it.

"Want me to call Ruth Avila?"

"See if she's got a half hour this afternoon," I said. "Be sure to mention Camille Sanderson's name."

"Sanderson? Not Camille North?"

"Suit yourself," I said. "Tell Ruth I'll walk over there."

Sandy left my office, and I picked up *Runner's World*.

"Boss," Sandy said from her desk in the outer office. "Lenny Stern on one."

I shoved the magazine in my brief bag and reached for the phone.

"Lenny," I said. "How's Emmet County's version of Woodward and Bernstein?"

"Busy, Russo. What do you want?"

"Got a client from Mackinac Island."

"Good for you," he said. "What do you want?"

"You know a guy named North, Conrad North?"

"No."

"He lives on the East Bluff. Successful industrial family from Chicago."

"Never heard of him. Can I go now?"

"Might be a story in it for you."

"You always say that, Russo."

"I tossed you the Bannister College story one step ahead of the *Free Press*, didn't I?" Stern spent a few years working for papers in Chicago and Detroit. He lived to scoop the big guys on an important local story.

I heard a sigh. "All right, all right," he said. "I'm listening."

I told him what little I knew about Camille and Conrad. "Heard any gossip?"

"Like I said, I never heard of him. Her either, but I'll nose around, see if anything turns up." The line went dead. Stern was always in a hurry.

I went out to Sandy's desk. The outer office was larger than mine because it had room for clients to wait. Our offices were on the second floor of a building I'd bought and renovated almost twenty years ago. I rented the retail space at street level to the Mackinac Sandal Company.

I sat in one of the client chairs next to three tall sash windows that looked down on Lake Street. A few visitors wandered the sidewalk glancing at store displays, but the tourist season was still several weeks away.

"Henri's voicemail picked up," Sandy said. "I told him to call your cell."

"What about Ruth Avila?"

"I just talked to her assistant."

"And?"

"She only has thirty minutes, and you can have it."

"Her office?"

"No," Sandy said. "Downstairs. She said don't forget your running shoes. What am I missing?"

I laughed. "She walks every day at lunchtime. For exercise. She has no office time available?"

"It's that or nothing," Sandy said. "I told her you'd take it." Sandy peered over the top of her screen. "You're not gonna wear those things, are you, boss?" She pointed at my well-worn deck shoes.

I shook my head. "Got a pair running shoes under my desk," I said. "A little beat up, but good enough for a walk."

We heard the cell vibrating noisily on my desk. I went to the other office and looked at the screen.

"Henri," I said. "How are you?"

"Good, Michael. Sandy said to call."

"You on the mainland or home?" Henri was, among other things, a landlord on Mackinac. A small apartment building in Harrisonville, the village it was called, and two condos downtown. He lived in a small house not far from Grand Hotel.

"On the dock," he said. "Margo just caught the ferry." Margo was Margo Harris. Henri met her during the trouble at Bannister College; they'd been "an item," as Sandy liked to say, ever since. She taught fiction writing with an intriguing twist. The Bannister catalog listed her courses as "*Erotic Romance*."

"You coming across any time soon?"

"Tomorrow or the day after. Why?"

"Need you to check on a guy for me."

"Who is it?"

"Name's Conrad North. Know him?"

"If you mean the East Bluff Conrad North, yeah, I know him."

"That's the man," I said. "What do you know?"

"A little I can tell you now. More than that, give me a day or two."

"I'll take highlights now," I said. "The rest when you come to town."

"Man's an arrogant prick, Michael. I don't like him. He belongs in an Erich Von Stroheim film. He's like a relic from the past. Thinks he's a big deal and acts like lord of the manor. I've even heard him fake an accent. For the effect, I guess. Talks down to damn near everybody. People don't like him for it."

"Run into him very often?"

"Here and there. Restaurants, an occasional party. Why you want to know?"

"How about Camille North?"

"Met her a few times," he said. "Mostly at social events or around town. Her family goes way back. I like her."

"Camille's filed for divorce."

"I hadn't heard that," Henri said. "Good for her."

I told Henri about the State Park lease and the bluff house.

"That house has been in the Sanderson family a long time," he said. "Her name just disappeared?"

"What she said. She doesn't know how it happened. But I need to learn about the leases. How they work. Know anyone I could ask?"

"Couple of people," Henri said. "One's at the real estate office. A friend at the State Park office, too. They'd help you out."

"Good to hear," I said. "I want to find out what happened to Camille's lease."

"Let me see what I can dig up," Henri said, and clicked off.

I looked at my watch. I traded my deck shoes for my old Brooks

Addictions, pulled a light cotton sweater over my head and went to meet Ruth Avila.

"Off for my after-lunch stroll," I said to Sandy.

"You haven't had lunch, boss."

"Details, Sandy, just details."

"I could pick up a couple sandwiches at Roast & Toast," she said. "You can eat when you get back."

"A turkey club sounds good. And a bag of chips, please."

"Your every wish is my command, boss."

I stared at Sandy.

"Not a word," she said, and wagged her finger in the air. "Just go down the stairs and take a hike."

3

"You're on time, Russo," Ruth Avila said. "I expected that."

Avila was five-eight, medium weight, with shoulder length gray hair pulled back tight under an Old English "D" baseball cap. She wore dark green wind pants and a matching jacket.

"You expected I'd be on time?"

"Let's go," she said. "I'm on a tight schedule." With that she was off towards Howard Street. I quickly caught up. "Two laps around the park. Then we'll see what time it is." We had a green light at the corner of Lake and Howard, and made our way to Pennsylvania Park. We turned up the sidewalk next to the shops.

"Of course I knew you'd be on time," she said. "If you weren't a runner, I'd never ask you to do this."

"I get it," I said. And I did. Exercise people respect the routines of other exercise people. "Do you put this on the schedule every day?"

"You bet," she said. "If I'm in the office, it's on the schedule."

Ruth picked up the pace as we headed towards Mitchell.

"I learned a long time ago, tell people I'm exercising at lunch, they have a million reasons why everything else is more important."

"So you put exercise on the schedule?"

"Not a chance," she said, and laughed. "Seems I have an important meeting every day about this time."

We turned at the end of the sidewalk.

"Camille North call you?" I said.

"Yes. She gave me a green light to talk with you. So what do you want to know?"

"For one thing, why didn't she want to talk about her divorce? Not a word. Why she'd leave it to you?"

"It's still pretty raw," Ruth said. "Don't take it personally, Michael. She breaks down every time. She probably didn't want you to see that."

"Well, start at the top," I said. "What's the official reason for the divorce? Did Conrad run off with two twenty-year-olds?"

"Haven't heard that line in a while," Ruth said, and laughed. "In fact he's had a string of affairs, always with older women."

"Older?"

"Yeah. As long as you think mid-forties is older."

"That wouldn't be you?"

"That wouldn't be me," Ruth said.

"Camille get tired of the affairs?"

"Sure," Ruth said. "Finally. She tolerated his philandering as long as it wasn't embarrassing."

"Isn't it always embarrassing?"

"Yes, but Camille convinced herself otherwise."

"Until?"

"Until Conrad and one of his women showed up on Facebook."

Ruth's workout completed one lap of the park. She looked at her watch.

"Let's go," she said, and we began a second lap.

"To make matters worse, the pictures were on her stepson's page."

"Ouch."

"Ouch, indeed," she said. "That's when Camille moved out."

"Moved out of her own house?"

"Uh-huh," Ruth said. "Conrad has two sons by a brief first marriage, born a couple of years apart in the early seventies. They don't like Camille and she doesn't like them. They live wherever their father happens to be at the moment."

"But they'd be in their forties?"

"Right."

"Isn't that a little old to be living with mommy and daddy?"

"Camille always thought so," Ruth said. "She has a daughter with

Conrad. Her name's Nicole. She's thirty-seven, thirty-eight. Nicole left home for college and never went back."

"She see her father?"

"She wants nothing to do with her father, or with Wolfgang and Wilhelm."

"Wolfgang?"

"And Wilhelm. His sons."

"Does Camille see her daughter?"

"As much as she can. They often meet in Traverse City, stay at the Park Place. They eat dinners, catch a concert at Interlochen. Nicole works for an ad agency in Chicago. She lives in Wrigleyville. Camille goes down in the winter. Mom-daughter time. Conrad doesn't care that his daughter is estranged."

"Sounds pretty unhappy to me," I said. "It's probably just as well. If Camille is right, Conrad's not a fun guy to be around if you're a woman."

"Especially if you're Camille."

"Especially that."

"I'd prefer not to call him misogynistic," she said.

"But it wouldn't be a stretch?"

"No, it wouldn't."

"When she moved out, where'd she go?"

"The Annex," Ruth said. On the west end of Mackinac lies a track of land, Hubbard's Annex to the National Park, filled with ornate Victorian cottages and open spaces.

"She lives at the Baldwin cottage. In the guest house."

"What happened to her house on the East Bluff?"

"Weren't you hired to find out?"

"Sure, but you must know something."

"Not much, I'm afraid. I've only seen copies of the paperwork."

"Conrad the name on the lease?"

"The one and only."

"And you have no idea what happened to her name?"

"Wish I did," Ruth said.

We turned and headed back towards Lake Street to finish lap two. The wind had picked up out of the north. It didn't help an already-damp spring afternoon.

"Did they have a pre-nup?"

"Pre-nup says equal compensation if the marriage dissolves. That's all."

"Conrad takes the bluff house because?"

"Because his name's the only one on the lease."

"So as long as Camille's compensated, so to speak, it's all perfectly legal."

"Sharp guy, Russo," she said. "Too bad AJ's got your heart. I'd make a run at you." Ruth slowed her pace, but didn't stop. "Sorry. I didn't . . . I mean, I'm sorry if that sounded, you know . . ."

"It's okay, Ruth," I said. "Forget it." We resumed our pace. "Your copy of the lease look legit?"

"Yeah, but that doesn't mean much."

"We need to know more about how they're written, specifically what it takes to make changes."

"Yes, we do," she said.

Ruth slowed to an easy walk. She looked at her watch.

"Good pace, Russo. I've just enough time before my next client meeting."

"I have an idea or two," I said. "Thanks for meeting me."

"Thank you for this kind of meeting."

Ruth Avila waved as she rounded the corner. I took out my phone and called Sandy.

"Hey, what's up?"

"Two messages," Sandy said. "They're on your desk. The sandwich is in the fridge. I have to run to the Clerk's Office and pick up some papers. You can catch me up when I get back."

"Okay," I said, and clicked off. But there wasn't a lot to tell. Not yet, anyway.

4

"I'm running late, Russo," Henri said. "Can't stop at your office."

"Where are you?"

"Northbound I-75. Should be in St. Ignace in an hour. Got a meeting on the island."

"When you coming back?"

"Not sure," he said. "How about you meet me at the dock? We'll talk on the boat."

"Not what I had planned for the day," I said. "But if you could find somebody to talk to me about leases?"

"I'll set it up," he said. "Get your ass moving."

"I'll be there," I said, and clicked off.

I hadn't been to Mackinac before the season cranked up in a long time. I love the anticipation of summer as the island changes from late winter's dingy mess to spring's cleaned up streets and sidewalks. Residents, workers and managers greet each other with handshakes and hugs and the annual spring question, "How was your winter?"

In April, the only ferry to Mackinac Island was the *Huron*, Star Line's steel-hulled mover of people and freight that can punch through ice still floating in the Straits. It only ran out of St. Ignace, and only a few times a day.

I punched Sandy's number.

"I'm in line at the Clerk's Office," she said. "What?"

I filled her in on the change of plans.

"I haven't been on the *Huron* in years," Sandy said. "It's so cool when it bumps the ice out of the way. Sure I can't tag along?"

"Next time," I said. "Somebody has to watch the office."

"Not much to watch."

"It's a lousy job," I said, and laughed. "But the pay is good."

"You got that half-right," Sandy said, with more than a touch of sarcasm. Then she clicked off.

I took my coat and brief bag and went to the car. I usually walk the three blocks from home to the office, so the car stayed in its parking spot behind my apartment building.

I took Mitchell, then Division to U.S. 31. Traffic was light through Alanson and Pellston. It was April, after all. There were more cars parked at the Pellston airport than on the road.

The Mackinac Bridge was down to one lane for maintenance on the center span, but I managed to drive across, park the car and walk to the ferry dock with time left over.

Henri was easy to spot. At six-three, he stood out in the small crowd of people at the boat ramp. He wore jeans and a tan Carhartt jacket, buttoned to cover the Glock holstered on his left hip.

"Russo. Good you made this work."

"Luck of the schedule," I said.

We boarded the *Huron* and went upstairs to the rear cabin. A teenage couple sat in the back corner, paying more attention to each other than they did to us. Only a few people occupied the forward cabin. The *Huron* would carry more freight than passengers this trip.

"Heard we're going the long way," Henri said. "Too much ice in the channel."

When the wind blew from the wrong direction, ice clogged the west entrance to the harbor like a jammed funnel. Traveling around the north side of the island added fifteen minutes to a thirty-five-minute trip (even longer, if the captain had to slow up too often for floating ice). Entering Mackinac's harbor from the east would give the ferry just enough room to slip inside the breakwater and away from the ice jamb.

"Give us more time to talk," Henri said as we settled into our seats.

"I take that to mean you tracked down our Mr. North?"

"Easy to do," Henri said.

The *Huron* backed away from the dock and turned slowly around for the leisurely trip along the far side of Mackinac.

"The man isn't very secretive. Pretty much does as he wants, out in the open. Likes to hang out at the bar at the Island House, or the Iroquois."

"Not exactly the Mustang."

"Certainly not," Henri said. "Eats in the Grill Room more often than anyplace else. Always at a window table." The front windows in the Island House dining room overlooked the harbor and the Round Island Lighthouse.

"Just like the tourists."

"Uh-huh," Henri said. "But tourists are nicer."

"Do tell."

"He rubs people the wrong way, and doesn't care. He acts like a petty dictator, bosses people around, points his finger in their face when he talks. That kind of thing. Restaurants, shops. Wherever he happens to be."

"Charming," I said. "How about his background?"

Henri pulled a slender reporter's notebook out of a jacket pocket and flipped it open.

"Conrad North was born in Stuttgart seventy-one years ago. That's the old West Germany, after World War II. His family was brought to America by the army. Conrad's extended family, uncles, aunts, already lived in Chicago."

"Why'd the army care?"

"Aircraft design. Fighters mostly. His father and two uncles. They worked for the Wehrmacht. In those days, the army needed anybody who was good. The Soviet Union was the new enemy."

"Thanks for the history lesson," I said, with some sarcasm.

"You're welcome," he said. "The military changed the family name from Hoffmann to North when the men went to work for American aircraft companies. Same for the kids when they started school. The rest of the family took the North name, too."

"I thought the family name was Nordschleife?"

Henri laughed. "That's part of Conrad's little fantasy world. He wanted people in Germany to think he was really important. He hated it when he had to give up the Nordschleife name. You get the reference?"

"Nope."

"Disappointed in you, Russo. And you call yourself a car nut?"

"Enough," I said. "What's your point?"

"Nordschleife is the Nurburgring."

"He liked having the same name as the German race track?" The "Ring," as it was called, was one of the world's premier motorsports tracks.

Henri nodded. "Tells you a lot, doesn't it?"

"Yeah. I almost need a program to follow the names. How'd the army get North out of Hoffmann?"

"Out of thin air. How do I know?"

"Think some American general's name was North?"

Henri shrugged. "Wouldn't surprise me."

We were only minutes out of St. Ignace when the *Huron* slowed and bumped heavy ice out of the way. We punched chunks of ice for maybe a half mile, then open water returned.

"Conrad can be charming if he wants to be, and he took Camille by storm. They met at a party on the island in the early seventies, three years before they married. She was a young, impressionable Birmingham school teacher who spent summers on the East Bluff. Her life had been quiet and uneventful until she met Conrad. He was dashing, handsome, educated at Groton and MIT. She was very impressed. Her wedding gift to him was to share the cottage."

"What did he give her?"

"Economic security."

"But the Sandersons must have had money," I said. "Bluff houses ain't cheap."

"They were cheap in the fifties," Henri said. "Many of them were empty and falling down. If you bought cheap and limited the costs to upkeep and the lease fee, a modest income might be enough. Besides, North money was serious money."

"How serious?"

"The Chicago branch of the family built several successful manufacturing businesses. Automobile parts. Demand for new cars exploded after the Second World War and the North family was right in the middle of it. The uncles finished their obligation to the army and joined the others."

"Any family money?"

"Yeah," Henri said. "Lots of it, but it's hard to trace. They had it before they left Germany in the 1920s."

"Wartime profiteering?"

Henri shrugged. "Be my guess. Conrad collects vintage cars, Porsche, Mercedes. Costs a lot of money. It ain't all from auto parts. Got to come from somewhere else."

"What about Conrad's sons?"

"Wolfgang and Wilhelm?" Henri said, and flipped to a new page. "From a short first marriage. A young woman who worked in one of his father's plants. The family did not approve. It was doomed from the start. They offered her a hefty settlement, and she quickly left town. She signed off and Conrad got the boys. He taught them to be bullies. Spitting image of dear old dad."

"They work for their father?"

"Hang out with their father is more like it. They tag along wherever he goes. Occasionally they show up at a company plant west of Chicago."

"Not real work?"

"Not that I can tell," Henri said. "They spend time acting tough, playing big shot. They don't seem to have any interests. No hobbies, no love life. Nothing."

"Conrad still chasing older women?"

"He shows up at island parties with different women. Lake Forest, too. Sometimes Petoskey or Traverse City. Nothing serious, but enough to irritate Camille."

"She talked herself out of it for a long time."

Henri nodded. "Until she'd had enough."

The *Huron* rounded the east end of the island at Mission Point Resort. We had our first look at the jammed-up ice at Round Island Lighthouse. The east end of the channel was open just enough for the *Huron* to slip by the breakwater and into the harbor. Its horn broke the chilly morning silence.

"Any idea what happened with Camille's lease?" I said.

Henri shook his head. "Nothing yet," he said. "Speaking of State Park leases." Henri wrote in his notebook and tore off a page. "Irma Renner at the real estate office. She's been doing this a long time. That's her cell. I told her you'd call."

"Thanks," I said, and put the paper in my pocket.

The *Huron* eased into the dock, pushing a few stray chunks of ice out of its path. The ropes were secured, and the ramp was dragged into place.

"Got time for coffee or a sandwich?" I asked.

"Another time," Henri said. "Have to get up the hill. Good chance to rent two of my apartments for next season."

We walked up the dock. Dirty snow melted slowly in the sunless corners of the buildings. The annual Christmas tree had been removed from its winter perch in the middle of Main Street, and several snowmobiles were parked on the dock, waiting for a ride to summer storage on the mainland.

"Walk with me," Henri said as he turned east towards Marquette Park. The sidewalk was more crowded with painters than visitors. No surprise for April. We went down the street and arrived at Doud's corner.

"This way," he said, and we went along the low cement wall that borders Marquette Park. Henri stopped when we came to the east end of the wall. "Up there," he said, and pointed at the houses on the East Bluff. "The gray one. With the turret."

"Next door to Carmine DeMio?" I said.

"Conrad North's cottage," he said. "But it's been Camille's home all her life."

"Actually seeing the place makes it more real," I said. "Can't tell you how many times I've run or walked right by that house."

"Just thought of something, Russo."

"And that is?"

"Give Carmine a call."

Carmine DeMio had run the Baldini crime family in Chicago until he retired three years ago and passed control to his son, Joey. The family owned, legitimately, the Marquette Park Hotel right in front of us at the east end of the park, as well as Carmine's house on the East Bluff. He was the same Carmine who was Camille North's special party guest.

"You talk to him?"

Henri shook his head. "I'm not welcome since I roughed up Joey and his pals." By pals he meant Santino Cicci and Gino Rosato, gunslingers who worked for Joey.

"Gee, that's too bad."

Henri laughed. "Yeah, I feel culturally deprived."

"Well, I'm not Joey's favorite private eye either," I said.

"True, but you and Carmine get along."

I'd helped out Carmine when Joey got himself tangled in a murder investigation a few years back. Carmine remembered the favor.

"You mean until I get in Joey's business."

"Until?" Henri said.

"It's only a matter of time," I said. "Why should I talk to Carmine?"

"DeMio knows lots of things, Russo."

"So do you."

"Yeah," he said. "But Carmine DeMio lives next door to the man in question. I do not."

"Good point," I said. "I'll give him a call."

"You carrying, Michael?"

I shook my head. "What am I gonna shoot, icebergs?"

"Funny."

"I'm just going to talk to the man, Henri."

"Be careful anyway, Michael."

5

"Have to go, Michael," Henri said. "I don't want to be late, and I have to stop at the post office."

"Thanks for the help."

Henri cut across the park toward Market Street.

"Good luck," I said, and he waved without looking back.

I sat down on the low concrete wall. A few people moved on the sidewalk or rode bicycles down Main Street. Two drays went by loaded with lumber and rolls of pink insulation. The marina was empty but for three men at the far end of the dock replacing sections of decking.

Henri had a point. Carmine DeMio had lived next door to Conrad North since he bought his cottage and the hotel four years ago. DeMio, retired or not, was acutely aware of his surroundings. Staying alive might depend on it. Besides, anything I learned about Conrad was more than I knew now.

I took out my iPhone and tapped DeMio's office at the Marquette Park Hotel.

"Vollini," a thick, gravelly voice said. Carlo Vollini was secretary to Carmine and Joey.

"It's Michael Russo."

Vollini hesitated, then said, "What do you want?"

"Been way too long, Carlo. I missed your charming smile, your . . ."

"What do you *want*?"

"A few minutes with Carmine."

I heard muffled talking. Vollini must have covered the receiver.

"Why?"

“Why do I want time with Carmine?”

“That’s what I said.”

“It’s not business, Carlo.” More muffled talking.

“Three o’clock,” Vollini said. “The front porch.” He hung up.

“He didn’t even say good-bye,” I said to a squirrel digging in the dirt a few feet away. “What happened to good manners?” The squirrel didn’t seem to care.

I put the phone back in my pocket and pulled out the note Henri gave me. Irma Renner would have to wait. I had not eaten since breakfast.

I walked down Main Street, dodging an array of ladders, carts and building materials crowding the sidewalk. Businesses were preparing for the season. With an early May deadline on the horizon, the pace of outside repairs had picked up. Men replaced windows and roofs and scraped paint as the April sun warmed the chilly air.

I turned up Astor Street and spotted several large cartons on the sidewalk at the Mackinac Sandal Company. Fran Warren came out of the door, opened a carton and picked up an armful of boxes.

“Hey,” I said. “Want some help?”

“Michael,” she said, and put down the boxes to give me a hug.

Fran Warren was a trim five-seven, in her early fifties with soft blonde hair, usually pulled back, and blue eyes. She was an avid bike rider on the hills of Mackinac or the streets of Petoskey. She opened the Sandal Company on the island in 1995 and rented the retail space in my building on Lake Street five years ago. “I need to earn a living,” she told me. “And I like Petoskey a lot better in the winter.”

“What brings you to town?” she said.

“Rode across with Henri.”

“How is my dear, sweet brother?” Fran said. Half-brother, actually. Henri and Fran shared the same mother.

“You being sarcastic, Fran?”

“Certainly hope so,” she said. “I haven’t seen him in quite some time.” Fran sat down on the front door steps and I sat next to her. The sun was warm by the time it came over the buildings.

"Why are you here, Michael?"

"You know Irma Renner?"

"Are you buying a house?"

"Might be interested in a house on the East Bluff."

"Nothing's for sale up there," Fran said. She turned and looked at me. "Now why are you asking? No bullshit about buying a bluff house either."

"Steady stream of traffic at the Mustang," I said, pointing at the bar on the other side of Astor Street. "Great name for a bar on Mackinac," I said. "Mustang."

"It's not a horse," Fran said.

"What's not a horse?"

"The Mustang. It's named after the car. You know, the Ford Mustang."

"You're making that up," I said.

"Not on your life," she said. "Guy named Butch Walters bought the old bar in the sixties. He was a Ford dealer in Cheboygan, and the Mustang was the hottest car in the country."

"Shatters my image of the place."

"You'll survive," Fran said. "Seabiscuit's busy, too," she added, talking about the restaurant a half block away. "Lots of lunch business right now. People are back at work." Fran paused for a second, then said, "Now what about Irma Renner?"

"Henri gave me her name," I said. "I need to talk to her."

"If you wait long enough, you'll be here when she comes out."

"The Mustang?"

"Like clockwork," Fran said. "Every day. Two beers and a sandwich for lunch."

"You saw her go in?"

"Didn't have to. I told you, like . . ."

"Clockwork, I know."

We sat quietly for a minute and watched two drays move slowly by and turn on Market Street. The first was loaded with huge bales of hay, no doubt going to the stables. The second carried four upholstered chairs and a matching couch tightly wrapped in heavy clear plastic. Someone had scribbled “Grand Hotel” on each piece.

“Fran,” I said. “Do you know Camille and Conrad North? Live on the East Bluff?”

“Are you handling her divorce?”

“Word gets around, doesn’t it?”

“Small world, Mackinac.”

“She’s got a lawyer for that.”

“It must be the house then,” Fran said.

“Sun sure is warm sitting here. No wind. Nice.”

Fran turned and looked at me. “It is the house, isn’t it, Michael? I heard she was going to lose it. The lease got screwed up. Michael? Say something.”

“Sure am hungry, Fran. I need some lunch.”

“I made a chicken salad sandwich. I’ve got chips, too, and coffee. I’ll split it with you if . . . wait a minute. That’s why you want Irma Renner, isn’t it? She knows about the leases.”

“Sandwich sounds good. Thanks.”

Fran started to say something but stopped. “There she is. Over there.” She pointed at a woman leaving the bar. “Hey, Irma. Got a minute?”

The woman waved and started across the street. Irma Renner was five-four and heavy through the middle. Her curly hair was a mix of gray and black, and she wore oval wire glasses. We stood as she crossed the street carrying a white Styrofoam cup of coffee.

“Irma, this is Michael Russo.”

Renner reached out and we shook hands. It was a firm handshake.

“You’re Henri’s friend,” she said. “You wanted to talk about Camille North’s lease.”

“I told you it was a small world, Michael,” Fran said.

“I would like to talk about the leases, yes. Not specifically her lease.”

Renner looked at her watch. “I have to make two phone calls,” she said. “After that, the rest of the afternoon I’m getting things ready for the season. You know where the office is?”

"I do," I said. "Fran just offered to share a sandwich. How 'bout I come over after that?"

"Fine," she said, and walked away without another word.

"Have you known her long?"

"Irma?" Fran said, and nodded. "A long time. She came here as a bride, barely out of her teens. Married Silas Renner. In the Twin Cities, I think it was. Sad story, really. Silas went through the ice a year later. They never found him. Irma stayed. Started drinking and never married. She's a little rough around the edges, but she's straightforward and honest. More so if she's sober."

"How about that chicken salad?"

"How about telling me what's going on?"

"Deal," I said. "Get the food."

6

Fran came out of the store with a thermos of coffee, two green ceramic mugs and a bag of chips. "Open the bag," she said. "I'll be right back."

I tore open the bag, grabbed a couple of chips and poured coffee. Fran put down a small, red-zippered cooler bag. "Our sandwich and some cucumber spears." She unzipped the bag and took out half a sandwich.

"Camille North hired you to get her house back. Right?" she said, holding the sandwich just out of my reach.

"Right," I said, and took the sandwich. I bit off a big chunk and enjoyed every moment of chewing it.

Fran open a small plastic container and put it on the step between us. I took a chunk of cucumber and popped it in my mouth.

"What have you heard?" I said.

"About Camille and the house?"

"The house, Conrad and the divorce. Anything."

Fran shrugged. "People have speculated about them for a long time. They haven't acted like a happy couple in years."

"Meaning?"

"Meaning, they snap at each other in public, a cocktail party, the next table at the Jockey Club. That kind of thing." Fran bit into her sandwich. "Those two sons of his," she said, and shook her head. "They're abusive toward Camille. From what I've seen."

"Physical? Shoving, hitting?"

"Never saw physical. But they despise her."

"Conrad tolerates behavior like that toward his wife?"

"As far as I can tell, yeah," Fran said. "Some of the other women think so, too."

"You ever seen Conrad be abusive?"

Fran shook her head. "Not physically anyway, but he's always verbally abusive. He's dismissive. Treats Camille with disdain."

"What about Conrad's women?"

"He's had affairs for years, if you believe the rumors."

"Do you?"

Fran nodded. "Women know these things, Michael. At the gut level. I don't know why Camille put up with it for as long as she did. She had to be embarrassed and hurt."

"Think she didn't know?"

"She knew," Fran said. "Wives always know. Even if they won't admit it."

"Did he see the other women around here? Before they separated, I mean."

Fran shook her head. "Not until after Camille moved out."

"Mostly older women, I hear?"

"So it'd be nicer if he ran off with a young bimbo?" There was an edge in her voice.

"That's not what I meant and you know it."

Fran put out her hand and touched my arm. "Sorry," she said. "That wasn't fair. Sorry." Fran looked up toward Market Street. "An older woman is harder. At least I think so. It's easy to rationalize a guy wants a tight body and lots of sex. Boobs are gonna sag sooner or later. I can't do anything about getting older, but what if I was never smart enough? Or funny enough. Then what?"

Fran ate the last of the cucumbers and put the container in the cooler. We sat quietly with our coffee for a few minutes.

"Have you met Conrad?"

I shook my head. "Never had the pleasure."

"I've seen what an affair does to a marriage. It survives or it doesn't. The husband tries to explain that the sex didn't mean anything. He's sorry. Blah, blah, blah." Fran drank the last of her coffee. "Conrad never apologized. I'd bet on it."

"That's because?"

"Conrad doesn't apologize, Michael, other people apologize. It's not in his DNA. It's arrogance, I suppose. He's got this air about him. An attitude, I guess."

"Thinks he's better than everyone else?"

"Yeah, sure," Fran said. "But it's something else. Conrad is certain he's right. All the time. It's like he had affairs because he was convinced it was the right thing to do."

"Sounds like a rationalization to me."

"Me, too," she said. "Even as I just said it. But he conveys the same damn attitude about everything. He's not offended or angry if you disagree with him. He's convinced if you'd gone through the same thought process you'd reach the same conclusion. You just didn't think it through like he did, that's all."

"If you say so."

"Yeah, yeah," she said with a wave of her hand. "I know that sounds muddled."

"And self-righteous, Fran. People don't behave that way without an elephant-sized ego."

"You need to meet the man, Michael. See what you think."

"You ever met Camille's daughter?"

"Nicole? A few times."

"You like her?"

"I do," Fran said. "Smart, friendly. She's quietly affectionate around her mother. They seem comfortable together."

"Ever heard Nicole be critical of her father?"

"I don't remember Nicole saying anything about Conrad one way or the other. I don't think she talks about her father in public."

"Good point," I said. "Think she has any interest in what happens to the East Bluff house?"

"I have no idea. Why don't you ask Camille?"

"I will. I was just curious. Nicole doesn't come to the island very often."

"Would you?" Fran said. "If Conrad was in the picture?"

"Probably not."

"Mackinac's too small to avoid people. It's not possible."

Fran poured the last of the coffee into our mugs.

"What happens now?" Fran said.

"Well, I'll talk to Irma Renner." I looked at my watch. "Could go up there now. See what she has to say."

"About Camille's lease?"

"Uh-huh," I said. "I need to know more about how they operate."

"Is it true Camille's name is not on the lease?"

I looked at Fran.

She shrugged. "That's the gossip, Michael. I've heard it a dozen times."

I nodded. "Her name is not on the lease."

"Conrad's?"

"Is on the lease," I said. "All alone."

"How did that happen?"

"Don't know," I said. "But I have to find out if I want to save Camille's home."

Fran leaned over and kissed me on the cheek. "I have faith in you."

"That's very sweet," I said. "Especially since I have no idea what I'm going to do next."

"That's an easy one, Mr. Russo," Fran said, and pointed toward Market Street. "You're going up to Mackinac Island Realty to talk with Irma."

"Yes, I am."

"And I'm going back to work, or this business of mine won't be ready for opening day."

A taxi moved smartly up Astor Street with two passengers and several large plastic containers on the rear shelf. Four large duffel bags were piled on the other bench seat. Workers headed up the hill to staff housing. The taxi turned at the corner and went out of sight.

"More people," Fran said as we stood up. "On every boat. In a couple of weeks, it'll be like nothing's changed."

"Thanks for the lunch," I said. "The conversation, too."

"You're welcome. Good luck."

A steady wind picked up out of the east. This time of year, even a light breeze off the very cold water dropped the temperature in town to uncomfortably chilly levels. The April sun would have a hard time keeping up.

7

I went to the corner, sidestepped a pile of slushy snow, and walked down Market Street. I needed to ask Camille some questions, and I need to do it soon. About Conrad, sure, about his sons. I'd built a picture of the North family and it wasn't pretty. But I knew almost nothing about Nicole. Did she have any role to play? I assumed she knew about her parents' impending divorce. Was she even interested in what happened to her mother's house?

Mackinac Island Realty occupied a small space between Lucky Bean Coffee Shop and the bank. A fortunate location if you sit at a desk all day and your clients need money. For more than thirty years, visitors have stopped to read a huge board of listings that hangs in the front window.

"Good timing," Irma Renner said as I came through the door. "Just finished up." Renner sat behind a desk at the rear of the small, square front room. The center of the space was filled with a round table and chairs. A smaller table near the door was covered with brochures and property information.

Renner stood up and came around the desk. She reached out and we shook hands. "What do I call you?"

"Michael is okay," I said. "Or Russo."

"Russo it is. Have a seat." Renner pulled out a chair at the center table and sat down. She put a yellow pad and pencil between us. "In case you want to take notes."

"Probably not, but thanks."

"Henri said you want to know about leases?"

I thought for a minute. "What do I need to know? Like, if I was a prospective buyer."

"Are you?"

I shook my head. "No."

"Didn't think so, but I had to ask."

"That's okay," I said. "Pretend I want to buy a bluff house."

Renner sat back, folded her arms across her chest and said, "All right. We'll call it 'State Park leases, 101.'"

"I'm ready and eager."

"I'll bet you are," Renner said, and laughed in a way that suggested her mind was elsewhere. But she stuck to business. "With the bluff houses, you lease the land, you buy the house. They're separate transactions."

"I buy the house from the current owner?"

Renner nodded. "It's personal property. Like an antique desk or an oil painting. It's a transaction between you and the owner. I make the paperwork happen."

I nodded. "Okay."

"You sign a lease with the Mackinac Island State Park Commission for the land."

"How long and how much?"

"The leases are twenty years and the fee depends on the size of the lot. These days, roughly twenty-five hundred to sixty-five hundred. Every lease must be approved by the Commission."

"How would I do that?"

"You'd go to the Park office," she said. "The Director recommends approval and takes it to the Commission for formal approval."

I leaned forward on the table. "What about changes to an existing lease? Adding or subtracting a name."

"You mean if a leaseholder gets married or dies?"

I nodded. "Like that," I said. "Or divorced."

Renner smiled. "This is where Camille comes in. Right?"

"More or less."

"Changes require Commission approval. It's the same process. Start at the Park office. But evidence is needed to make the changes."

"Like a dead body?"

"Funny man," Renner said. "A death certificate would work just fine, I'm sure."

"Divorce papers, or a notarized statement from the ex?"

"Yep."

"Is it easier to add names?"

"Sure," she said. "Especially if the surname's the same. Like for children. But if you want to add a spouse, you'd need a marriage license."

I thought for a minute. "What do you know about the North lease?"

Renner shrugged. "We have files on all the leases," she said, jerking her hand hitchhiker style over her shoulder. "What do you want to know?"

"How many years are left on the current lease?"

"Let me check." Renner got up and went into an even smaller back room. I pulled out my iPhone and hit the home button. Henri had texted, "call me."

Renner returned with an open manila folder. She put it on the table and slid it over to me. She pointed to a sheet of paper. "Renewed almost two years ago."

"A fresh twenty years."

Renner sat down. "Yep."

"Both Camille and Conrad named?"

Renner picked up the sheet of paper. "It doesn't say. It's just a notice of renewal."

"How does renewal work?"

"The leaseholder applies for a new twenty-year lease with the Commission. It's usually a formality."

"Would it not be a formality because of a divorce?"

Renner shrugged. "Can't tell you that."

"Anything else I should know?"

"That's it, Russo. Not much to it, really, even though buying a bluff house is a house-buying experience like no other. It might seem strange from the outside, leasing property from the state. But around here, it's just part of the deal, that's all."

"Ever run into trouble?"

Renner shook her head.

"Nothing out of the ordinary?"

She shook her head again. "Nope."

"Is that a 'no' for real estate generally, or the island in particular?"

Renner laughed. "You're a sharp guy, Russo. Henri was right about you."

"Henri's right about a lot of things."

"Henri's a good man," she said.

"Suppose I wanted to know more. Wanted to get into the weeds. Who would I see about that?"

Renner scratched her forehead. "Well, the Park Commission runs the place. The assistant for the Commission or the Park Director."

"Got any idea how a name might be removed from a lease?"

"A lease can be rewritten. A few hoops to go through, but it's easy to do."

"What if you didn't want anybody to know?"

Renner smiled. "So we finally get to the sixty-four-dollar question."

I shrugged.

"Then the gossip is true?" Renner said. "Camille's name really did vanish from her lease?"

I hesitated.

"She hired you to figure it out, didn't she?"

I waited.

"Look, Russo, Henri LaCroix told me to trust you because he trusts you. Was Camille's name removed from the lease?"

"Yes," I said. "You have any idea how that might happen?" I leaned forward and put my elbows on the table.

"You want to know if Conrad could get his wife's name off the lease without her knowing about it."

I nodded. "Conrad had the most to gain."

Renner sat back. I wasn't sure if she was thinking about her answer or didn't want to answer. I took a deep breath. I'd try the easy way first.

"All right," I said, "you're the expert on this. Speculate on how it might happen."

Renner sat up straight and thought for a minute. "I'm only guessing, you understand."

"I understand," I said. "But you see the process from start to finish every time you ink a deal."

Renner nodded. "Yeah, I do."

"Well?"

"Look, Russo, it could have been something illegal, possibly bribery or blackmail." Renner shook her head. "But if I were a betting woman, I'd bet on a good old-fashioned screw-up."

"A screw-up?"

She nodded. "A left-hand-right-hand kind of screw-up. Papers are shuffled, names mixed up. Hell, Russo, it's more likely a clerical mistake than bribery."

"Seriously. A mistake?"

"It happens all the time. Buy a car, buy a house. Fill out papers anywhere these days. It happens. Nobody pays attention. They're on autopilot when it's something they do over and over again."

"A clerical error?"

"It's not very sexy, I know. It'd be a lot more fun if Conrad cooked up a plot to steal the house from his wife. People would love to gossip about that."

I shook my head. "I don't know."

"You don't believe it could happen?"

"It's not that. Believing Conrad would steal the house isn't hard. But how did he do it? He couldn't just walk into the Park offices and ask to see the lease files . . . in private, please, so I can change some names."

"Wish I could be more helpful."

"You have been helpful," I said. "I have a better understanding of the leases. For that I thank you."

Renner stood up and we shook hands. "Let me know if I can do anything else," she said.

"I appreciate that," I said, and left the office.

8

The wind blew sand over the street. It came out of the east, off the cold water. The air was chillier now, and clouds dotted the sky. Renner had been helpful enough, but if there was a way to alter documents, she either didn't know it or wasn't talking. On the other hand, I was in good shape if I ever wanted to buy a house on the bluff.

I walked down Market Street toward Marquette Park. Painters were erecting scaffolding on the tall west wall of the Stuart House Museum. I only had a few minutes to get to the Hotel and meet Carmine DeMio. I took out my phone while I walked and punched Henri's number.

"Russo," he said.

"What's up?"

"Funny thing about my apartments."

"Mackinac apartments are funny?"

"Shut up, wise-ass, and listen to me."

"If you say so."

A family of four stood at the edge of the curb in front of the post office. Mom and dad huddled over a map while the two children ran around, pushing each other and laughing. The snow was barely off the ground, but tourists were already here looking for adventure. Good for them.

"The guy didn't take one apartment, let alone two."

"Sorry to hear that," I said. "Why am I interested?"

Henri passed over my question and said, "He'd never been to Mackinac before. He wanted something closer to town, not up the hill."

"Heard that one before. So?"

"Said he wanted to be closer to his work."

I waited. There had to be a punch line.

"He was hired by Conrad North."

"That right?"

"Guy said he's remodeling several rooms in North's house."

I crossed Fort Street and went into Marquette Park. The grass was flat and brown; a few piles of crusty, dirty snow hid in shaded corners. Three men raked the grass at the base of the wall at Fort Mackinac.

The Marquette Park Hotel, Carmine DeMio's legal business, sat on the other side of the park. The four-story hotel was a beautifully restored Victorian structure, originally built as a private home before the Civil War. Of course, DeMio'd given it a first-class renovation when he turned it into a hotel. I walked slowly toward the top of the long, curved drive.

"I don't imagine Camille'll be happy Conrad's building a man cave the minute she's gone."

"Camille's not the problem," Henri said.

"Then what is?"

"The man's a gunslinger, Russo."

That was Henri's punch line. No doubt about it.

"You know this how?"

Silence on the other end of the line. "Sorry, Henri. Dumb question."

"Yes."

"Describe him," I said.

Henri didn't hesitate. He knew I'd ask. If I didn't ask, he'd still remember every detail. That's how he'd survived tours as an Army Ranger in Iraq and Afghanistan.

"Caucasian. Mid-twenties. Six feet, could be a little less, one-seventy with long dull blond hair curled behind the ears. No facial hair, green eyes and two small scars over his left eye. Hard to see at first. Got to look close. Clean hands, smooth. This guy doesn't do sheet rock."

"Armed?"

"Shoulder holster, left side," Henri said.

"You see it?"

"Didn't have to," he said. "But it's there. Something else in the small of his back. A small gun, a knife maybe. He's light on his feet, Russo. He moves easily."

"This man have a name?"

"Ben Miller."

"Ben Miller?" I said. "A gunslinger named Ben Miller? Is brother Frank Miller on the noon train?"

"Probably not," Henri said. "Doubt he's heard of the movie."

"Wonder why Conrad North of Mackinac Island and Lake Forest, Illinois, hired a kid with guns?"

"Only one reason I can think of, Russo. Be careful," he said, and clicked off.

I stopped at the front steps of the hotel and turned around. The wind blew hard and steady off the cold water. A lone sailboat bounced unhappily, tied to a dock in the harbor.

Remodeling, my ass. Conrad North had somehow learned that Camille hired me to investigate the lease. And he didn't like it.

Somebody moved in behind me. I turned around.

"Russo." It was Santino Cicci, one of DeMio's gunmen. He was six feet, trim even behind a heavy jacket, with a chiseled face and a small, neatly trimmed goatee. Along with his pal, Gino Rosato, he'd worked for Joey DeMio since Carmine's retirement three years ago.

"Santino," I said, and grinned. "Nice to see you again. Still roughing up the locals?" Cicci and Rosato had a long, unpleasant history with the folks who lived on the island. They enjoyed rousting the residents for their own amusement, and just to make sure everyone knew they were tough enough to do it.

Cicci moved closer. "You been needling me a long time, asshole," he said. "Do it again, you're not gonna like what happens."

"You tried that already, tough guy," I said. "Hope you got a better plan this time."

Cicci hesitated. He wouldn't try anything stupid at the hotel. Unless DeMio told him to.

"Let's go," he said. "Mr. DeMio doesn't like to be kept waiting."

Cicci turned on his heels, went up the steps and down the east end of the long porch. The hotel had not yet opened for the season. Two rows of white Adirondack chairs and small square tables were bunched up against the wall of the hotel. Clear plastic roll-up awnings hugged the front railing the entire length of the porch. They shook in the stiff wind.

Two Adirondack chairs and a table sat alone near the end of the porch. Behind the chairs was a tall propane heater that looked like a skinny tree made of tin. I felt the heat as I moved closer.

Carmine DeMio looked up from one of the chairs.

"Come closer," he said, waving an outstretched arm in my direction. "Get warm."

Santino Cicci walked beyond DeMio and sat in a small folding chair a discreet distance from his boss.

"Sit," DeMio said, pointing to the other chair. He did not stand or shake hands. DeMio dictated protocol, not the other way around.

Even seated, DeMio was an imposing figure. He was easily six-three and in his mid-seventies. He was heavier than I remembered, likely from too much good food and good wine. His skin was olive-colored, and his thin black hair was combed back tight. DeMio was born in Naples, but grew up in Chicago. He'd methodically worked his way to the top of the Baldini crime family, until finally turning the reins of the family businesses over to his son.

DeMio held a large mug of coffee.

"You want something, Russo? Coffee? Wine?"

"No, thanks," I said. "Just had lunch."

DeMio shrugged and put down his mug. "Carlo tells me this is personal," he said.

I nodded. "Yes," I said. "I need information for a case I'm working. It has nothing to do with your business."

DeMio nodded, but he kept his eyes on the harbor. Each gust of wind shook the vinyl blinds, straining the short ropes that held them down.

"My case involves your neighbor, Conrad North."

"Ah, the Nazi next door," he said, and laughed hard. "Well, what about him?"

"I know a little, but you live next door to the man. He was there before you bought the Hayden house, and . . ."

"He'll be there alone from now on," DeMio said. "Since he kicked the broad out."

I started to say something, but DeMio cut in. "She your client? The wife? She hired you to get the house back, didn't she?"

I was beginning to think I was the last person in northern Michigan to have heard about Camille, Conrad and the State Park lease.

"I'd prefer not to talk about my clients, Carmine."

"Bullshit, Russo. What am I gonna do, tell the cops?" DeMio laughed again, just as hard. "She your client or not? Sure you don't want anything to drink? A nice cab?"

I shook my head. "Camille North is my client, yes."

DeMio glanced my way for the first time since I'd sat down. He had an exasperated look on his face, like I was wasting his time.

DeMio shrugged. "What do you want to know?"

"Tell me about Conrad," I said. "As a neighbor on the East Bluff, as a resident on the island. Anything you want."

DeMio looked over at Cicci, then back at me. He picked up his mug, and said, "I don't like the guy. Lousy neighbor."

"Wild parties, lots of drunken noise? Stuff like that?"

"You disappoint me, Russo. You come all the way here to be a smart-ass? To talk about parties?"

I waited.

DeMio sighed loudly, like he was growing more disappointed by the moment. What a shame.

"Dinner parties, Russo. Sedate, pompous dinner parties."

"Ever go to one?"

DeMio nodded. "Right after I moved in. North had twelve of our neighbors over for dinner so I could meet them."

"Must be a big dining room."

"These old cottages are all alike," he said, gesturing with his right arm at all the houses on the bluff above the hotel. "Clapboard and bailing wire, wrapped up in 19th Century architecture."

For a godfather of the Chicago mob, this man had a few surprises.

"Architecture your new hobby in retirement, Carmine?"

He turned my way again. "Mackinac Island, yeah," he said. "Started with Phil Porter's book on the cottages."

"*A View from the Veranda*."

DeMio offered a thin smile. "You know it?"

"I'm a fan of Mackinac, too," I said. "Learn anything about Conrad North at dinner?"

"Only that I wouldn't go to another one," DeMio said. "Man thinks he's Hitler. I don't like that. He tells people what to do. Mackinac doesn't need a petty dictator pushing people around. But it's got one. I don't need to live next door to Hitler, but I do."

"Hitler's a bad analogy, Carmine."

"That so?"

"Time for a history lesson."

DeMio sat up straight. "You gonna give me a history lesson? Me? You got balls, you do, Russo. I told you that before. You gonna tell me about Hitler and the old country?"

"No," I said, and shook my head. "I'm not talking about mid-20th Century history, Carmine, I'm talking about Hitler. Everybody and his dog gets called Hitler these days. Senators, governors, presidential candidates. It's always a bad analogy."

"That so?"

"To call any contemporary character 'Hitler' diminishes the evil created by the real German Chancellor." I leaned in, toward DeMio. "It demeans his crimes and the hell he dropped on Europe. On the Old World. If any asshole can be Hitler, the real Adolf Hitler gets off the hook. That's bad history."

Carmine DeMio picked up his mug and drank some coffee. He pointed at something in the harbor. Don't know what.

"Mussolini signed the *Pact of Steel*, with Hitler before the war . . ." DeMio shook his head but never finished the thought. "You're a pretty smart guy, Russo."

We sat quietly in our chairs, Carmine and me, with Santino Cicci a short distance away. The wind had eased up again, but it still slapped the blinds against the wood pillars of the porch.

I sat forward and put my elbows on my knees. "What can you tell me about Wolfgang and Wilhelm?"

Carmine glanced my way. "Nothing to tell. They're pussies, those two. Spoiled rich kids."

"Those kids are in their forties."

"They're still spoiled," he said. "The Nazi wasn't tough enough on them. Didn't raise them to be men."

"They ever bother you?"

DeMio shook his head.

"That because of who you are?"

"They leave me alone. Who cares why?" DeMio looked the other way. "Santino?"

"They're punks," Cicci said. "They don't know how to fight. They stay out of our way. But when they're together, they act stupid."

"How stupid?" I said.

"Threaten people, push 'em around. Act tough."

DeMio picked up his mug and finished the coffee.

"Did you ever meet Nicole?"

"Only once," he said. "A long time ago, with her mother. Before college. Seemed like a bright kid. Pretty. Haven't seen her since."

"What can you tell me about Camille?"

DeMio shifted in his chair, like he'd been sitting too long.

"Nice enough. Quiet. I forget how many generations on Mackinac."

"Four."

DeMio shook his head. "Four generations of family in that house. Then the Nazi steals it." He crossed his legs and pulled his coat tighter around his shoulders. "It ain't right."

Carmine DeMio had softened (if that's the right word) now that Joey ran the family business. The Don of the Baldini family would've never taken the time to wonder about four generations of Sandersons, or anybody else.

"You know a guy named Ben Miller? Mid-twenties, blond hair. He just showed up on the island. North hired him."

DeMio looked over at Santino and nodded. Cicci got up and went into the hotel. He returned a few minutes later, followed by Carlo Vollini. He was a big man, six-six at least, heavy and soft. He wore tan wool slacks and a navy cardigan sweater that pushed against his middle. He carried a manila folder.

"Carlo," DeMio said.

Vollini opened the folder. "Gunnar Lundberg," Vollini said in a thick, deep voice, "was born in Lexington, Ohio, 1992."

"Gunnar?" I said. "That Miller?"

Vollini ignored my surprise.

"Dropped out of high school his last year. Juvenile trouble, stealing cars, vandalism. Ran away from home, Cleveland, before he turned eighteen. Hooked up with bad guys in Cleveland and Toledo. Freelance gun these days. Northern Ohio, Detroit."

"Where'd the 'Ben Miller' come from?"

"Lundberg uses several names," Vollini said. "That one most of the time."

"That's all, Carlo," DeMio said.

Vollini nodded, closed the folder and left the porch.

DeMio stood, and so did Cicci. My appointment was clearly over, so I stood up too. To my surprise, DeMio reached out to shake hands. He'd never done that.

"Thank you for the time, Carmine," I said.

"Come back when the hotel opens. We'll have breakfast. The Eggs Benedict, remember?"

I'd first met Carmine DeMio over breakfast four years ago in the hotel dining room. Joey had been accused of murder at Cherokee Point Resort, and I was there trying to prove the cops wrong.

I turned to walk down the porch.

"Russo." It was Santino Cicci. I stopped and looked back.

"Lundberg," he said. "Ben Miller? He wears a shoulder holster."

"I know."

"He carries a Ken Onion."

"A fighting knife?"

"Hooked on the back of his belt," Cicci said. "He knows how to use it."

I glanced at Carmine. He was smiling as he stared out over the harbor.

9

I stepped off the porch. The wind had dropped off and the sun again warmed the air. I made my way down the long drive to the sidewalk. A dray lumbered up the drive delivering cedar shrubs and two six-foot maple trees. Preseason landscaping at the Marquette Park Hotel was underway.

I had enough time to make the *Huron's* last trip of the day to St. Ignace. The four-trip April schedule required more attention to the clock. Workers crowded aboard the first and last ferries of the day. I didn't want to get caught with an unexpected overnight any more than they did. As I neared Doud's corner, I saw Henri sitting on the cement wall that fronts Marquette Park. I sat next to him.

"What'd the Don have to say?"

I filled Henri in on what I'd learned about Carmine's East Bluff neighbor.

"Doesn't make North sound any more charming," Henri said.

"It certainly does not."

The *Huron* sounded its horn as it rounded the breakwater.

"You know Ken Onion knives?"

Henri turned my way. "You talked fighting knives with Carmine DeMio?"

"Ben Miller carries one," I said.

Henri smiled. "So it's not an extra gun behind his back."

"Good thing to know."

"Uh-huh," Henri said. "Must be a serious guy."

"Santino Cicci thinks so." I told Henri about Miller.

"Well, I got more news for you about Miller, or Lundberg, or whatever he's called."

"Yeah?"

"He's been following you."

I've been at this long enough not to react when I heard news like that. Instead I watched a gray dray loaded with bright tan lumber move slowly by us, the driver's head down, fixed on his cell phone.

"You see him?"

"I've been following him following you."

The *Huron* pulled into the dock. Passengers would come off first, then freight.

"Now we know for sure."

"Yes, we do."

"You see him now?"

"He was on the porch at the Parish Hall when I sat down a few minutes ago." Trinity Episcopal Church and its Parish Hall were a block up the Fort Street hill behind us.

"Good spot for Miller. He'd pick you up easy enough when you left the hotel," Henri said. "He's got a line of sight on us, if he's still up there."

"Any idea what his game is?"

"We could ask him."

I shook my head. "Let's see what he does," I said. "Think he'll get on the boat when I go?"

Henri shook his head. "No place to hide. You'd see him."

"Guess he can pick me up on the mainland if he wants."

"You're easy enough to find in Petoskey," Henri said.

"I need to get a good look at him."

I looked at my watch. We had time. "Got an idea," I said. "Come on."

I was up and off the wall. Henri, too. We moved quickly across Fort Street as if we were headed straight down the sidewalk toward the old Arnold dock. As soon as we got to Doud's front door, we were out of Miller's sight.

I caught Henri's arm. "Inside," I said, and we ducked into "Michigan's Oldest Family-Owned Grocery Store."

"You need a sandwich for the trip home?" Henri said.

I ignored him and moved to the other side of the checkout lanes. We'd be hard to see from the sidewalk, but if Miller came around the corner, we'd spot him easily through the market's big windows.

"That's him," Henri said. "Green parka."

"Got him," I said. Miller looked young enough to be just another college kid working on Mackinac for the summer. He moved smartly past the windows, his long blond hair sticking out under a blue Tigers cap. He was looking straight ahead, trying to find us.

"Let's have some fun," I said. Henri and I were out the door fast. Miller was little more than thirty feet ahead of us. There were only a few people between us.

"He'll stop when he doesn't see us," I said. "Go right by him."

Henri unbuttoned his tan Carhartt coat for faster access to his gun. Odds were that Miller would be surprised and do nothing, but Henri never took chances.

We kept pace with Miller, but did not close the gap. When he came to the Murray Hotel, he stopped almost as if he was about to enter the hotel. Instead he turned around and looked back. He saw us. We went by him without looking and crossed the street to the top of the dock. If Miller knew we were on to him, he gave no sign of it.

We walked down the dock just like we would have done even if a man with a handgun and knife wasn't following me. Henri and I stopped at ramp two and stood facing each other so Henri could see up the dock. The *Huron* was loading passengers.

"Only got a couple of minutes," I said. "He back there?"

"No," Henri said. "He figures you're leaving."

"Think he knows we're on to him?"

"Hard to tell," Henri said. "If he's a careful man, he'll assume we are."

"I'll pay attention," I said, "just in case."

"You do that," Henri said. He turned and we moved closer to the ramp. "Want me to roust him tonight?"

"No. Leave him alone."

"I'd have fun."

"I'm sure you would," I said. "Just keep an eye on him. See what his next move is."

The ship's horn sounded a long, clear blast.

"They'll pull the ramp in a minute," I said. "Gotta go."

"I'll let you know if anything changes," Henri said.

"See ya," I said, and walked onto the *Huron*. I made my way to the top deck. The rear cabin was crowded with workers. The nightly card game had begun, and tall cans of beer, covered with paper bags, had been pulled from backpacks.

I stopped outside the front cabin door and leaned against the railing as the *Huron* backed away from the dock. I pulled out my phone, and punched AJ's number.

AJ Lester was editor of *PPD Wired*, the online version of the *Petoskey Post Dispatch*. She'd arrived in Petoskey in 2000, two years after I did. An experienced journalist, we first met when she interviewed me for a story on downstate professionals who'd moved north to live and work. We'd been together ever since.

"Michael," she said. "Where are you?"

"Just leaving the island. You have plans for dinner?"

"Where do you want to go?" she said. "I'm buying."

"You treat, you pick."

"We haven't been to Chandler's in a while."

Away from the dock, the *Huron* started a slow turn. I looked at my watch. "Should be there by a quarter to seven."

"Unless you get hung up on the bridge."

I laughed. "Okay. Make it seven." I clicked off and put the phone in my coat pocket. The cabin was jammed with people holding backpacks or coats or both. I wedged myself into a small opening on the bench seat and turned to look out the cabin window.

Henri was leaning up against the pop machine, arms folded, like he was waiting to pick up supplies. The real reason he waited for the *Huron* to leave the harbor had nothing to do with supplies and everything to do with a man named Ben Miller, who carried a handgun and a fighting knife.

10

I've taken the *Huron* to Mackinac often enough over the years to appreciate the onset of the regular ferry schedule in early May. There's something quaint about the old, steel-hulled carrier, but the thirty-five to forty-minute ride from St. Ignace seemed longer with each trip. I'm not even counting extra time to cross the bridge.

As the *Huron* inched its way to the mainland dock, the nightly ritual had begun. Commuters gathered their gear and headed down to the main deck before the *Huron* was tied up. They were eager to disembark as soon as possible. I let them go. I wasn't in a hurry to get to my car only to sit in line waiting to leave the parking lot.

When the cabin was almost empty, I made my way off the *Huron* and walked to the far end of the lot. I beeped the locks, opened the door and sat down. I hit the start button and the twin-turbo six growled to life.

Ever since Henri told me about Ben Miller, I'd wondered why Conrad North needed a gunslinger just to find out what I was up to. He could have asked me. He could have sent his two sons to ask me. Okay, so I'd have told them to shove it. Maybe North knew I would do that, and preferred someone tough enough to get answers. Or tough enough . . . for what? To scare me off? He didn't know why I was nosing around, unless Camille had told him. Another reason to contact her soon.

I pulled out of the lot and followed State Street to I-75. The BMW moved swiftly and smoothly through the long on-ramp at the north end of the Mackinac Bridge.

Miller followed me during my short stay on the island, but he didn't travel to the mainland. Henri was likely right that Miller didn't want to tip his hand. Or that I'd not done enough to jeopardize North's plans. Not yet anyway.

Only a few cars were lined up at the tollbooths. I swiped my commuter card and moved onto the southbound lanes. Work on the bridge had stopped for the night and only a small section, just shy of the north tower, narrowed to one lane. I left 75 at the U.S. 31 exit for the trip to Petoskey.

Traffic was light as I hit town, so I stayed on 31 through Bay View, cut off at Lewis and parked behind my apartment building.

It was almost seven when I walked through the door at Chandler's. A delightful restaurant, Chandler's is tucked into a courtyard behind Symon's General Store. It's a one-block walk from my office in one direction, and one block from my apartment in the other. Living downtown added to the reasons I moved to northern Michigan in the first place. I liked a life that included moving on my feet every day. And this from a lifelong car guy.

"Good evening, Michael," said a voice from behind the bar.

"Hello, Jack," I said to the bartender, a small, wiry man in his fifties who looked much younger except for his salt-and-pepper hair. The bar was on the left side of the rectangular room, with tables on the opposite wall and on the floor. Two women in their twenties sat talking at the bar.

"In the back," Jack said, and pointed to the rear of the room. I saw AJ waving from a four-top on the side wall.

I walked back, leaned over and kissed her, gently, on the lips.

"Hello, darling," I said.

Audrey Jean Lester, who disliked both Audrey and Jean, was tall, about five-nine, with an angular face, green eyes and slightly curly black hair, which was pushed behind her ears. She wore a classy outfit typical of the successful businesswoman: a simple dark gray two-piece suit with a rose silk blouse, open at the collar.

"Hello to you, too," she said, and kissed me back.

"That was nice," I said, smiling.

"There's always more where that came from."

"Good to know," I said, and sat down. "How was your day?"

"It gets better and better," she said, referring to *PPD Wired.* "There'll always be kinks, but now I expect them. They're not a surprise anymore, I'm happy to say."

"Good evening, AJ, Michael," our waiter said. "Something from the bar this evening?"

"Hello, Andrew," I said.

We ordered Chardonnay, and listened as Andrew explained the evening's dinner specials.

"Be right back," he said.

"You still think the electronic edition has a clearly defined role?"

AJ nodded. "Yeah, we're there. But we have to adapt as fast as possible. Our online audience doesn't know what it wants half the time."

"It's been that way since you started."

AJ nodded again. "Yes, it has."

Andrew placed two glasses of wine on our table. "Back in a few," he said, "to see if you're ready to order."

"Now tell me about the island. Did you meet Conrad North?"

I shook my head. "Too soon," I said. "I need to know more about the man before I knock on his door." I told AJ what Henri had to say, and about my visit with Carmine DeMio.

AJ laughed.

"What?" I didn't get where she was going.

"Well," she said, still laughing. "Who would you rather have as your neighbor, Carmine or Conrad?"

I laughed and said, "Beats me."

"One's a killer, the other's, what, a petty dictator?"

"I choose Carmine," I said. "The man's a genuine tough guy."

Andrew returned to the table.

"I'll take the lamb shank," AJ said. "And another glass of wine with dinner."

"Michael?"

"The salmon special, please."

I'd waited a little bit to tell AJ about Ben Miller. She never liked it when a case turned dangerous. She accepted it, but didn't like it. I could tell by the look in her eyes that she wasn't happy with the news.

"I'm not worried about Miller," I said.

"You never worry about men with guns, Michael. Even when you should."

I drank some wine. "We don't know why North brought Miller here. Maybe he's just an errand boy."

"He's got two good-for-nothing sons for that," AJ said. "No, Miller's here for a reason, Michael. Conrad North needs a gunman because he's worried about you."

"I haven't done anything, AJ."

"You're snooping around. You're asking questions. North's hiding something, and doesn't want you to find it. I'd bet on it."

Andrew arrived at the table with our dinners. He put the plates in front of us and left another Chardonnay for AJ.

"Bon appetit," he said.

I raised my glass. "A toast."

AJ clinked my glass. "To what?"

"You," I said. "Because I love you, and I have not told you that today."

AJ smiled, clinked my glass again. "That's very sweet,"

We ate a few bites of dinner quietly, with only the low din of the restaurant in the background.

"How's your lamb?"

"As good as I remember," AJ said. "The salmon?"

I nodded. "Two thumbs up." I drank some wine.

"North has his reasons, Michael," AJ said.

I thought maybe she'd left Ben Miller alone for the rest of the evening.

"Camille might know what her husband's up to. Why don't you ask her?"

"If she had anything else to make her husband look bad, she'd have told me already."

"Maybe, maybe not. Besides, you don't know how aware she is of his business, or his life apart from her."

I drank the last of my wine as Andrew approached the table.

"Another glass, Michael?"

"I'll pass," I said. "Just the check."

Andrew cleared our plates and went away.

"How about the daughter?" AJ said. "Nicole?"

I nodded. "She doesn't spend time on Mackinac. Not sure what she knows."

"You should find her and ask," AJ said. "See if she has any interest in the bluff house."

Andrew left the bill in the middle of the table. I put down a card.

"Whatever you say, ma'am. Does the press have any other suggestions?"

"Yes," she said. "Come stay the night. I'll make it worth your time. Promise."

"Hmm."

"Is that all you can say, 'hmm?'"

"How about I say yes?"

"That's the ticket," AJ said, and smiled. "Let's get out of here."

AJ started out of her chair, then sat back down.

"What?"

"One more thing before we change the subject."

"Okay." It wasn't okay, but there you go.

"A freelance gunman from Cleveland or Detroit? To follow you around a small island? Seriously?"

"You said that already."

AJ shook her head. "That's not what I mean."

"Can we go now?"

"No. I have one more suggestion."

"I'd rather talk about you and me."

"That can wait."

"Really?"

“Be quiet a minute, will you? Call Marty Fleener. See what the State Police know about Conrad North.”

“Can it wait ‘till morning?”

AJ smiled. “Yes, darling,” she said, and took my hand. “It can wait ‘till morning.”

11

I moved my hand around the bed. It didn't find AJ. "You up already?"

"Shh. Go back to sleep," she said from someplace in the room.

"What time is it?"

"Almost six-thirty," she said. "I'll make coffee."

"Okay." I pushed the pillow against the headboard and inched my head up.

I must have dozed off, but I heard AJ come back to the bedroom. She was wrapped in a white terry robe two sizes too big.

"Going to the shower," she said, pointing at the bathroom.

"Want me to join you?"

"No."

"Want to reconsider?"

"No," she said, and closed the door behind her. I heard the water come on.

I found my clothes on the chair by the door. Khakis, a long-sleeved T that read "Taste of Chicago" across the front, a brick red crewneck sweater and scruffy brown deck shoes. I kept basic clothes at AJ's, even a navy blazer and wool slacks, just in case. But I'd have plenty of time to stop at home before I went to the office.

I sat at a small wrought iron table in AJ's kitchen with a mug of coffee and banana slices. Her house on Bay Street overlooked the ravine. She'd been renovating the two-story Victorian since she bought it five years ago. I turned on the floodlights perched high on the back of the house. Huge trees, elm, maple, oak, lit up in the darkness. A squirrel, no doubt surprised by the lights, sat frozen on the railing of the deck.

AJ walked in, poured coffee, grabbed a napkin from a basket on the counter, and sat down. She still wore the massive robe, but her hair was curly wet from the shower. She drank some coffee and popped a banana slice into her mouth.

"Remember to call Camille," she said. "And Marty Fleener."

I smiled. "Good morning to you, too."

She reached out and touched my hand. "Sorry, sweetheart, busy day ahead. I didn't want to forget to tell you."

"I'll remember," I said, tapping my head. "Memory like an elephant."

"Bullshit."

"Is that any way to talk to the man who whispered in your ear last night?"

She rolled her eyes. "Sarcasm will get you nowhere."

"Wanna bet?"

"No," she said. "More coffee?"

"No, thanks. I'm out of here in a minute."

"Do you have a busy day?"

"No. Not unless calling Camille turns into an all-day chore."

"I think there's more going on with her divorce, Michael."

"Conrad's just another husband being a prick 'cuz she's the one who wants out of the marriage."

"That's as good a motive as any for a prick to be a prick," AJ said, and put her mug on the table. "But why does a prick husband need a gunslinger?"

I shrugged. "Mackinac's a tough league?"

"Michael, I'm serious. If this Miller guy is as bad as he seems, it might be a good idea to find out if there is anything else to this divorce."

"I hear you, AJ," I said. "I'll call Camille as soon as I get to the office."

"I have a better idea."

"But you said . . ."

"Call Fleener first. It's the reporter in me, Michael. I can smell it. Something else's going on. See if Miller's got another connection to Conrad North."

"Like what?"

"How the hell do I know? Do I look like State Police?"

"You certainly do not," I said.

AJ got out of her chair and put her mug in the sink. "I'm going to be late." She leaned over and kissed the top of my head as she went by. "Let me know."

I put our mugs in the dishwasher, grabbed my coat at the back door and went out into the morning air.

The early light in the eastern sky silhouetted the tree tops on Bay Street. It was chilly, but the sun would warm the April day quickly enough. I enjoyed the ten-minute walk to my apartment, especially since I hadn't planned to run this morning.

Walking, like a good run, gave me time to think. AJ's instincts, a reporter's instincts for a good story, were usually right. I seldom questioned them, and I wasn't about to this time.

I took a quick shower, put on a pair of khakis sharply creased from the cleaners. I added a blue button-down and a navy fleece, picked up my brief bag and headed for the office.

I went up Howard, cut through the parking lot behind the Lake Street stores and stopped at McLean & Eakin to pick up the *New York Times*. I had a standing order so the paper would be held for me every day. I read most publications online, but a hard copy of the *Times* remained a treat.

"Good morning, Sandy."

"Morning, boss," she said from behind her desk.

"Anything?"

"If you mean new clients, the answer is no," she said. "There're two messages on your desk. I don't think either one's urgent."

I hung my coat on the rack at the door. "Did I give you Camille North's number the other day?"

"Right here," Sandy said, picking up a business card. "Haven't filed it yet. Want me to call her?"

"Yes, but find Marty Fleener first."

"Something happen?"

"Right now, just a couple of questions," I said, and went into my office.

Sandy followed me. "I don't believe you," she said from the doorway.

I nodded slowly. "All right. Find Marty, then come on in."

"Be right there," she said.

Sandy returned to my office and put down two mugs of coffee. She sat in her usual spot on the sidewall, next to the desk.

"Thanks," I said, and drank some coffee. "Tastes good."

"Fleener's out of the office," she said. "They'll get him a message."

"Okay." I brought Sandy up to date on my trip to the island.

"AJ's got a point, boss."

"About Ben Miller?"

She nodded. "Even if Conrad North's a wannabe dictator, a hired gun? For what?"

I shook my head. "I don't know."

"Fleener could have another angle on the guy," she said.

I nodded. "AJ thinks so, too."

"Like minds," Sandy said, and smiled.

"So you've said before."

"What'd you say Miller's name was?"

"Lundberg, Gunnar Lundberg. Why?"

"I just wondered," she said.

"Why he picked that name?"

"Should I start singing?"

"Want to get fired?"

"Do not forsake me, oh my darling . . ."

"Enough," I said. "You'll scare the dog."

"We don't have a dog. Just listen to me for a minute. Suppose Miller, I mean Lundberg, suppose he chose that name for a reason."

"Such as?"

"I don't believe in coincidences any more than you do, boss. Lundberg has an alias, and it comes out of *High Noon*?"

"You don't know he was thinking about movies, Sandy."

My phone buzzed on the desk. "It's Marty," I said, and tapped the screen.

"I've got work to do," Sandy said. She walked out.

"Marty, thanks for the callback." Captain Martin Fleener was a detective with the Michigan State Police. A twenty-year veteran from Grand Rapids, he'd been reassigned to the Petoskey post in 2010. His reputation as an interrogator was legendary with the cops and in the jailhouse. We had an easy, though sometimes contentious, friendship.

"Make it quick, Russo. I'm on stakeout."

"Stakeout. In northern Michigan? Are you kidding?"

"I'm serious," he said. "What?"

"I want to know where you are."

"Across from the hospital. Off 31."

"Near Johan's?"

"Parked outside," he said. "It's glazed or fried cakes. Have to decide before I go in the front door."

I laughed. "You suckered me on that one."

"I'll say. What do you need?"

"Go get your donuts and call me back."

"I'll survive another five minutes."

"You know a hired gun, Gunnar Lundberg?"

"Don't think so."

"Goes by Ben Miller?"

"Doesn't ring a bell," Fleener said. "Do we have a gunslinger in the neighborhood?"

"We do."

"Spell it. I'll check him out."

I did.

"Are you working a case, or just chasing bad guys around town?"

"Working a case," I said. "My client's husband hired Miller."

"Who's your client?"

I hesitated.

"Tell me the name," Fleener said.

"Not sure I want to do that, Marty. Not right now, anyway."

"Then tell me who hired the gunslinger."

"Name's Conrad North."

It was Fleener who hesitated this time.

"Marty?"

"From Mackinac Island?"

"That's the guy," I said. "Recognize the name?"

"I need that donut. And some coffee. Call you back," Fleener said, and clicked off.

I knew Fleener pretty well. Conrad North rang a bell. So why the brush-off? I went to the front office.

"Did Fleener help?" Sandy said.

"Not much." I told her about the call.

"If the captain's cagey, there's a reason."

"Be my guess," I said. "Question is, why?"

12

I revised some paperwork for a client in Traverse City and took care of my messages. I was seriously thinking about changing my mind and going for a mid-day run when Fleener called on the office line.

"How were the donuts?" I said.

"What's your interest in Conrad North?"

"He hired Ben Miller."

"Besides that."

"Why, Marty?"

"Who's your client?"

"I'd rather not . . ."

"Russo, who's your client?"

"How 'bout I . . ."

"We looked at North five years ago after his wife disappeared."

"Camille North went missing?"

"No," Fleener said. "His first wife, Annora. The case is still open. Now who's your client?"

"Camille North."

"Small world, isn't it?" Fleener said.

"You think North was responsible for his wife's disappearance? What'd you say her name was?"

"Annora. She was called Annie," Fleener said. "Conrad was suspect number one, but we couldn't prove he had anything to do with it. No evidence pointed at anyone else either."

Fleener asked about my work for Camille. No point not telling him now. I ran it down for him, but there wasn't much there.

"So you haven't figured out how her name dropped off the lease?"

"No, not yet," I said. "Think there might be a connection between the disappearance of wife one and Camille's house?"

"I always look for links," Fleener said. "But I don't see one here. You?"

"Maybe Conrad buried Annie in the backyard. Doesn't want the body found."

"Don't give up your day job, Russo. You'd make a lousy mystery writer."

"Don't worry," I said. "Having enough trouble figuring out how Camille lost her house."

"If I stumble on anything, I'll let you know."

"Appreciate that, Marty," I said. "How about Ben Miller?"

"Yeah, I can help you on that one," he said, and I heard him shuffling papers. "Hold on a second."

I swung my chair around and put my feet on the window sill. The bright blue sky silhouetted the leafless trees along Bay View Road. Buds had sprouted, but that was all. Marty came back on the line. I grabbed a yellow pad and a pencil.

"Lundberg was born in Lexington, Ohio. He's twenty-six, but looks younger. I sent two photos to your phone."

I put my feet on the floor and grabbed my phone. I opened messages and Miller's cheery face looked back at me. One photo was a mug shot. He wasn't smiling. The other was a surveillance photo of Miller dated six months ago, a close-up of him getting out of a taxi in downtown Detroit.

"Lundberg worked his way up as a juvie. He's got an older brother, Nils, very protective. Taught him to boost cars, burglary . . ."

"Thought Lundberg was a shooter?"

"Coming to that," Fleener said. "Cleveland PD's sure he killed his first man before he turned sixteen. Never proved it in court."

"Gang history?"

"Some contact here and there, but nothing permanent."

"This a State Police file?"

"Organized Crime Division in Lansing. I work with a guy down there, we help each other out."

"Miller's a made man?"

"He's a freelancer," Fleener said. "Doesn't work for anyone in particular. Never seems to be out of work very long. OCD says he's good with a gun and a knife."

"So I've heard."

"He's a black belt in Karate, too. You got a belt in Karate, don't you?"

"Yeah, few years ago."

"Any good at it?"

"If I have to be."

"You might be interested to know that Lundberg's worked for the Baldini crime family."

"Well, how 'bout that?" I said. "He's worked for DeMio."

The world just got even smaller.

"I talked with the old man. He never mentioned Miller was a hire."

"Could be Joey's hire," Fleener said. "Might explain how a guy like North found a shooter when he needed one."

"Yeah, but Carmine doesn't like Conrad North, Marty."

"I doubt Joey checks every move with his father."

"Don't be too sure about that," I said. "Of course, Joey might have a reason to play nice with his father's neighbor."

"Could be they got something going, and he wanted to help out."

"Think I'll have a chat with Joey," I said. "I'll accuse him of holding out on me. See what he has to say."

"Don't get too cute, Russo," Fleener said. "You may have access to the DeMios, but don't push your luck. I don't want to drag your soggy ass out of Haldimand Bay."

"Yeah, I hear you. Is Miller still on the island?"

"OCD thinks he'll stay awhile," Fleener said. "They'll let me know if he leaves permanently."

"Well, Miller's there, North's there and our favorite Mafia family is there."

"Going up to join the club, are you?"

"Yep," I said. "Want to come along for the ride?"

"No," Fleener said. "Be more fun to see who chases you first."

13

"What'd Fleener have to say?" Sandy stood at my office door.

I pushed my chair back and put my feet on the corner of the desk. I told her about Conrad and Annie and Ben Miller.

"If it turns out that Lundberg's brother uses 'Frank Miller' as his alias, you don't get to hush my singing. I might just play Tex Ritter all day."

"Spare me, oh god-of-movies, spare me."

Sandy didn't react to that one. "Did you know that North had a first wife?"

I nodded. "Uh-huh, but Camille never said much. She was mother to Wolfgang and Wilhelm. That was about it."

"You think she's aware that wife number one is missing?"

"How would she not know that, Sandy?"

"Beats me, boss, but when you're dealing with wives, ex-wives and husbands, I never assume a thing."

"Good point," I said. "You find Camille?"

She nodded. "I talked to her while you were on with Fleener. I said you'd call back."

Sandy handed me Camille's card.

"Thanks," I said, and picked up the phone.

"Before you do that, boss, Lenny Stern's downstairs. He wants a few minutes."

"Lenny's in the sandal store?"

Sandy rolled her eyes. "What am I going to do with you?" she said. "He's at Roast & Toast."

I dropped my feet to the floor with a thud and followed her out of my office. "Going downstairs. Want anything?"

"How 'bout a stiff drink?" she said, with sarcastic edge.

"I'll ignore that. Would you like something from Roast & Toast?"

"No, thanks," she said. "What about Camille?"

"Do it when I get back." I headed down the stairs and walked three doors to the restaurant.

Roast & Toast felt like an urban café. High tin ceilings, bright neon, tables and a few booths along one wall. Lenny Stern sat at a two-top at the rear of the room. I went to the counter, got a mug and filled it with an organic Sumatra.

"Morning, Lenny."

Stern was small, about five-four, wiry and in his late sixties. He was nearly bald except for a few wisps of gray scattered around his ears. I'd never seen him in anything other than a two-piece black suit, a white cotton shirt, not ironed, and a skinny black tie. There was a gray sharkskin suit. Once.

"Russo," Stern said, and pointed at the other chair like there was more than one option. He moved a spoon around a large mug.

I sat down and drank some coffee. "How's things? Scooped the *Free Press* lately?"

Stern shook his head. "Not often enough, is all I can say." He put down the spoon and picked up the mug.

"Your meeting, Lenny. What can I do for you?"

"You said you had a story I'd be interested in. That still true?"

I nodded. "You said you'd nose around about Conrad North."

"When you asked about North . . ."

"Didn't seem like you recognized the name."

"Not at first," Stern said. "But it nagged me the rest of day. So I did some digging."

"Uh-huh."

"Annora North," he said. "Didn't connect the names at first. Annie's been gone five, six years now."

"Did you know the first Mrs. North?"

"Never met the woman, but there were plenty of stories."

"Before or after her divorce?"

"Mostly after," he said. "After she ended up in Traverse City."

"I didn't know about that."

"She wanted to be closer to her sons."

"They're all in Chicago in the winter?"

"Apparently Lake Forest wasn't big enough for both of them, if you know what I mean."

"Conrad and Annie?"

"Uh-huh," Stern said. "Annie turned into quite the party girl."

"You can do that in Traverse?" I said.

Stern looked over his mug.

"Be a party girl, I mean."

"I knew what you meant, Russo," he said. "She hung out with a younger crowd, mostly singles working on careers. One woman in particular she was close to."

Stern took out a small notebook, wrote something and tore off the page. "Here," he said, and handed me the paper. "You might want to talk to her."

"Got an address or phone?"

Stern shook his head. "Lives in downtown Traverse. On West 7th. She works for one of the banks."

I put the paper in my pocket. "Want more coffee?" I said. Stern shook his head, so I got a refill and went back to the table.

"What's my story?" Stern said.

"I'm just getting into it," I said. "Seems to have more layers than I thought."

"Such as?"

"Chicago industrialist who's lived on Mackinac for years."

"Conrad North?"

I nodded and told him about Camille, the lease, and Ben Miller.

"I didn't realize you were such a dangerous guy."

"Not sure what Miller was hired to do, Lenny."

"You're the one kickin' up dust, Russo. North must be hiding something."

I shrugged.

"Well, when you find out, I want to be the first to know." Stern took in air and let it out slowly. "I think you're right, there's a story in there."

"AJ thinks so, too."

Stern smiled. "Not surprised," he said. "That woman's a born reporter. Too bad she's wasting time on the desk."

"Wouldn't mention that, if I were you."

"Already have."

"What'd she say?"

Stern laughed. "Let's just say it ain't printable in a family newspaper."

I laughed this time. "Sounds like AJ," I said. "Time to get back to the office."

I got up, put my mug on the counter with the other dirty dishes and came back by the table.

"Thanks for the tip, Lenny."

Stern nodded. "Don't mention it. You know how to find me."

14

"Well, that almost makes it unanimous," Sandy said, looking up from the screen. "This may have started with a house on the East Bluff, but . . ." Sandy's voice trailed off like there was no need to state the obvious.

"While I call Camille, see if you can find this woman." I handed Sandy the slip of paper. "She works for a bank in Traverse City."

"Patricia Geary," Sandy said, reading the name. "I'm on it."

I sat at my desk, swung my chair around to see Little Traverse Bay, and tapped out Camille's number. She picked up.

"Michael," she said. "I was hoping you would call."

"Hello, Camille," I said. "How are you?"

"Well enough, thank you. Have you any news?"

"Some," I said, and told what I'd learned. "It's more complicated than it seemed at the start."

"That's always the case with Conrad," she said. "He makes everything more complicated than it needs to be, I assure you."

"I'm beginning to understand that," I said. "Camille, we need to sit and talk. I have more questions."

"Of course."

"Are you coming to the mainland in the next day or two?"

"I was in Grand Rapids for a week," she said. "I just returned last night. I'd rather not turn around and leave the island so soon."

"I'll come up, if that's all right with you."

We agreed to meet the next day.

"You know the Baldwin cottage?" she said. "In the Annex?"

"It's on the park, right? Dark green two-story. Next to the old Gunn Cottage."

"That's the one," she said. "Oh, and Michael, bring your rain gear. It looks like we have a storm coming in."

I clicked off and put down my phone. I looked out at the bay. A scattering of dark gray clouds hung low in the sky, and the wind was calm. But that meant nothing at the Straits. The convergence of two lakes, Huron and Michigan, in the narrow channel between Round Island and Mackinac Island could cause trouble quickly. Add tricky currents and a dose of heavy wind, and conditions were unpredictable.

Sandy came into the office, sat down and looked at a yellow pad.

"Patricia Geary . . ."

"You found her already?"

"That's what you pay me for, boss," she said. "Besides, she was easy to find. Three pages on Google."

"Three pages?"

Sandy nodded. "Geary's a Senior Vice President at Boardman Bank & Trust. She's been actively involved in city affairs over the years. Downtown Development, Cherry Festival, that kind of thing. She works at the main office on Front Street, near the parking ramp. Bank has branches in Northport, Suttons Bay and Interlochen. She was born in Gaylord in 1961, that'd make her fifty-six, fifty-seven. Spent most of her career at the bank."

Sandy tore off two sheets of yellow paper and handed them across the desk.

"Her number's at the top of the first page."

"Thanks."

"Want me to get her on the phone?"

"I'll do it," I said.

"I'm going for a sandwich in a bit. Julienne Tomatoes, probably. Want me to bring back a sandwich or salad?"

"Not sure," I said. "I'll let you know."

I called Boardman Bank & Trust and reached Patricia Geary. I explained who I was and why I'd called. When I finished, I tapped out a message to AJ. I didn't have to wait long for her to call.

"Hi, sweetheart," I said. "Want to have dinner at Red Ginger?"

"Red Ginger?"

"Been a long time since we've had sushi."

"Too long," AJ said. "But Traverse City?"

"I'm running down for a late afternoon appointment. Come along and we'll stay for dinner."

"What's the appointment?"

"I'll explain on the way."

"Give me twenty minutes. I'll meet you at the back door."

I went to Sandy's desk and told her about my unscheduled trip.

"You can't talk to a bank dressed like that."

I looked down at my khakis and navy crewneck. "I'm casual but neat," I said. "This is all right."

"Only old people say 'casual but neat,' boss. The least you can do is ditch the sweater and put on a blazer."

"You my fashion consultant now?"

"I'm your 'chief cook and bottle washer,' that's what I am. The blazer?"

"Talk about old people lines, Sandy."

"I am old," she said. "Older than you, anyway. Leave. I have work to do."

I grabbed my brief bag and walked home to dress in my best hedge fund blazer. A few minutes later, I threw a rain jacket in the back seat of the 335 and got in for the four block ride to the paper.

I waited for AJ in the parking lot behind the *Post Dispatch*. She came through the door like a woman on a mission. She put her briefcase and coat in the back and hopped in.

"Hi, darling," she said, and leaned over for a kiss. I drove down Mitchell to U.S. 31. "Don't you want to stop for a danish?" she said as we passed Johan's Bakery. "You know, one for the road."

I shook my head. "I seem to be surrounded by sarcasm today."

"Only today?" AJ said, trying to sound coy. It didn't work.

At the stoplight, we took U.S. 131 south to Kalkaska. Traffic was light. It was the middle of an April work day, and only a scattering of tourists slowed our drive. The ground was a flat, uninteresting brown; only the pine trees were green.

"Tell me about your meeting."

I did.

"So, I guess I missed the part about why you think the banker . . ."

"Patricia Geary."

"Right. Why you think Geary can help you with Camille's lease."

"Not sure she can," I said. "But Lenny thought she's worth a look. You said it yourself, AJ, something's going on. Lenny thinks so, too. Let's see what she has to say."

Traffic picked up at Mancelona, and we rode with it to Kalkaska. I took a right on M-72 west for Traverse City.

"What about Camille?"

"Haven't talked to her yet," I said. "Meeting her tomorrow on the island."

"Did you talk to Fleener about the kid with the gun?"

"He was helpful," I said, and told her about Gunner Lundberg.

"That still doesn't explain why North employed a man like that."

"No, it doesn't, but DeMio's holding out on me. I need to ask Joey about it."

We approached the twin roundabouts inserted in the Kalkaska road.

"Careful there, Mario Andretti," AJ said. "Time to slow up."

"I don't know what you mean, darling."

"Don't 'darling' me, Michael. People have no clue how to drive a roundabout. One of them's going to hit you some day. You won't like a big, fat dent to your fender very much."

We somehow managed to survive our adventure in the roundabouts and turned south on 31 for the slow trip downtown, along the bottom of East Bay.

"When're you going to get a sensible car?"

"This is a sensible car, AJ. All-wheel drive, manual transmission, winter tires when I need them."

"You're not listening, are you?"

"No."

I went straight onto Front Street and inched my way along to the parking ramp across from the bank.

We parked the car and took the stairs to street level. The sky was filled with clouds, but they didn't hold rain. Just another cloudy spring day in northern Michigan.

"What are you going to do?"

"I'll happily wander through the stores," AJ said.

I pulled her close and we kissed.

"Text me when you're done talking to the bank."

15

The lobby of Boardman Bank & Trust looked like the 1970s if it were a suburban ranch house with twenty-foot ceilings. Chrome, glass, and brown leather. It seemed out of place in northern Michigan. The directory near the elevator put Patricia Geary on the third floor. I found the stairs tucked away on the far side of the lobby and pushed the heavy door.

On the third floor, I wound my way through two short hallways and ended up in a large waiting room that featured more leather and chrome. A receptionist sat in the middle of the space under a huge tinted skylight. Her desk was sandwiched between two tall palm trees. Office doors were evenly spaced around the room, but they were unmarked, no name, no number. Must be tough filling in for an absent receptionist.

"Hello," I said to the woman behind the desk. She was about thirty, with an angular face and curly brown hair that touched the shoulders of her sweater.

"Yes, sir?"

"Michael Russo to see Patricia Geary."

The receptionist tapped a keyboard twice and looked at the screen. "Have a seat, please," she said, and picked up a desk phone.

Before I decided which leather and chrome chair would be the most comfortable, I heard a door open behind me.

"Mr. Russo," a voice said, and I turned around.

"I'm Patricia Geary." She walked over and we shook hands. Geary was in her mid-fifties, five-seven, stocky, with salt-and-pepper hair pulled back into a tight ponytail. She wore a black two-piece suit over a soft green camisole.

"Thank you for making the time to see me."

She nodded. "This way." I followed her to door number four (if I counted from the elevator I didn't use).

Geary's office was a perfect square with a wall of windows overlooking West Bay. Nice view. The room was furnished like the lobby, except for two cheerful watercolors on a side wall and a large mahogany desk in front of the windows.

"Have a seat, please."

"Thank you," I said, and sat down. "How did you manage it?"

"Pardon me?"

"The desk. Everything else around here is leather and chrome. But you," I gestured, "have this beautiful desk."

Geary smiled, and gazed at the desk. "It's mine. I was on the way home from our Interlochen branch two years ago and found it at an estate sale. They practically gave it away. It cost me more to get it here than to buy it." She placed her hands on the desktop, palms down. "It was worth every penny."

She pulled her hands back, folded her arms across her chest and said, "But you didn't come down here to talk about furniture."

"No."

"I didn't realize anyone cared much about Annie. Have the police reopened the investigation, Mr. Russo?"

"Not that I'm aware of. As I explained on the phone, Annora North's name came up in a case I'm working . . ."

"Is her . . . disappearance part of your case?" Geary had leaned forward, on her elbows. "Have you any new information?"

"No, I don't," I said. "Her disappearance is still an open case, but that's all I know." Geary's eagerness made it feel as if Annie went missing six days ago, not six years ago.

"Is Conrad North part of your case?" she said.

"I'd prefer not to discuss details about . . ."

"Of course he's part of your case," Geary said. She sat back, her eyes narrowed. "You wouldn't be here if he wasn't."

I'd obviously hit a nerve. Wonder why?

"Have you met Conrad North?" she asked.

"No. I've not had the pleasure."

Geary scratched her forehead and glanced off to one side of the office. Like she was looking at the watercolors. Or buying time.

She took a deep breath and said, "How can I help you?"

"Annie North. I'd like to know more about her. I'd like to know about the woman. Who she is, what's she's like. I know she married Conrad when they were young, and that they had two sons. But that's about all I know."

Geary leaned forward again, but she was more relaxed this time. Some of the tension was gone.

When she didn't respond, I tried a different question. "How did you meet her?"

"Here," she said. "At the bank. She needed help. Her accounts were complicated to set up. Annie wasn't just young when she married Conrad, Mr. Russo, she was a kid. He was handsome, rich, well-known. Annie was taken with his style, his life, his charm."

I've heard that before.

"Apparently she wasn't charmed for very long, since they divorced a year after Wilhelm was born. That was '74 or '75. She left Chicago . . ."

"Lake Forest."

I nodded. ". . . and moved here in '75 or '76."

"1976."

"She had an apartment."

"She bought a condo. On the river."

"To be closer to her sons."

"It didn't quite work out that way," Geary said. "Conrad worked hard at turning the boys against their mother. Then along came Camille. Lake Forest quickly became uncomfortable, almost unlivable. Living here, she seldom had to deal with any of that."

"A reliable source told me that she developed a reputation as a party girl after she moved here. That sound right to you?"

Geary laughed. "If by 'party girl' you mean she was single and met other singles at one bar or another, then I guess the answer is yes. Traverse City may seem big to you folks up north, Mr. Russo, but it's still a small town. We meet to eat, drink and talk because, well, it's what we do after work. Nothing wild or crazed about that. It's how you meet people if you're new in town. Annie joined in like the rest of us. That's all there was to it, I assure you."

You know lots of details, Ms. Geary. I wonder . . .

"Did you know Annie well?"

Geary clasped her fingers together and rested her chin on her hands. She remained silent for a good minute.

"Ms. Geary?"

Small tears appeared at the corners of her eyes.

"I'm not trying to pry, Ms. Geary. I'm just trying to understand my case. I'm not sure if Annie North fits in or not, but I need to find out."

The tears rolled down her face slowly. "He killed her, Mr. Russo. I'm sure of it."

"Annie North?"

Geary nodded.

"Who killed her?"

Geary's eyes drilled me hard. "Who? Conrad North, that's who."

"There's no evidence to support that."

She shook her head. "Doesn't surprise me a bit. Conrad's too smart for that. The man covers his tracks. Or other people cover for him. Annie's dead, Mr. Russo. I hope I'm wrong. I mean, do people just disappear these days? Do they? Everybody's got a camera in their pocket. How do you just go away?"

"It's not easy," I said. "It'd take planning."

"Yes, it would." Geary's eyes went someplace, for a moment. "Annie's only plan was to be here." Geary pointed out the window. "She wanted a life, here, with friends, a comfortable place to live. Her plans were here, Mr. Russo."

I hesitated. "Were you and Annie partners, Ms. Geary?"

She reached for a tissue to dry her cheeks. "You couldn't get married in those days, Mr. Russo. Not here anyway. In Michigan. We kept our relationship quiet. Annie worried about my career. You know, if the bank found out. Only a few friends knew."

"Was Conrad aware of your relationship?"

Geary shrugged and wiped her eyes another time.

"Probably. Sometimes I thought we were being followed, but it was different in those days. Maybe I was paranoid. I have friends who are harassed all the time. It's a little easier today. I don't know."

"Would he have been annoyed?"

"About us?"

I nodded.

"Conrad would've hated that Annie found love at all, Mr. Russo. But with a woman? Can you imagine him saying, 'My wife left me for another woman?'" Geary was animated as she talked, with just a hint of a satisfied grin. "Can you imagine him explaining that to his buddies?"

"Or his sons?"

She nodded. "Or his sons, yes. He used me as a wedge."

"You sure about that?"

Her face was serious, stern. "You want me to run off a litany of vile words they used when I ran into them? I could start with 'lesbo' if you like. Or 'dyke.'"

"No," I said, putting my hand in the air, palm out. "I'm sorry for the question. Seems clear Conrad knew about you and Annie."

Geary picked up a pen and began tapping the desktop. She glanced at the watercolors, then back at me. "You're not looking into Annie's disappearance, are you?" she said, moving the conversation back to an earlier place.

"No."

"Why not, Mr. Russo?"

"I was hired for a specific reason." We'd already covered this ground, but Geary was obviously in pain. It was her partner who'd disappeared, after all. And she was quite certain her partner was dead.

"But if you learn something about Annie . . . while you're working on the other matter, I mean. You'd tell me, wouldn't you?"

I nodded. "Right after I tell the police."

I asked a few more questions about Annie's life in Traverse City, how she spent her time and with whom, but I'd gone about as far as I could.

"Thank you again, Ms. Geary, for seeing me on such short notice."

She stood up and we shook hands. "Good-bye," she said.

16

I stopped on the sidewalk in front of the bank. The clouds hadn't gone anywhere, but the wind had picked up. Still no sign of rain.

Patricia Geary couldn't help me with Camille's problems, but I'd learned that Annie seemed to be a pleasant woman, not unlike Camille. Both of them were damaged by their association with Conrad.

Geary also confirmed the portrait of North I'd painted. I'd like nothing better than to stumble on more information about Annie North's disappearance, solid information that would solve the mystery for the cops and bring resolution to Patricia Geary.

I pulled out my iPhone and texted AJ. In a moment, my screen lit up: "at horizon." I put away my phone for the short walk down Front Street to Horizon Bookstore.

Over the years, I've sharpened my investigating skills as surly as I trained for Karate or practiced on the shooting range. I would say the same thing about working hard in law school. It got me a good job with a white-shoe firm in Birmingham before I struck out on my own in Petoskey. Some skills develop from experience.

But some skills come without training or practice. Like trusting my instincts. I've learned that when my gut and my head are in conflict, I should trust my instincts. If I did that, I came out all right. If I didn't, well . . .

I'd only walked a short distance, not half-way to the bookstore, when the first small jolt hit my gut. No mistake. I felt it.

Someone was watching me.

I've been followed before and I know how to spot the tail, even good ones. I had no reason to suspect a tail. That's the thing about gut instincts. Reason doesn't help.

Whoever it was knew I was in the bank. Did he follow me there, assuming it's a man? Or did he know where I was going? Either way, he had me now.

I kept moving at the same pace, like nothing had changed, but I stopped at the window of the Grand Traverse Pie Company like I was trying to see how busy the place was. I glanced over my shoulder, back where I'd come from. Nothing. Nothing obvious anyway. I started up again and glanced across the street. Nothing.

I went into Horizon Bookstore. The main floor of the two-story building revolved around a large, square sales counter in the middle of the room. It was surrounded by tables and shelves, all stuffed with books. A meeting area was tucked into the rear of the store, and a small coffee bar took up space near the front door. AJ was off to one side, in the fiction section, with a hardcover in her hands.

I walked up to her. "Hi," I said. "We've got a problem."

She looked at me for a moment. "Okay," she said slowly, and closed the book.

I took the book out of her hands, opened the cover like I was interested, and told her of my suspicions.

AJ picked another book off the shelf and opened it. "You only have one case, dear," she said. "So who would it be?"

"Well, it's not Conrad North or his sons. They couldn't follow a horse down Main Street. They'd be too easy to spot."

"You haven't spotted anyone?"

"Not yet," I said. "Tried on the way here, but no."

"Your instincts are usually right, Michael. This isn't an amateur."

I nodded.

"Then it has to be Miller," AJ said.

I nodded again.

"Wasn't Henri watching him?"

"That was the plan, yeah."

"Give him a call."

"Let's go over by the window," I said, and pointed toward the coffee bar. AJ put the two books back on the shelf.

We walked to the front window and stopped at a small table. AJ sat facing the street, I watched the front door. I took out my phone and punched Henri's number.

"Russo?" Henri said.

"Where are you?"

"Seabiscuit. A nice booth by the window with Margo and two glasses of wine."

"Where's Miller?" I said. "Still on the island?"

Henri was quiet for just a moment. "Why are you asking?"

"He's tailing me," I said.

"Tailing you?"

"Yeah. He give you the slip, Henri?"

"You on the island?"

"Traverse City. Front Street with AJ."

"Traverse?" That caught him off guard. It didn't happen very often. "Sure it's Miller?"

"Haven't seen him yet, but he's here."

"You have to find out."

"Yes."

"You said AJ's with you?"

"Yeah. We're in Horizon Bookstore."

"Run a two-man on him," Henri said. "He'll have to follow you."

I put my phone away and said, "You up for a little cops-and-robbers?"

"It's your call," she said.

"I'm gonna walk out of here. If I'm right, he'll follow me."

"Even if he knows I'm here?"

"He'll go with me. He has no choice."

"So I wait a little and see if I can spot him watching you."

I nodded, apparently with a quizzical look on my face.

"Once a beat reporter, always a beat reporter," she said. "Tell me what he looks like."

I described Miller in as much detail as I could remember.

"Funny," she said.

"What is?"

"Other side of the street."

A pedestrian walkway crossed the street in front of the bookstore. Two benches sat near the sidewalk on the far side.

"What about it?"

"A guy on the park bench," she said. "Blue jacket."

I moved my chair to get a better look.

"Is that your guy?"

"Could be," I said. "Right build, blond hair."

"Only one way to find out," AJ said.

"Yep."

"How far are you going?"

I shrugged.

"Fustini's is two blocks from here," she said. It was a specialty shop, featuring vinegars and oils. "How 'bout that?"

I must have had that look again, because AJ smiled and said, "I remember the old days. We used to do shit like this all the time, Michael. Only we wanted to catch Councilman so-and-so with the bad guys."

"Should be far enough," I said. "Want some basil olive oil?"

"Go," she said.

I got up. "I'll stop at least two times. Ought to make it easier for you."

"Okay. Buy the oil," she said. "I'll meet you at Amical."

"You're thinking about dinner?"

AJ almost looked irritated. "You're the one not thinking. The bar's in the front window. With a wide open view of the sidewalk."

I chose not to say another word and went for the door.

The *Idiot's Guide for Private Eyes* says if you want to spot a tail, you can't act like you're trying spot a tail. I walked casually down the sidewalk, making two stops along the way for window shopping. I might see Miller, I might not. It was AJ's job to spot him. If he stopped when I did, all the easier for AJ.

Before I arrived at Fustini's, my cell buzzed and I took it out. It was Henri. It would be perfectly normal to stop on the sidewalk, at least for a minute, and take the call. And a good opportunity to glance around without arousing suspicion.

"Talk to me, Henri."

"He left the island."

"Permanently?"

"No. Had a look around his apartment."

"You bust in?"

Henri ignored my question. "He's still living there."

I casually looked around as if I had nothing better to do while chatting on the phone. One guy a few doors down might have been Miller. The jacket was the right color.

"How'd you miss him?"

"Don't know yet," he said. "But I will."

"Okay."

"I'll let you know," he said, and clicked off.

I went into Fustini's and bought a bottle of basil olive oil. A light rain had started by the time I made my way back up the street toward Amical. I walked quite deliberately this time, and saw no one who looked like Miller. AJ was sitting on a barstool in the front window of the restaurant when I came through the door.

Amical had been on Front Street since the mid-nineties. A small, cozy bar occupied the front of the room. Tables filled the long, narrow space all the way back to large windows overlooking the bay.

I handed AJ the Fustini's bag.

"Thanks," she said, and pointed to glass of Chardonnay on the bar. "For you."

I sat down, picked up the glass and tipped it toward AJ. "Thanks," I said, and sipped some wine. "Well?"

"Mr. Blue Jacket, from the bench?"

"Yeah?"

"He's our man."

"No shit."

"You weren't out of the bookstore ten seconds, he started down the sidewalk. On the other side of the street." AJ drank some wine. "I waited a little, but I figured it had to be our guy. He sure didn't expect anyone following him. I got a good look. Baseball cap and long blond hair. I watched him from this side. It was a cinch. When you stopped for the phone . . . was that a real call?"

I nodded. "Henri. Tell you in a minute."

"He stopped when you did. He pretended to browse in store windows," AJ shook her head, "but he watched you. When you went into Fustini's, he waited." AJ shrugged. "That's when I decided it was time for wine," she said, and picked up her glass.

"I wonder if he followed me back here."

AJ smiled. "He's over there," she said, and pointed across the street. "Trying to keep dry."

I turned on the barstool. Miller was in a doorway across the street, trying to stay out of the rain and out of the way of customers. He moved slowly two doors down and did the same thing.

"Hard to be invisible," she said, "especially when it's raining."

I turned back to AJ. "You should have been a PI. Have I told you that?"

AJ nodded. "More than once," she said. "I take it as a compliment, but one of us is enough."

The maitre d' walked up. A thin man with a thin face, in his thirties, wearing skinny black pants and a mauve shirt, untucked. "Your table is ready," he said, gesturing toward the middle of the room. He walked away. We took our wine and followed him.

We sat at a two-top thirty feet from the front door. I sat with my back to the wall. We were close enough to see Miller if he came through the door, far enough away to enjoy our dinner even if he did.

"Do you think Miller'll come in the restaurant?"

I shook my head. "Not if he's careful."

A waiter stopped at our table. "Good evening. I see you have wine," he said. "Let me tell you about our specials this evening."

After the waiter left, AJ said, "Why is Miller following us?"

"It's me he's following," I said. "You happen to be with me."

"Okay. Why's he following you then?"

I shrugged. "I'm on the island, it's easy to figure. Maybe Petoskey, but here?" I shrugged again, like I thought it would help.

"What'd Henri have to say?"

"Miller got off the island under the radar. Henri missed him."

AJ shook her head. "Unusual for Henri."

"Yes, it is."

"You think he's pissed off?"

"Guaranteed."

Our waiter returned.

"The Alaskan halibut for me," AJ said.

"Roasted chicken, please," I said.

"An appetizer or salad for either of you?"

We both said no, and he left the table.

"Chicken? Really, Michael? You never order chicken out."

"Sounded good. Besides . . ." My phone buzzed in my pocket. "Hold on a second," I said. "It's Henri." I got out of my chair and went to the bar so I could see across the street.

"What'd you find out, Henri?"

"Miller gave me the slip when I went to meet a prospective tenant. For the apartment he didn't take, for crissakes."

"You ask around on the dock?"

"Yeah. Miller caught the first boat this morning."

"You think he knew I'd found Geary, or was he just following me?"

"Not sure it matters," Henri said. "Either way, he tells North."

"So North figures I'll find Geary at some point."

"And learn more about him. Maybe learn too much," Henri said. "Geary say anything interesting?"

I told Henri about my conversation with Patricia Geary.

"I think North figures the more you know, the more dangerous you are. Where are you?"

I told him.

"Can you still see Miller?"

I looked up and down a rainy Front Street as best I could from inside Amical. No sign of Miller.

"Where's your car parked?"

I told him.

"He'll watch your car," Henri said. "He knows you'll end up there sooner or later, and it's better than standing in the rain."

"Okay, thanks."

"Russo? Be careful in the parking ramp. Easy place for an attack."

"Okay," I said, and clicked off.

Our dinners were on the table when I sat down.

"Glad you started eating," I said.

Our waiter came to the table immediately and lifted a stainless steel cover from my plate. I dug in.

"Chasing bad guys with you makes me hungry," I said.

"Stop with the smart-ass routine long enough to tell me what Henri said."

I did, and finished with, "How's the halibut?" AJ looked at me a little impatiently to say the least.

"Henri's right about one thing, Michael."

"Only one thing?"

"Will you please shut up."

I nodded. "Sorry."

"Look, Michael, you know a lot about Camille, about Conrad."

I shrugged. "So . . ."

"The more pieces you have, the . . . the . . . like Henri said, Michael, you're more dangerous."

I took my eyes off what remained of my tasty chicken.

"Be careful of Miller, will you?"

I put my fork on the plate. "Chicken was a good choice for dinner, even if I do say so myself."

"Michael?"

"Yes, darling?"

"Don't 'darling' me, Michael. Miller's gonna make a run at you."

"Yes."

"Tonight?" she said.

I thought for a minute while I ate more roast chicken. "Maybe. But I doubt it'll be during the ride home."

AJ started to say something, but I cut in. "Most people can't drive a car like the movies. Takes a lot of practice."

"Like when you take your car to racetracks downstate?"

I nodded. "Exactly like that. If he comes at us, it'll be here or at home." I ate the last of my dinner and picked up my wine. "He'll count on surprise."

The waiter put the check down and I dropped a card on the tray.

I thought about how Miller would come at us.

"On the other hand, if he knows we're on to him, he might not try at all."

"Meaning what?"

"I have an idea," I said. "Come on."

I zipped my coat and we left Amical. The rain was lighter, but still coming down. AJ pulled up her hood and put her arm through mine.

"Let's go over to State Street."

"Okay," she said. "Any particular reason?"

"Yeah," I said as we walked. "Miller might be in the parking ramp, but if he's following us . . ."

We turned on State, walked a half-block, then cut back toward Front Street on Park.

"Sure is fun," AJ said. "Whatever it is we're doing in the rain."

We moved faster. "Soon as we turn the corner, duck into the Run Fit store."

Through the doors we went. "Away from the windows. Let's see if he's back there." The sales clerk said "hello" and went back to texting. We stood behind a rack of exercise clothes on sale.

We didn't have to wait long. Miller turned onto Front Street a few seconds after we dropped into the store. He stopped and glanced around, trying to find us on the street.

"Wait here," I said. Miller was still on the sidewalk when I bolted through the door and stood in front of him.

"Evening, Gunnar."

Surprised him. I saw it in his face.

"Nasty weather tonight, don't you think? Want to come inside where it's warm?"

I watched his hands, but they didn't move any more than the rest of him.

I moved in closer. "Tell you what, Gunnar. When we're done here, we go to the car and back to Petoskey. I'll take the Kalkaska road and 131. That make it easy enough for you?"

Miller's hands were still in sight. Without a word, he turned away from me and went back around the corner.

"See you, Gunnar."

AJ came out of the store. "You should have told me you were gonna do that."

I turned toward her and put my hand on her arm. "Didn't know what I was going to do 'till I did it. Seemed like a good idea."

"What if he'd pulled a gun?"

I shook my head. "Street's busy, rain or no rain. He's been careful so far."

"Let's go home," she said, and we started down the sidewalk.

We found the 335 in the parking ramp and got in. I pulled out on State Street, hit the wiper switch and headed for U.S. 31 out of town.

AJ changed the radio to Interlochen classical music and put the volume low. Traffic was light in both directions.

"What about Miller?"

"We'll be all right," I said. "Miller won't try anything tonight. He knows we're watching."

"He won't make the same mistake next time, Michael."

17

"You really weren't worried on the way home?" Sandy said. I sat in the front office, in a chair by the window. Sandy was at her desk. It was a little after nine-thirty and a stiff wind blew rain against the glass.

"I was careful," I said. "Very little traffic all the way back. Would've been easy to spot him."

"I'm surprised you didn't stay at AJ's."

I shook my head. "Enough excitement for one day," I said. "Besides, she had a budget meeting first thing."

Sandy glanced at her screen. "Unlike you, who waltzed in here ten minutes ago. I suppose you got a run in this morning."

I nodded. "Thirty minutes of intervals," I said. "Just to get the blood moving."

"Figured a guy with a knife and gun would've taken care of that."

"You'd think."

Sandy got up and went to the antique walnut table near the door. She slid the carafe out of the coffeemaker. "Want some?"

I shook my head.

Sandy sat down with a fresh mug of coffee and took a sip. "I think North sent Miller to the mainland to see what you were up to."

"Me, too."

"You going to Traverse didn't matter," she said.

"It didn't?"

"No. You'd made yourself a big headache for North before Traverse City."

"What about Geary?"

"North knew you'd find her, sooner or later," Sandy said. "It's what you were doing in the meantime he couldn't predict."

"So he put Miller on me," I said. "Makes sense."

"Of course it makes sense," she said. "Would I make stuff up for the hell of it?"

I smiled and quickly added, "Of course not, Ms. Jefferies. Perish the thought."

"You bet your ass," she said. "When are you leaving for Mackinac?"

"Hoping to get rid of me?"

"Perish that thought, too," she said, with a heavy dose of sarcasm.

"Leaving in a few minutes," I said. "Rain gear's in my office."

"Are you going to see the godfather after you're finished with Camille?"

"You talking the movie or Joey DeMio?"

"Why do I put up with you? The pay's so-so, the hours are lousy . . ." Her voice trailed off. Good thing her mug had coffee in it. I could see it sailing by my head before it crashed through the front window. "I'll try again. Why would Joey acknowledge having hired Miller if his father didn't last time?"

I leaned forward in my chair, scratched the side of my face gently with the back of my fingers and said in a heavy voice, "Because I'll 'make him an offer he can't refuse.'"

"Out." Sandy's arm shot out, pointed at me. "Get out of here. Now. Before I quit, or, or, throw my mug at you. Go."

I kept my mouth shut, got up and went into my office. I put on my MSU-green Gore-Tex rain suit and grabbed my brief bag.

"I'm leaving now," I said. Sandy didn't look up from her screen. She busied herself at something. "Good-bye," I said at the door. Nothing. "Shoot a text to Henri, will you. Tell him I'm on my way." I opened the door. "Please."

"Boss," Sandy said.

I turned around.

"Take your gun."

I stayed at the door, holding it half open. "I don't think . . ."

"Boss," she said, and pointed to my office, slowly and gently this time. "The gun."

I let go of the door and walked to my desk. I kept a .38, a box of shells and a well-worn leather holster in the lower left drawer, right next to the tape dispenser. It was well-cared for and loaded. I unzipped my jacket and clipped it to my belt, left side.

"Okay," I said.

"Be careful, boss," Sandy said. "Call or text if I can help."

I went down the stairs and outside. I left my car in the lot behind the Lake Street stores, so I cut through Roast & Toast to avoid as much heavy rain as I could.

I got in, hit the start button and the motor growled to life. I slipped out of my jacket and dropped it on the floor in front of the passenger seat. I went up Bay, turned left at Perry Hotel and took Lewis over to 31. There wasn't much traffic in Bay View, but what little there was crept along like they'd never seen rain before. It opened up once I passed Oleson's Market, so I picked up speed. The wipers swept rhythmically across the window, barely keeping up with the rain.

Camille wasn't much help at our first and only meeting. She needed help, so I took the job. I'd learned about State Park leases, and Patricia Geary had given me some helpful details about Annie and Conrad. Now I needed context, information only Camille could provide. The whole picture was coming together, but it was still out of focus.

I cruised effortlessly through Alanson and Pellston despite the often heavy rain. By the time I reached the Straits the rain had let up, but the electric sign at the base of the Mackinac Bridge read "High Winds." It often said that, high winds or no high winds. In the foggy distance, I could make out a single line of cars and trucks snaking its way up the northbound lane. No need to hurry. I'd given myself plenty of time. A lesson learned long ago.

Back to Camille. What did she know about Conrad's business affairs? Anything? She had to have opinions about Annie. What of Nicole? Was she interested in the bluff house, or would she maintain her detachment from all things Mackinac?

The parking lots on the dock were crowded, but not full. By the end of April, it'd be tough to find a space until all the ferries started running from here and Mackinac City. I parked the 335 away from other cars and walked to the dock. I sat in the back cabin on the upper deck of the *Huron.* Two women in their twenties, bundled up in heavy parkas, sat on the other side of the cabin. They busied themselves texting and sharing.

I thought about calling Joey DeMio's office, but talking to Camille first was more important. Whatever Joey might tell me about Ben Miller could wait.

The rain was steady and the wind still blew out of the west, but it didn't roil the waves. Not today anyway. The ferries out of St. Ignace hugged the west shoreline of the island, so it was easy to see the cottages in the Annex and on the West Bluff. Much easier than crossing from Mac City. Trees were still bare this early in the spring, so the view was even better.

The *Huron* was slow, taking more than double the time it takes other ferries to make the trip. I pulled a dog-eared copy of Robert Parker's *Early Autumn* out of a jacket pocket. Following the adventures of Spenser the private eye was a pleasant way to spend the extra time.

When the *Huron* rounded the west breakwater, it blasted its horn and slowed. I put Spenser away and put on my jacket. My traveling companions, phones in hand, hurried out of the cabin and down the stairs.

I spotted Henri on the dock. He stood under the overhang to keep out of the rain. His tan Carhartt coat was zipped and the collar turned up. His black cap with a bright orange Old English "D" above the brim was pulled down tight. I made my way off the boat and stood with him out of the rain.

"Michael," he said. "You taking a taxi to Baldwin's?"

"Thought I would, yeah. Maybe walk back down."

I pulled out my phone and called for a taxi. "Fifteen minutes, give or take," I told Henri. "Pickup at Seabiscuit."

"Let's go," he said.

I put up the hood of my parka and we started up the dock for Main Street.

The dock was jammed with carts filled with lumber or shingles or overstuffed chairs tightly wrapped in several layers of plastic, all waiting to be unloaded onto drays for delivery around the island.

"Do I have a welcoming committee?" I could usually count on one of DeMio's men waiting to tail me when I landed on the island.

Henri laughed. "Not this time, but he knows you're here."

"Of course he does," I said. "His people work the docks. He knew before the *Huron* left St. Igance."

We turned at Main Street, but had to walk in the street to stay away from scaffolding blocking eighty feet of sidewalk. Two men scraped the old clapboard siding two floors up, but the rain kept their paint cans tightly capped.

We entered the Seabiscuit Café and sat at the bar. The Seabiscuit was a square room with brick walls, a high ceiling and a large, heavy bar on one side. Big screen televisions and horsey memorabilia decorated the space. The place was busy but not crowded; that would come later, when the tourists arrived.

"Gentlemen," the bartender said. "What can I get you?" She was forty-ish, tall, with a square face and shoulder length brown hair.

"Coffee," Henri said. I nodded and held up two fingers.

"See anything of Ben Miller?"

Before Henri could answer, the bartender put two white mugs in front of us.

"I'm catching a taxi," I said, and put a ten on the bar. "Keep the change."

"Thanks," she said, and went back to drying wine glasses.

"Haven't seen him," Henri said, sipping his coffee, "but he got back first boat this morning."

"Probably stayed in the city last night after he was through with us." I drank some coffee and glanced out the window. "Think he knows I'm here?"

Henri shrugged. “He’ll sure as hell know when you show up at Baldwin’s. Don’t imagine Camille makes a move without Conrad getting an update.”

“Think Miller’ll make a move here?”

“On you?” Henri said.

“Yeah.”

“It’d be tough. No place to hide. Especially this time of year, one ferry running.” Henri shook his head. “Mainland’s a better bet.”

“I’ll keep that in mind.”

“How ‘bout we roust him?” Henri said. “Get his attention.”

“I got his attention last night,” I said. “That’s good enough for now. He tries something, I might change my mind.”

“Taxi’s here,” the bartender said, pointing out the front window.

I slid off the barstool and zipped my parka. “Time to go, Henri. See you later.”

“Let me know when you leave Baldwin’s.”

“Checking up on me?”

“Playing it safe,” he said.

18

I climbed aboard an empty taxi. Another benefit of the off season. Clear plastic blinds were tied down to keep passengers dry, and several wool blankets hung over the seats.

"Am I the only one going?"

"Drop you first," the driver said in a gruff voice. "Then I pick up." He was well covered in warm, heavy pants and coat. Only his bearded face peeked out from under a heavy hood.

The driver said something to his two-horse team I didn't understand, and off we went. He cut up Hoban, turned on Market Street, then up the hill. The shutters had been taken down at the Gate House, which was scheduled to open in a few days. We swung in front of Grand Hotel, scheduled for its "soft opening" this weekend, too, then up the West Bluff. Rain or no rain, workers busied themselves at the hotel and a few of the bluff houses.

We went left on Grand Avenue and into Hubbard's Annex, or just "The Annex." The area was created in the 1880s by Chicago native Gurdon Hubbard, who bought a large chunk of land and sold lots to wealthy friends. Like many of the original cottages, the Baldwin house was on the "Common," or park area.

The driver pulled up. Like the other cottages around it, Baldwin's was an ornate Gothic style with tall windows, peaks in the roofline and a long porch. It was built by Charles Caskey, builder of Grand Hotel.

I paid the driver and gave him a generous tip. As I walked up the stone path, Camille North came out on the porch with another woman just behind her.

"Michael," she said. "Hello." Camille wore black tights, a red poly turtleneck, black fleece vest and Brooks Addiction running shoes.

I climbed the four steps to the porch and shook hands with Camille.

"Michael, this is Althea Baldwin, a dear friend and my host." Baldwin was in her late seventies, five-one with short gray hair and a pleasant smile. She wore navy slacks, a camel V-neck sweater and Cordovan penny loafers.

"Welcome to 'Serendipity Cottage,'" she said, and shook my hand. Folks with huge buildings they referred to as cottages often gave them cute names only family members understood. The Baldwin choice appeared on a small carved wood sign that hung discretely above the front door. "Shall we go inside where it's warm?"

Althea Baldwin took my coat. We stood in a large foyer with a twelve-foot ceiling. Just ahead was a staircase and a short hallway to the back of the house. To the left was the living room, to the right a small parlor. Oriental rugs in muted shades of red, blue and green covered most of the wood floor.

"This way, please," Baldwin said, and we walked into the parlor. "Mr. Russo, there's ice and water over there," she pointed to a sideboard next to double doors that led outside, "and coffee in the silver service. Make yourselves comfortable. I'll leave you now."

"Thank you," I said.

Althea Baldwin smiled and left the room. Camille poured a glass of water and went to a settee with wood legs and upholstery that looked a lot like the Oriental rugs. I poured a cup of coffee and sat on a matching settee on the other side of a coffee table from Camille.

"Thank you for coming to see me, Michael," she said. "I've been across several times in the past few weeks. I need to be here for a little while."

"You're welcome, Camille. I always like my time on Mackinac." I sipped some coffee and said, "By the way, I'm just curious, are you a runner?"

She looked a bit surprised.

"Your outfit," I said. "Especially the shoes. People don't wear Addictions as street shoes."

"Unless they're retired running shoes," she said. "Do you know Ellie St. James?"

"She live at Woodbluff?

"She does. I'm helping her train for the Detroit Marathon. We're scheduled to go out later this afternoon. It's another reason to stay planted here for a while, if you know what I mean."

"Even if it's not in your house?"

Camille's shoulders sagged. "That would be my first choice, of course." She sipped some water and held the glass. "But I love the island, Michael, all of it. Besides, I've loved my time with Althea. We grew up here, you know, in the summers. I was much younger, so she didn't pay me much attention until college. We went to Bannister. You're familiar with Bannister College."

I nodded and smiled. Bannister was a small Liberal Arts school in Petoskey. I'd been drawn into some nasty business there a while back.

"Althea and I rode back and forth together, until our cottages closed for the winter." She put down her glass and smiled. "We've been good friends ever since."

"Did you and Conrad spend time with Althea and her husband?"

"That would be William Baldwin," Camille said. "William died, it must be fourteen or fifteen years ago now." Camille took a deep breath and let it out slowly. "No, William did not like Conrad."

"Did Conrad like Mr. Baldwin?"

"Conrad doesn't like anyone, Michael. He's quite judgmental. You don't make many friends that way." Camille leaned forward and put her elbows on her knees. "It doesn't help to make passes at their wives, either."

"Conrad made a pass at Althea?" I said, pointing in the general direction of the doorway as if she were standing there.

"She wasn't the only one." Camille looked down, as if to study the Oriental rug in front of her. "I'd call him on it. He'd behave for a while, but nothing changed, nothing ever changed."

I imagined rotten husband, Conrad, was fair game for gossip at the Mustang. Time to move on.

"What can you tell me about your husband's work?"

Camille shrugged. "Not much, I'm afraid. He never talked business when I was around. He said it didn't concern me, that he didn't want me to worry about such things." She shook her head. "Condescending bastard." Camille put her hands out, palms up. "I let it go. He really wanted to keep me away from his work. I knew that. He didn't want me to know anything about it."

"Did you know?"

"What Conrad did?"

"For a living, yes."

"The stock market. Gold, silver, that sort of thing. Family money. He didn't actually go to a job, if that's what you mean. He was trained as an engineer. Worked for, you know, Boeing, Lockheed."

"But not recently?"

Camille shook her head. "I don't pay much attention." There was an edge to her words. "Is this really important? Will this get my house back?"

Her voice mixed frustration and fear.

"I have to learn all I can about him, Camille. He covered his tracks with the lease. If I can figure out how he pulled it off, I'll have a better chance of changing things."

She leaned back on the couch, rubbing her eyes with both hands. "All right," she said, but it was not convincing.

"How does Nicole feel about all this? You said she didn't want anything to do with her father or her brothers . . ."

"Half-brothers," she said, with more than a touch of annoyance.

"Half-brothers, yes," I said. "Is she involved?"

"I'm not sure I understand."

And not happy I asked either. "Well, is Nicole interested in the fate of the cottage?"

"I don't see what . . ."

I sat forward. "Camille. Let me do my job. I'm trying to get your house back. I don't know how the pieces fit together. Hell, I'm not sure I *have* all the pieces. But I ask questions. That's how I learn things. That's how I help you."

Camille sat quietly. She stared in my direction, but she wasn't looking at anything in particular.

"Nicole has mixed feelings about our cottage. Her affection for Mackinac and our home is as strong as mine, but she detests Wolfgang and Wilhelm. They treat her like a whore, and she hates them for it. She wasn't shocked when I told her about the divorce. That was the first time she'd talked about the cottage in a very long time. About it being hers someday."

"Until the lease happened."

"She was angry, Michael, but she wasn't surprised Conrad would do that to me. Not surprised at all. I always said I wanted the cottage for Nicole. I wanted it to stay with the Sandersons."

"Conrad agreed?"

"Yes, he did," she said. "A long time ago, anyway."

"Was Nicole aware of that?"

Camille nodded. "Sure. But I never . . . we never talked about it. Not that I can remember."

"Does Nicole know I work for you?"

"I talked with my daughter before I called you, yes."

"I'd like to talk to Nicole," I said. "That all right with you?"

Camille nodded. "I'll give you her contact information." She reached for her phone on the coffee table. "Give me your email." I did, and she tapped a few times. "Done," she said, and put the phone down.

"Thank you," I said. "One last thing, Camille. What can you tell me about Annora?"

"Annie," she said, and offered a faint smile. "She was nice enough, I guess. I never had much contact with her. She didn't like me very much, to tell the truth."

"You know why?"

"She always believed I took Conrad away from her."

I waited. I didn't want to ask the obvious question.

"That was years ago, Michael . . . I don't know, maybe I was part of why they split up. Once Conrad turned her sons against her, well, she wasn't around much after that. I don't know."

There wasn't much more to ask. Not now anyway. I started to get up.

"Is Annie still missing? Have you heard anything?"

"No."

"Some people thought Conrad had something to do with her, you know, just vanishing like that."

"Do you think Conrad . . ."

"No, of course not," she said. "He's not capable, I mean, Conrad wouldn't do . . ." Her voice trailed off. She'd been asked the question before. She shook her head.

I got off the settee this time. "Thank you, Camille."

She stood. "You didn't call for a taxi," she said as we walked to the front door.

"The rain's let up. I'd rather walk down. Enjoy your run, and say goodbye to Althea for me."

"I'll do that. I hope to hear good news soon."

"Yes," I said as I went down the steps and walked toward Lakeview Boulevard.

19

I wanted to hear good news, too. And soon. I pulled up my hood and shoved my hands in the jacket pockets. The rain was lighter now, barely more than a heavy mist. I looked out as I walked along the bluff. A thin breeze ruffled the surface of the Straits, but the wind had played itself out. I turned into the trees and went to the top of Pontiac Trail, a narrow path that snakes its way in front of the West Bluff cottages, high above the water.

I came off the Trail onto West Bluff Road, and stopped at the overlook. I pulled out my iPhone and tapped Henri's number.

"Michael," he said. "On your way down?"

"Yeah."

"Any sign of Miller?"

"No."

"Good to hear."

"But I've been at Baldwin's. He'd be easy to spot out here."

"You calling DeMio?"

"Uh-huh."

"Want me to tag along?"

"To keep an eye out for Miller," I said. "Joey's no problem."

"You say."

I ignored him. "Later," I said, and clicked off.

I tapped Joey DeMio's office. Carlo Vollini picked up.

"It's Michael Russo. How you doing, Carlo?"

After a moment of silence, Carlo said, "What do you want?"

I thought about offering Carlo my usual repartee, but I wasn't in the mood. Carlo's never in the mood for it, which is why I liked to needle him.

"Your boss have ten minutes for me?"

"What do you want?"

I let it go, again.

"Let's start over," I said. "I'd like ten minutes with Joey. A few questions about the case I'm working on. That's all. I'm a short walk from your office."

I heard muffled voices – Carlo had covered his phone. After a few moments he came back on the line. "Be at Seabiscuit. Front door. Now."

"On my way."

I moved quickly down the West Bluff. In front of Grand Hotel, a small tractor and trailer sat at the curb while two men moved a load of shrubs to the grass. Other workers scurried around the hotel's gardens below the street level. In a few days, the grounds would be free of workers and ready for guests.

By the time I reached Market Street the mist had stopped, and I pulled off my hood. The rain or mist – or both – were sure to return. April in northern Michigan.

Santino Cicci. As soon as I turned on Astor Street, I saw him leaning on the doorway at Sander's, across from Seabiscuit. That meant Joey was close by. As I walked past him, Cicci raised his arm and moved away from the building. Gino Rosato stood at the curb in front of the restaurant. Even a casual trip downtown required DeMio's gunmen to tag along.

I arrived at Seabiscuit, and stopped. Rosato knocked on the glass. I saw Joey at the big round table just inside the front window. Carmine DeMio sat with him.

Rosato came over to me and said, "Wait right here."

I nodded.

Joey came through the door. He wore no coat, just a black V-neck sweater over a gray turtleneck and jeans. This was going to be a short conversation.

He pushed his hands into the jeans pockets. "Russo," he said. "Make it fast, we're watching the playoffs."

"Hockey?"

He tossed me a what-a-stupid-jerk look. "NBA."

I couldn't help myself. Had to needle somebody. "The *Pistons*?"

"*Bulls*," he said. "So? Why am I out here, not watching the game with my father?"

"Gunnar Lundberg. AKA, Ben Miller."

"What about him?"

"Carmine didn't tell me you knew Miller, that he'd worked for you."

"You didn't ask."

"Miller works for Conrad North."

DeMio nodded. "Can I go back to the game now?"

I don't remember Carmine ever being as annoying as his son. More often than not, Joey was a prick.

"You put North onto Miller?"

"Why do you care?"

A dangerous prick, but a prick nonetheless.

"Did North ask you for a shooter?"

DeMio glanced down Main Street, like he was expecting a taxi at any minute.

"Joey . . ."

He looked back at me.

"North needed a guy who could handle himself. Lundberg was available."

I put my hands on my hips. "Give me something, you're back to watching the game."

Joey hesitated, then said, "Lundberg on you?"

"You could say that."

DeMio turned and looked in the window, where his father sat watching us. Carmine nodded.

"Lundberg's good with a knife or gun."

"So I heard. What else?"

DeMio looked over my shoulder and nodded at Santino Cicci. I stepped aside and turned to watch Cicci cross the street.

"Sir?" Cicci said to DeMio.

"Santino, *che cosa sai* Gunnar Lundberg?"

Cicci nodded in my direction.

"*Si,*" DeMio said. "*Lui e dopo il nostro amico qui.*"

The two men continued to speak Italian, intentionally cutting me out. Felt like I was stuck in a Fellini film, but I waited, with my mouth shut.

"*Grazi,*" DeMio said, and Cicci returned to his post at Sander's.

"Lundberg's brother, Nils," DeMio said. "Taught Gunnar how to kill."

I nodded.

"If Nils shows up, the brothers mean to kill somebody, probably you."

"Okay."

"One more thing. Gunnar likes to attack daytime. No rainy streets at midnight. When you least expect trouble."

I started to say something, but I heard a whistle from behind me. DeMio heard it, too. It was Cicci. I turned in time to see Cicci nod down the block. By the time I looked back DeMio had turned around, as had Gino Rosato.

Coming down Main Street, walking right up the middle of the street, was Henri LaCroix. His coat was open, his hands at his sides.

"Gino," Henri said, offering a fake salute to Rosato. "Santino. How you doing?"

When he got close enough, Henri came toward DeMio and me.

Rosato moved closer, and Cicci started across the street.

Henri watched both men as he walked up to us and stopped. "Joey, my man. It's sixty-five and the sun's out in the Windy City. The hell you doing up here?"

DeMio put his hand up, palm facing outward, and his henchmen slowed.

Henri smiled and said, "What's the matter, godfather, you worried? About me?"

"Can we do something for you, soldier boy?"

Henri shook his head. “Not unless you want to rustle me up a bowl of whitefish chowder. Man, am I hungry. You and the boys want to join me?”

“Be nice to the gentleman, Henri,” I said. “He just gave me a couple of tips about Lundberg.”

“Is that right?” Henri said. “And all these years, Joey, I thought you read too many Mario Puzo novels.”

“Easy, Henri,” I said. The only thing holding Joey back was the small group of locals who'd gathered to watch our every move once Henri arrived on the scene.

“Michael my friend,” Henri said smilingly, “let's get some chowder.” He moved toward the front door. “This way.”

I followed him inside, stopping at Carmine's table in the window. “How the *Bulls* doing?”

Carmine shrugged. “They need Jordan.”

I nodded, then went to the far end of the bar and sat next to Henri.

“Joey was getting a little hot out there, Henri.”

“Couldn't happen to a nicer guy.” Henri smiled. “Unless it's Conrad North.”

The bartender came up and placed two coasters in front of us. “Afternoon, Henri. What'll it be, guys?”

“Whitefish chowder for two.”

“Hold on a second,” I said. “Nothing for me. The *Huron* leaves,” I looked at my watch, “in ten minutes. Don't want to be here all night.”

“Chowder for me then,” Henri said.

The bartender nodded and went down the bar. Joey had joined his father. Rosato and Cicci sat at other end of the bar, where they could watch us.

“Got enough time to tell me about Camille?”

I shook my head. “Send you an email from the boat. Any sign of Miller?” I asked as I got off the barstool.

“He's on the island. Saw him at the post office this morning. Don't think he's following you.”

"You don't think? That mean you don't know?"

"You don't pay me enough to tail the guy all day."

"I don't pay you anything."

"What I said."

"You kept me from getting killed a while back."

"Make sure I don't have to do that again, will you?"

"See what I can do," I said, and walked away.

I leaned in on Rosato and Cicci. "Fellas, don't bother to get up. I'm going to the boat. Not sure when I'm coming back. Want me to let you know?"

For some odd reason, Rosato and Cicci kept watching the game and paid no attention to me.

I stopped near DeMio's table. Joey and Carmine looked up.

"Joey," I said, and nodded.

Joey went back to his sandwich and the game.

I went through the door and headed for the dock.

20

I settled into a bench seat in the main cabin. People were tightly packed, holding coats, backpacks pushed under the seats. The rear cabin of the last ferry is usually filled with workers enjoying the trip across by playing cards and drinking beer. No such frivolity in the main cabin, but lots of talk about children, sports and better jobs.

I pulled out my iPhone and texted AJ. I didn't have to wait long for a response: "my house. wine chilled. pick up something for food." How could I refuse an invitation like that from the woman I love? Did I ever mention that she's smart, savvy, thoughtful, sexy and funny? Okay, so she never met a kitchen she liked unless it had to do with the décor. I tapped, "ok," then wrote Henri a brief email summary of my time with Camille. Henri might have an idea how the pieces fit together. My picture was still fuzzy.

My phone vibrated, and I looked at the screen.

"Hey, Henri," I said.

"You on the boat?"

"Yeah."

"Can you talk?"

"Hold on," I said, and went out the starboard door. The wind was cold and damp. I pressed up against the outside cabin wall as best I could. "Go ahead."

"Read your email. Call Nicole and get her take on this. Her mother, the cottage."

"Conrad, too?" I said. "And Patricia Geary?"

"Whatever she'll talk about. Camille didn't say much about Nicole 'till you asked. Wonder why?"

"Might not be a reason, Henri."

"Maybe."

"Camille knew Conrad was trouble, then the divorce became trouble. She might have wanted to keep her daughter out of it."

"One more thing," Henri said. "Miller's on the island. At least until the first boat in the morning."

"Good to know. Thanks."

I clicked off and went back inside the cabin. I pulled out Parker's book and returned to the adventures of Boston's favorite private eye. Maybe William Kent Krueger next, or Michael Harvey.

The *Huron* sounded its horn and slowed as we entered the harbor at St. Ignace. The evening trek to the deck below began as if signaled by the ship's horn. I suppose I'd be in a hurry to leave the ferry, too, if I'd worked all day. But I hadn't, so I waited.

I tapped AJ, "what sounds good to eat?"

"you decide," came back. Should have guessed.

The boat emptied out pretty quickly once it was tied up and the ramp was down. I made my way off the *Huron* and took the boardwalk along the water to the far parking lot. I kept a careful eye on people, even though Henri said Miller remained on the island. Just being careful. Once a gunslinger like Miller is involved, another one, especially brother Nils, could show up anytime.

I left the parking lot for the slow trip through town to I-75. Traffic was backed up at the toll booths, even the commuter lanes. I got in line, patiently waiting my turn. We were lucky on the bridge. The road narrowed to one lane for only a half mile. Traffic broke open after that.

The rain had started up again, but I knifed through the cars and trucks on 31, happily forgetting about Conrad and Camille and the house on the East Bluff. At least for a few minutes, I could think about AJ and me. Our lives were busy and interesting, so we didn't get much time together. Especially when I was on a case or she was working on a feature piece.

I turned off 31 near Conway and went the back way to Toski Sands Market for salads and a couple of sandwiches. It was 6:45 by the time I pulled into AJ's driveway. The rain was steady, but the air was warmer than in St. Ignace.

AJ opened the kitchen door. She wore baggy running shorts and a tattered white sweatshirt with with a huge "S" in the middle and paint stains, well, all over it. Her black hair was still shiny damp from the shower, and she wore no makeup.

"Hello darling," she said. "You brought food, I see."

Wait? What?

I leaned in and kissed her. "I take my assignments seriously, you know that." I handed AJ the large shopping bag. She put it on the kitchen counter while I hung up my coat and kicked off my shoes.

AJ took an open bottle of Chardonnay from the refrigerator and picked up two glasses. "Meet you in the living room."

The living room was a rectangle, with tall sash windows fronting Bay Street and one window looking out on the driveway. A red brick fireplace (it burned real wood) was on the opposite side of the room from the three-seat couch that held us. We had our feet on the coffee table.

Matching stuffed chairs framed each end of the coffee table. A small plate with chunks of Dubliner cheese and a few crackers sat next to our wine glasses.

I picked up my glass. "A toast."

"To anything in particular?" AJ said as she lifted her glass.

"Yes," I said. "To us. Let's enjoy our evening, and forget everything else for a while."

We touched glasses and sipped some wine.

"But you'll still tell me about Mackinac?"

"Sure," I said. "How about after dinner?"

AJ shook her head slowly.

"No? Not after dinner?"

"I plan to rip your clothes off and make mad, passionate love to you after dinner."

"Oh."

"'Oh?' Is that all you can say, 'Oh?'"

Think fast here. I drank a healthy gulp of wine.

"I meant, I wasn't thinking about making love, I . . ."

"There was a time, not so long ago, when making love with me was all you thought about, all you talked about."

Oops. I drank more wine.

"You used to tell me I sounded like a broken record."

"Well, yeah, I did say that, I guess."

"More than once."

"Uh-huh. But I've been, you know, thinking about you since I knew you were on your way home. You know, thinking about you."

"You were?"

AJ nodded.

"Do I get to rip your clothes off, too?"

AJ looked down at her baggy shorts and paint-stained sweatshirt. "If you want," she said. "This is all there is. I'm not wearing any underwear." She stood up and pulled the sweatshirt over her head, dropping it on the floor. "See?"

"I do see."

AJ stuck a thumb in each side of her shorts and pushed down. She took one step, then kicked the shorts in the air toward me.

She pointed up, toward the second floor. "Put the sandwiches in the refrigerator and follow me."

21

AJ was in the shower. I eased my way out of bed, put on nylon running pants and an old fleece jacket, and went down to the kitchen. I filled a large glass with water and drank half of it. I unwrapped the sandwiches, put them on plates, opened the salad containers and arranged everything on the counter.

AJ came into the room, walked up and kissed me. I kissed her back. She was wrapped in that oversized white terrycloth robe. Her hair was damp again.

"I forgot to ask what we're having for dinner."

"You had other things on your mind, I'm happy to say."

AJ smiled. "Yes, I did."

"Sandwiches are chicken salad, with lettuce and tomato."

I pointed at the salads. "Red-skinned potato salad and broccoli salad."

"You fix the plates here," AJ said. "I'll get the wine and napkins and meet you on the couch."

I added a generous portion of each salad next to the sandwiches on our plates, took them to the living room and sat next to AJ. I reached around the end of the coffee table and picked up her running shorts. "These yours?"

She grabbed the shorts out of my hand, folded them and put them behind her. "Wise-ass."

"Thank you," I said. "Always appreciate a compliment. How's your sandwich?"

"Very good," she said. "Thought I was hungry before, I'm really starved now." She picked up her wine and smiled. "Thank you, darling."

I picked up my glass and sipped some wine. We sat quietly for a few minutes, enjoying our food and each other.

“Are you ready to tell me about Camille now? Especially since it was my idea to talk to her.”

I could only nod because I was enjoying a huge bite of broccoli salad. By the time I’d polished off half the sandwich and most of the potato salad I had finished describing my time with Camille.

“So Conrad’s a skirt-chaser, huh?”

“Appears to be the case,” I said. “You must have been hungry, you’re almost done.”

“I’ve been eating and listening, darling. You’re the one talking.”

“True,” I said. “You know, I’m trying to figure something out.”

“What’s that?”

“Well, I’ve talked to Camille twice.”

“Your office and today?”

“Right,” I said. “She found me, AJ. She hired me to do a job, so why does it feel like pulling teeth to get her to talk? Doesn’t seem to matter what I ask.”

“She’s embarrassed, Michael. She lives in a very small place. People gossip.”

“Do people care that much? About her and Conrad?”

“They lived in a big house on the East Bluff. Their troubles are like reality television if you live in a very small place.”

I folded up my napkin and put it on an empty plate. “I guess so.”

“Her circle of friends is even smaller. Conrad hit on some of those women. Of course she’s embarrassed. Talking about it hurts. Then she lost the cottage and, well, she’s having a tough time, that’s all.”

“I haven’t been much help,” I said.

AJ reached out and touched my arm. “You’re doing your job, Michael. It’ll come together. It always does.” She leaned back and put her feet on the coffee table. “Think about Nicole for a minute.”

“What about her?”

“She can’t be very comfortable talking to her mother about any of this.”

“Because it’s still her mother and father?”

AJ nodded. “Nicole can despise Conrad all she wants, it doesn’t matter.” She tapped my arm. “Didn’t you tell me she knows about you, that her mother hired you?”

“Uh-huh.”

“Do you think she would be comfortable talking to you?”

I shrugged. “Don’t know.”

“I’m only guessing. But if I were writing this story, I’d call Nicole first thing in the morning and find out.”

“I can do that.”

“If nothing else, she ought to have plenty to say about Conrad.”

“I bet she would,” I said. “Be nice if it helped.”

“Maybe you’ll get lucky.”

I picked up our dishes and went to the kitchen. AJ followed me, napkins and glasses in hand, and we cleaned it all up.

“Darling,” AJ said, as she wrapped her arms around me. “Have you decided to stay with me tonight?”

“Haven’t thought about it one way or the other,” I said, putting my arms around her.

“Don’t worry. I’ll push you out early enough to get your morning run in.”

“You have something, ah, interesting in mind for us?”

AJ nodded. “*Out of the Past* is on in ten minutes. Robert Mitchum, Jane Greer.”

“Kirk Douglas?”

“Uh-huh. Corruption, betrayal . . .”

“And a private eye. Do I really need to watch a private eye?”

“Think of it as work prep for solving your case.”

“Work prep?”

“I have every confidence, darling.”

22

I sat in AJ's kitchen with a mug of coffee and a sliced banana. I'd eased my way out of the bedroom to let AJ sleep a bit longer.

I ate two slices of banana and opened my iPad to search Conrad North in the archives of the *Chicago Daily News* and the *Chicago Tribune*. I got several hits, but they were mostly civic or personal. His home in Lake Forest had made the city's annual home tour twice over the years. Searching his primary employers, Boeing and Lockheed, wasn't any more helpful. Typical public relations pieces on new government contracts, or awards for innovation in North's area of responsibility. I ran North's old family name, "Hoffmann." Very few hits this time, but one of them described a family vacation to visit old friends in, of all places, Mackinaw City.

"Morning, darling," AJ said, coming up behind me. She leaned down and kissed my cheek. "What're you doing?"

I explained what I was up to. She was wrapped up in that overgrown robe again.

AJ filled a mug with coffee and said, "Mackinaw City?"

"Uh-huh. Rented a cottage at Wawatam Beach. Know it?"

AJ nodded. "Interesting coincidence, isn't it?"

I looked up and grinned.

"How could I forget?" she said, and rolled her eyes. "This from the man who doesn't believe in coincidences."

"A little melodramatic, don't you think?"

"I must be groggy after you made mad, passionate love to me last night."

"You had pretty good game yourself."

"Of course I did," she said. "What'd it say about the people in Mac City?"

I shrugged. "Not much. Only a family name, Weber."

"The Mac City part bugs you, doesn't it?"

"Yes, it does. I emailed Sandy the article. She can check it out later." I finished the banana and drank some coffee. "I'm outta here in a few minutes. Want to do a short run before the office."

"Are you running alone?"

I nodded.

"Be careful, please."

"Nobody gets mugged in Bay View, AJ."

"Funny man."

"Not being funny. Bay View's a busy place in the spring. Somebody'd see an attack."

"Watch yourself anyway." She put her mug in the sink. "Time for a shower."

I grabbed her sleeve as she went by. She leaned in and kissed me. "I'll call later," I said.

I put our dishes in the dishwasher, got my coat and left by the kitchen door. I gave the backyard a quick glance as I beeped the door locks. The four block ride to my apartment was no different than any other morning, but I paid extra attention anyway.

There's a small antique dresser in my bedroom reserved for running gear. I changed into a pair of wind pants and a long-sleeved T without writing on the front. I pulled on an old, beat-up Spartans hat to help with the light rain. Once outside, I took the shortcut up Rose to Arlington to Bay View.

The Association is always as busy in April as it will be in the middle of July, but it's all maintenance and construction. Trucks were parked everywhere, in the street, on flat brown grass, in the alleyways. Fresh paint, new roofs, a new addition here and there. Running on the Association's streets was more difficult because of all the activity, but I was safer running here because of it.

Once I settled into a pace, I pushed out the clutter of daily life. With fewer distractions, it was easier to see a case, or its players, from a different angle, a helpful angle. More often than not, I discovered something.

This wasn't one of those times.

I took a hot shower, put on a fresh pair of khakis, a plaid button-down shirt and navy cotton crewneck. The rain finally blew itself out, so I only took a light jacket and my brief bag. It felt odd driving to the office, but I needed the car for an appointment in Charlevoix.

"Morning, boss," Sandy said, and handed me several messages.

"Good morning to you, too. Anything I need to do right away?"

"One thing requires your undivided attention," she said, pointing to the sideboard. "Over there."

"You stopped at Johan's."

"Wish I could claim credit," she said. "Henri dropped them off."

"Didn't know he was in town."

"He stayed with Margo last night. He's on his way to Gaylord. Said he'd call later."

I hung up my jacket and opened the Johan's box.

"You get the J-bun," she said. "I claim the cinnamon donuts. Both of them."

"Whatever you say."

"I should be so lucky," Sandy said, with more than a touch of sarcasm. "Don't forget Charlevoix."

I took coffee and a J-bun to my desk.

"Look through the green folder first. The Zielinski file," Sandy said from the doorway. "Then give her a call. You have anything for me?"

"As a matter of fact. Did you see my emails?"

"From Camille North? Her daughter's contact information?"

"That's the one."

"It's logged in," she said. "What'd you want me to do with that *Chicago*

Tribune article? I assume it has something to do with Conrad North's family."

"Dig around," I said. "Find out what you can about the family in Mackinaw City and their connections to the Hoffmanns."

"Okay."

"And see if you can get Nicole Sanderson on the phone."

"Will do," Sandy said, and went back to her desk.

My phone buzzed. A face with a kiss. That was AJ's not-very-subtle way of making sure I was okay after my run. I tapped back a thumbs-up.

I'd just finished the Zielinski file when Sandy came to the door. "Nicole Sanderson on line one. I wonder why she goes by Nicole 'Sanderson' and not Nicole 'North?' It's her father, after all."

"Maybe I'll ask her," I said, and picked up the office phone.

"Nicole, hello."

"Mr. Russo."

"I appreciate you taking the time. Please, call me Michael."

"Yes," she said. "What can I do for you?"

Not exactly warm and fuzzy, but workable.

"Your mother told you that I would call?"

"She did, yes. But she wasn't clear why you wanted to talk to me."

"I thought you might help me better understand what happened with your father and the lease."

"What do you mean 'what happened?' My mother lost the cottage, Michael. Isn't that why she hired you? To get the house back?"

"Yes," I said, "that is why she hired me."

"You've learned nothing, is that correct?"

This wasn't going well. Have to shift focus. Shift something.

"Nicole, I learn by asking questions. No one can explain how the cottage on the East Bluff went from your mother's name to your father's name without anyone noticing."

"Conrad North is my father, biologically, but that's the extent of it. Keep that it mind, please."

Well, that explained why she went by "Nicole Sanderson." Great. Let's see if I can antagonize her more.

"Nicole, I will find out how the names got switched. I'll find out because that's what I do. I hope we get your mother's name back on the lease, but I can't guarantee that will happen."

"So I gather."

Shit.

"Nicole, I'm not trying to pick a fight. You don't know me from a hole in the ground, but your mother didn't hire me until after she'd done her homework."

I waited for a response that didn't come. Like mother, like daughter. I tried again.

"Talk to me for a few minutes, will you, please? Help me understand all this from your point of view. You're detached from the island. From your father, from the house, even from the divorce."

I waited this time. Why not?

Nicole's voice was softer when she spoke. Not much, but enough. "Do you really think mother will get the cottage?"

"I won't lie to you, Nicole, I just don't know. But I'm a long way from quitting, a long way."

She paused, then said, "What would you like to know?"

"For starters, did you expect to inherit the cottage?"

"Of course I did."

"But your half-brothers?"

"My mother meant the cottage for me, not them, not the three of us. But that's a moot point, isn't it? My attorney tells me I got screwed right along with my mother."

"You're angry about that?"

"You're goddamn right I'm angry. For me, for my mother." Her voice trailed off. She was lost in a thought, far away from our conversation. She went quiet again.

"I left for Princeton at eighteen and didn't go back home," she said at last. “Not to Lake Forest, or to Mackinac. Chicago’s been home for a long time. My life is here.”

Sandy came into the office quietly and put a sticky note on my desk. “Camille,” it read. Sandy pointed at the desk phone. The light for the second line blinked quietly. I mouthed “two minutes” and Sandy left the office.

“Nicole, do you have any plans to visit the island?”

“None,” she said. “I have plans with my mother for a long weekend here next month. But that’s it.”

I tried to finish the call on a hopeful note, but Nicole wasn’t having any of it. Her trust in me was limited by circumstances and geography. But she could have hung up on me. Might as well be grateful for small victories.

“Sandy,” I said, without leaving my desk. “Camille still waiting?”

“Line two, boss.”

I picked up the phone and punched the button. “Camille? Sorry, I was on with Nicole.”

“You didn’t answer your cell, Michael. I need to talk to you.”

She never heard (or perhaps didn’t care) that I’d been talking with her daughter.

“Go ahead, Camille.”

“No, I’m . . . not sure this works.”

“What works? I don’t understand.”

“The phone.”

“What about the phone?”

“I only have a cell.”

I wasn’t sure where she was going. Unless . . .

“You think someone’s listening in?”

“I just don’t want to take any chances, you know. This is important.”

“All right,” I said. “How should we do this?”

“Come to Althea’s.”

“I have to be in Charlevoix this afternoon, Camille. Too late to make the last ferry.”

"Tomorrow?"

"Will you be all right 'till tomorrow?"

"Certainly, Michael," she said. "I'll be fine. I would rather talk about this in person, that's all."

"I can be on the first boat."

"I'm going out with Ellie in the morning. Seven miles."

"Around lunchtime, then," I said. "Will that be okay?"

"Fine, Michael, that'll be fine. Until tomorrow."

I said good-bye and put the phone down.

"She okay?" Sandy said.

I nodded. "Yeah. She thinks her cell isn't safe."

"Nobody's cell is safe."

I shook my head. "She meant her phone."

"Somebody's listening?" Sandy said. "Conrad?"

I shrugged. "Suppose I'll find out tomorrow."

"Has to be him."

"Did Henri say when he'd head back to the island?"

"Didn't sound like today."

I picked up my cell and texted Henri.

My phone buzzed right back. "Hey, Henri."

"What's up?"

I told him about Camille's call.

"Thought if you were home, you could check on her."

"Sorry," he said. "Margo's got some free time, so I'll be down here for a few days. Think Camille's in trouble?"

"Same old trouble would be my guess," I said. "But she insisted we talk in person."

"Let me know if she has anything new."

"Will do."

"Margo and I are eating in Harbor Springs. Seven o'clock at The New York. Want to grab your favorite editor and meet us?"

"Yeah," I said. "Pretty sure AJ's free."

Sandy rapped on the doorjamb. She pointed at her wrist as if she wore a watch.

"Have to go, Henri."

"Shoot me a text if you need to," he said, and clicked off.

"You can't be late," Sandy said. "Zielinski's a paying client."

"Yes, she is." I put the green folder in my bag, took my coat and left the office.

23

Cruising the Lake Michigan shoreline on U.S. 31 from Charlevoix to Petoskey is never a speedy trip. Even if I try. It's usually quicker in the off-season, but this ride back from Charlevoix felt more like June than April. Too much traffic, all of it moving sluggishly. The season starts earlier every year.

I told AJ that I'd pick her up for dinner in Harbor Springs, so I returned the car to the parking lot behind the office. I found several empty spots. I took my coat and brief bag off the passenger seat and opened the door.

Crack.

The door's window caught me in the side of the head. Hard. The door was closed again.

"What the . . ?"

I looked out the side window and got an eyeful of somebody's belt buckle and a 9mm automatic. Ben Miller. And another man.

The door opened a few inches, but I didn't do it.

"Get out, asshole," Miller said. "Slow." He opened the door and I came out slow, just like he said. Miller grabbed my bag and coat, threw them back in the car and slammed the door. He then slipped the gun into a big side pocket of his jacket, but left his hand there. I assumed the knife was hooked to the back of his jeans.

The other man was tall, had to be six-six, trim and dressed in an expensive two-piece black suit covered by an equally expensive charcoal topcoat.

Conrad North.

"You know who I am?" he said.

"The meter maid in better clothes?"

Miller swung sideways from the hip, his elbow catching my solar plexus. The blow knocked me back against the car, and I gasped for air. I wrapped my arms around my abdomen like it might help. It didn't.

"Mister Russo," North said, stretching out both words. "Shall we try again?

I glared at North. I tried to see if it was just the two of them.

"Mr. Russo?" he said again.

I nodded. Didn't have another option.

"Answer the question. Do you know who I am?"

I loosened the grip on my midsection and stood straighter. I had just enough air to talk evenly. "Conrad North."

"Indeed I am, Mr. Russo, indeed I am. I believe you know my associate?"

"We've met."

Miller grinned. He was enjoying himself. Never a good sign.

"Do you know why we've dropped by to see you this afternoon?" North said.

"They threw you off the island?"

North grabbed Miller's arm before he could swing. The older man shook his head, like a father disappointed yet again by his idiot son.

"Mr. Russo, must you act stupid? You're not that tough."

"Neither are you."

North looked away, and Miller's left fist crashed into my ribs. I slid down the side of the car and sat on the tarmac. Not having enough air was suddenly becoming an issue.

"Stand him up," North said with disdain. Miller lifted me off the ground. He pushed me hard against the car door. He leaned in and held me there with a stiff arm, exerting all his body weight. For just a moment, Miller was off balance, vulnerable to the right move, but I struggled just to keep steady.

"Go ahead, Mr. Russo," North said. "Try it. I can see it in your eyes.

You're looking for an edge, a way, any way." North shook his head, and smiled. "There isn't one."

North gestured at Miller, and he took his arm away. I stayed on my feet, but it wasn't easy.

"We need to have a little chat, you and me."

"Is that right?"

"Indeed it is."

I was tired of the guy already, and we'd just met. Imagine how Camille felt?

"What'd you want, North?"

North slipped his hands into the pockets of his topcoat. "My wife, Mr. Russo."

I waited.

"Stay away from my wife. Do not contact her again."

I didn't respond. Wonder if he remembers Camille's name?

"It's over, Mr. Russo. Do I make myself clear?"

I stayed quiet.

"Do I have to do this again?"

He took in a lot of air and let it out slowly.

"One more time then. Stay away from my wife. Am I making myself clear?"

I nodded toward Miller. "Why'd you bring Gunnar into this? To fuck with tourists?"

North smiled. "No, Mr. Russo. He's here to fuck with you. Stay away from my wife, or I will have him kill you."

Miller smiled and caught me with another fist to the midsection. Should have seen that one coming. I slid down the car to the tarmac. Again.

North and Miller stepped back, paused for a moment to look at me, then turned and walked away. They were out of sight by the time I pulled myself off the ground and leaned against the car. My ribs would be sore for a few days, but Miller hadn't done any real harm. Joey DeMio had warned me Miller liked to attack during the light of day. Too bad I didn't listen.

I took a few deep breaths to move air to sore muscles. I reached in the car for my bag and coat and walked slowly to the office.

24

"He really said that?" Sandy asked. I sat in a chair in the outer office with a bottle of water and a very sore midsection.

"He hired a gunslinger because of you?"

I swallowed some water, wishing it were a single malt. "That's what he said."

"Sure you don't want me to take you to the emergency room? Just to play it safe."

I shook my head. "Been hit before. I'll be all right in a couple of days."

"Okay. But if that grimace on your face doesn't go away, I'll insist."

I nodded. "Fair enough."

"Something must have changed, boss. Following you around's one thing. Punching you out's a lot different."

"I wasn't exactly 'punched out.'"

"Oh, yeah? How're the ribs?"

"They've felt better."

"Uh-huh. Want some aspirin?"

"Maybe later," I said. "I'd rather hear about the *Chicago Tribune* piece."

"Ah, yes. Summer vacation at Wawatam Beach."

Sandy hit a few key strokes and settled back in her chair. "Lord love the internet," she said. "And Google. Did you know that Father Marquette went to Mackinac Island . . ."

"Does Father Marquette have anything to do with the Hoffmanns?"

"No, but . . ."

"Get on with it, Sandy. You're talking to a man with sore ribs."

She put her hands in the air. "Okay, okay. I'll start again. I tried different combinations, you know, played around, using 'Hoffmann' or 'Weber,' that's the name of the other family, or 'Mackinaw City.' As it turns out, the Hoffmanns spent quite a few summers at the Beach Association. Conrad would've been a kid."

"How 'bout the Webers?"

"Emil and Lena Weber, yeah. Lived in Chicago. That's how Emil and Conrad knew each other. It's unclear if they met in the Windy City or in the old country. In any case, Weber goes to Mac City, so does Hoffmann. Weber eventually bought a cottage at Wawatam Beach. Hoffmann rented each summer."

"Weber have kids?"

"Three, two daughters and a son," Sandy said, scrolling with her mouse. "Helene, Lara and Rolf, born a few years apart. They'd all be in their mid-sixties. Rolf's the oldest."

"Close to Conrad's age," I said. "Wonder if they all grew up together?"

"Seems likely, since the families were friends." Sandy tapped a few keys and scrolled again. "The Webers died a year apart. Her first. Rolf retired from state government, Department of Agriculture in Lansing. Nothing on the daughters."

"Think they're still alive?"

"Not sure, but I assume so. Their names are not on the Social Security Death Index."

"Could have married names."

"Yeah, but Social Security tracks that. As far as I'm concerned, the daughters are alive until proven otherwise."

"What do you make of the Webers and Hoffmanns?"

"It's a little hazy. Emil and Conrad had business dealings, that's for sure."

"What was Emil's work?"

"Let's call it 'import-export' for lack of a better term."

"Ah, the always suspect 'import-export' business."

Sandy nodded. "It seems likely he supplied Hoffmann's company with something. Parts, money, workers: it's not clear. I don't know if it's all nice and legal, but it doesn't pass the smell test."

"That's not a lot to go on," I said, "but at least we've put Conrad North in the Straits area."

"Did Conrad meet Camille up here?" Sandy said.

I shook my head. "She taught school in Birmingham. They met down there."

Sandy nodded. "Okay."

"Keep digging about the daughters, what're the names again?"

"Helene and Lara."

"Yes, keep digging. The business connection, too."

"Because there's nothing else to do?"

"You're a cynic, you know that?"

"Yes, boss."

I stood up and quickly grabbed the back of the chair to steady myself.

"Want that aspirin now?"

I glared at Sandy, trying to look annoyed. "Yes, mother."

She shook two aspirin out of a plastic bottle in her desk and handed them over.

"Now go home. Take a hot shower, change clothes. You'll feel better."

I shrugged.

"You know I'm right. Go."

I picked up my coat and brief bag. "See you in the morning."

"Watch yourself in the parking lot, boss."

25

Sandy was right about the shower, especially a hot shower. I did feel better. Too bad I couldn't say the same for my ribs. Pulling a sweater over my head was, well, let's just say my ribs were yanked in awkward directions.

I texted AJ that I was on my way. I drove up Bay Street and pulled into her drive. AJ came out the kitchen door and climbed in.

"Hello, darling," she said, and leaned over to kiss me.

"It's nice you could leave work early," I said.

"I think so, too. We've had too many long days lately."

I went over from Mitchell to Division, then down the hill to 31 North. AJ asked me about Charlevoix, of course. I offered a brief description of my client appointment, but I put off any talk of my unscheduled appointment in the parking lot. I wanted to tell it only once, probably at dinner. We took 119, then Beach along the water into Harbor Springs.

The New York restaurant began life as a hotel run by the Leahy brothers in 1904. Still located at the corner of Bay and State Streets, it survived Prohibition and the Depression. By the late 1970s, it had evolved into a restaurant and bar serving tourists and locals alike. It featured two large rooms, with high ceilings, tall windows and an interesting menu.

Henri and Margo waited at a four-top in the front room. "Hellos" were exchanged all around. I noticed that Henri had exchanged his usual Carhartt coat for a black blazer to hide the shoulder holster.

Margo Harris was a trim five-eight, with a fair complexion, blonde hair cut to the neck and green eyes. Like AJ, she was dressed like a professional woman on a casual evening out: jeans, a sweater, and in Margo's case a dark leather bomber jacket.

"How long has it been?" AJ said.

"Since we've all had dinner?" Margo said. "Late February, I think."

"Good evening, ladies and gentlemen," our waiter said. "A drink this evening?"

Margo and AJ ordered wine, Henri a draft. Then it was my turn. "An Oban, neat."

After the waiter left, Henri said, "Tough day, Michael?"

AJ shot me a look from across the table. She'd picked up something in my behavior on the ride over. I'd winced at every bump and pothole in the road. Plenty of those in Michigan, after all. And AJ was ever the observant journalist. I didn't fool her one bit.

"Had some trouble this afternoon," I said.

AJ shot me another look. "In Charlevoix?" she said.

"When I got back."

No one said a word. Very unusual for this crew. I plunged ahead and told them about my parking lot visitors.

The waiter dropped off our drinks and took our order. Homemade lasagna for AJ and me, hanger steak for Henri and a beet salad for Margo.

I expected AJ to react first. She usually did when things got dicey. But it was Henri this time.

He leaned forward, put his elbows on the table and said, "Think I'll stick around a while longer." He touched Margo's arm. "If that's okay with you."

Margo put her arm around Henri's shoulder and kissed his cheek. "Of course, it's okay with me. But a question, Michael?"

"Yes?"

"I'm delighted to have my house guest stay on, but I'd like to know why these two gentlemen messed with you? Especially since Henri's about to jump in."

"Sure, Margo. But Henri, go home if you need to."

It was AJ's turn. "No, Henri, don't go."

"It's okay," Henri said. "I didn't want to go home 'till the end of the week anyway."

"Michael?" Margo said. "*S'il vous plait.*"

I gave Margo the short version of Camille, Conrad and the lease.

The waiter put our dinners on the table. We all stopped talking and dug in. After a few minutes, the initial hunger had passed.

"Sandy's right," AJ said. "Something must've happened."

"I think so, too," Margo said.

"It doesn't matter," Henri said.

"But it'd be nice to know what I did that pissed them off," I said. "In case we want to stick it to Conrad again."

"It was you," Margo said, "going to see Camille. On the island, I mean."

"But North knew she'd hired me."

"What Margo means, Michael," AJ said, "is that you invaded his territory. So to speak."

"Oh."

"Like I said, it doesn't matter," Henri said. "We need to be ready next time, that's all."

"Next time?" Margo said.

Henri nodded. "There was a first time, so there'll be a next time."

"Will it be more dangerous?"

"It usually is," I said.

"Henri?" Margo said.

Henri nodded slowly. "Michael's right."

We finished our dinners, and the waiter cleared the dishes.

"Didn't you say you were going across to see Camille tomorrow?" AJ said.

"I believe the operative phrase is 'invading Conrad's territory.'"

"Fuck his territory," Henri said. "How 'bout we invade his house? Set the old boy on the right path."

I started to laugh, "Let me see what Camille wants first, Henri. We can always roust Conrad another time."

"She didn't give you any idea what was on her mind?" AJ said.

I shook my head. "Only that she needed to explain it to me in person."

"That's not much to go on."

We paid the tab and left The New York. It felt a little more like spring had decided to show up. The air wasn't warm. It simply wasn't as cold as the last several days had been.

"Call me when you get back tomorrow, Michael," Henri said. "Watch yourself up there."

After a round of hugs and good-byes, Margo and Henri walked around the corner and AJ and I went for the car. I took Beach Drive through Wequetonsing Association on the way out of town. A mix of very big cottages and normal-big cottages lined the street on the bay. Shorter streets ran off Beach for a long block to Pennsylvania Avenue. They were every bit as ornate as the bluff houses on Mackinac.

"I love the big old houses," AJ said.

"Cottages, darling. We must call them cottages."

"Right," she said. "I always forget to do that."

"Not hard to see why."

AJ reached over and put her hand on my knee. "I always worry when a case turns ugly. I mean, it's okay, it's what you do. I just . . . I'd love to have you stay tonight, darling," she said. "But . . ."

"Early meeting?"

"Yeah. Sorry."

"It's all right," I said, and squeezed her hand. "I need to catch the second boat. Mackinac'll eat up most of my day."

"Let's plan on dinner when you get back," AJ said. "Sound okay?"

"Yes, it does."

26

I sat at the kitchen table with a plate of scrambled eggs and a mug of coffee. I was reading the *Times* on my iPad when the phone buzzed. I wouldn't have taken the call, but I saw the name on the screen. Martin Fleener.

"Morning, Marty."

"Your client's dead, Russo."

"The hell you talking about?"

"Camille North, Russo. She's dead. Shot twice."

"Jesus, Marty. Where are you?"

"Mac City. The trailhead at the overpass."

"Behind the IGA store?"

"That's it. I thought you'd want to take a look." He clicked off.

I took one last drink of coffee and left my dishes on the table. I grabbed a rain parka and went out the back door to the parking lot.

I drove over to 31 North and headed out of town. Traffic was lighter than I expected. I hit the high speed wipers and pushed the 335 hard through the driving rain. Forty minutes later, I pulled into the IGA lot. Patrol cars, light bars flashing, and two ambulances crowded together at the I-75 overpass. Curiosity slowed traffic to a crawl on Nicolet, and cars filled the Burger King parking lot across the street. They all sat facing the overpass, with wipers swinging fast to move away the rain.

I tugged on my parka and pulled up the hood. The rain pounded the ground. A patrol officer stopped me when I got to the yellow tape. Before I could explain why I was there, Fleener came up. He wore an ankle-length black rain parka and an oilskin hat.

"This way," he said, and turned away without another word. I followed him through the maze of cops and EMTs. The south approach to the Mackinac Bridge splits Mackinaw City. From the overpass, the North Western State Trail runs to Petoskey in one direction, the North Central State Trail runs to Gaylord in the other. At the side of the trail was a black nylon tarp on the ground.

"Officers," Fleener said, and pointed at the tarp. Two officers, both in their twenties, gently lifted the tarp but held it up to protect the body. Camille North was on her back, her left leg twisted awkwardly against the low concrete wall at the side of the trail. Her left arm was tucked under her torso. She wore blue nylon running pants and a gray camisole over a black sports bra. The laces on one Addiction running shoe were untied. A large red smear stained the center of her chest. Her clothes and hair were soggy from the rain.

"Two in the chest," he said. "Small caliber probably. We'll know more after they finish."

"Think she was killed here?"

"Hard to tell. Lot of rain overnight."

I strained to see as much of Camille's body as I could. I loosened the hood on the parka and wiped the rain off my face. I squinted most of the time. Something wasn't right.

"What?" Fleener said. "See something?"

He signaled the officers to replace the tarp.

"What's your theory, Marty?"

Fleener shrugged. "Until we know differently, the woman goes for a run and is shot. Could be a stranger, but I doubt it. Could be a set-up. The shooter knew her route. He picked the overpass to stay out of the rain until she jogged by."

"Maybe," I said, "but I don't think she was killed here. Too many things are wrong."

"Such as?"

I wiped my face again. It didn't help.

"For one thing, why run here? She lives on the island. You called me at eight. No ferry leaves the island before eight each morning, so she was here last night. We had a meeting scheduled for noon today. On the island."

"So she stayed overnight in the city."

I shook my head. "Maybe, but how would the shooter know her running route? On the island, sure. Same for Lake Forest in the winter. But she didn't make a habit of running here."

"We'll check the motels anyway. Restaurants, too. What else?"

"I don't think she was out for a run. The April temperatures are okay, so no parka, but no hat? In this rain? Not likely. If she was shot during a run, why is one shoe untied? She's not wearing a watch either. Camille was a serious runner. It doesn't fit, Marty. She was killed someplace else."

"Okay," Fleener said.

The steady rain had eased into a heavy mist. A woman from the ME's office came up to us.

"All set, captain."

Fleener nodded and we moved out of the way. Two men put a stretcher on the ground and unzipped a black body bag.

We heard Fleener's name shouted out. He turned around.

"Hold on," he said.

Fleener walked back toward Nicolet, but I stayed behind, watching them put Camille North in the body bag. All she'd wanted was her family home back.

And it got her killed.

27

I edged back under the overpass, trying to stay dry. When Fleener returned, we watched quietly as they took Camille's body away.

"Bad scene, Michael. Mac City cops aren't happy. The tourist season's almost here. You can imagine the Chamber's reaction."

"And one very nice woman is dead."

Fleener paused and turned my way.

"You want to fill me in?" he said. "Last I heard, the woman was getting a divorce. Her soon-to-be-ex is on our radar screen because wife number one is missing . . ."

"Annie," I said, "her name is Annie."

Fleener nodded. "Then you told me the husband hired a professional."

"Ben Miller."

"Right, Miller," Fleener said. "What happened after that?"

I took deep breath, let it out slowly and brought Fleener up to date.

"You have any reason to think she was in danger?"

I shrugged. "Not at the time. In hindsight? I don't know. Annie North is missing, Conrad hires a gunman, now Camille's dead."

"Do you think Miller killed her?" he said.

"Be my first guess."

"But it's only a guess?"

"Yeah. If it turns out she really was shot with a small caliber, well, Miller carries a 9mm."

"Shooters usually have more guns."

"I'll have to ask Miller about that," I said.

"No, you won't," Fleener said. "You don't have a client anymore. You're done with this, Russo. Understand? I'll run the murder investigation."

I started to talk, but he cut me off.

"I have more help than I need. Mac City cops, Mackinac Island cops. I don't need you." Fleener stopped. "Or him," he said, jerking a hitchhiker's thumb off to our left.

I turned just as Henri LaCroix walked up the muddy road.

Fleener looked at him with a blank expression and said, "How'd you get in here?"

"Told the officer I work for Russo," Henri said. "He let me through."

"Of course, you did," Fleener said. "But how'd you know about the crime scene?"

Henri looked over at me.

"I texted him, Marty."

Fleener scowled. "I'll tell you what I just told our friend here: it's a murder investigation now. Russo leaves it alone. That goes for you, too."

Henri knew when to be quiet.

Fleener looked back at me. "It's bothering me, what you said."

"What I said?"

"Why did North and Miller rough you up in the parking lot? You hadn't even met the guy."

"AJ figured out why," I said.

"AJ?" Fleener said. "What's she got to do with this?"

"AJ's right," Henri said.

"AJ's always right," I said.

Fleener glared at me. "I'm sick of your smart mouth, Russo. You know that? There was a dead woman right here in the dirt a few minutes ago. Don't you take anything seriously?"

I leaned toward Fleener, angry too. "That dead woman's my client, goddamn it. Don't tell me how to act. If I don't smart-mouth once in awhile, I just might kill somebody."

Fleener started to move closer, but we heard a noise. Henri was clapping his hands just loud enough for us to hear.

"Gentlemen," Henri said. Fleener and I looked at him. "Walk it back. Both of you. Nobody's gonna get killed."

"That's good to hear, coming from a trained killer," Fleener said.

Henri shook his head slowly, but he refused to get caught up in our anger. "Ease up, Marty. You, too, Russo. Not another word. Take the temperature down."

We stood quietly for what seemed like a long time, but probably wasn't.

Calmer now, Fleener said, "One of you explain it to me, and do it now. I have to head back to the office in a minute and I . . . what did AJ figure out?"

Henri kept quiet. Marty had backed off; now it was my turn.

"AJ's sure I did something to piss off North."

"Like what?"

"Like going to the island to do my job. 'Invading North's territory' is what she called it. I pushed him too hard. Something like that."

"That's it?"

I nodded.

"Henri?" Fleener said.

Henri shrugged. "Until something better comes along."

"Look," I said. "Fact is we don't know why he upped the ante in the parking lot, but it doesn't matter now. He changed the game for good when he killed Camille."

"We don't know Conrad North killed his wife," Fleener said. "Or that Miller did."

"You want to bet on someone else, Marty?"

Fleener shook his head.

"So Conrad's at the top of your list?"

"The husband always is," he said.

Fleener glanced at his watch. "Have to get back. We okay, Michael?"

I nodded. "Yeah, we're okay."

Fleener nodded.

"Before you go."

"I'm listening."

"She wasn't killed at the overpass, Marty, and she sure wasn't running when she was shot."

"I remember you said that."

"Why was Camille in Mac City? What was she doing here? I was supposed to meet her on the island. Why didn't she call me or meet me here?"

"Maybe it didn't have anything to do with you, Russo," Fleener said.

I shook my head. "Camille North didn't strike me as secretive. Embarrassed about her life being a mess, sure, but I was trying to help her, remember?"

"People do strange things under pressure, you know. From what you've said, she had plenty of that these days."

Fleener looked at his watch again, distractedly. "I'm late."

We moved out from the shelter of the overpass. The mist was gone, but heavy clouds made the rest of the day uncertain.

"I'll be in touch," Fleener said, and walked away.

"On the other side of the IGA," I said to Henri.

We went around the building and found my car. We watched cars and trucks speed by on I-75 as they climbed their way toward the center of the Mackinac Bridge.

"Lot of traffic for this time of year," Henri said.

"Sure is."

We were quiet for a minute.

"Michael?"

"Yeah."

"You ready?"

"Yeah. Want to come along, Henri?"

"Yes."

"Who's first?"

"Miller," Henri said. "Unless Conrad's a shooter."

"He's not."

"Then we take the shooter first."

28

"Get in the car." I beeped the locks and we climbed in. I started the motor, adjusted the temperature and turned down the radio.

"No," Henri said. "The music's good."

"Didn't know you liked classical."

"Didn't used to," he said. "Grew up on rock, any kind of rock. Kept the adrenalin pumping for work. The money guys made fun of me for it." Henri had spent several very lucrative years in the financial houses on LaSalle Street in Chicago.

"How'd you get to classical?"

"Iraq. First tour. Firefights moved the juices. You know Michael Herr's *Dispatches*?"

"The journalist? Wrote about Vietnam?"

Henri nodded. "Said he went to cover the war, but the war covered him. Still true. I needed to bring it down, not pump it up. I didn't eat pills like some of the guys." Henri shrugged. "Been listening ever since."

The traffic sped along, and we sat quietly and listened to the music.

"When'd you see Miller last?"

Henri thought for a minute. "Four days ago. Downtown on my way to the boat. I'll make a couple of calls, see what he's been up to."

"If he's not on the island, he'll be hard to find."

"Hard, but not impossible," Henri said. "If Miller drops off the radar, he can't keep you away from North."

"No, he can't," I said. "If we don't find him, let's give him a reason to come out of the weeds."

"Be fun to fuck with Conrad," Henri said, and smiled.

"It would be. Any luck at all, we could rough up the boys, too."

"That'd be a waste of my time."

I nodded. "Yes."

Beethoven's *7th Symphony* started playing on Interlochen Public Radio. We listened for a minute.

"Did you know Tom Hooper used that . . ."

"In *The King's Speech*," Henri said. "Second movement."

"You're good, Henri."

"Yeah? I lost Miller twice. Two fucking times, Russo. That's not good."

"Then let's find him. Where're you headed?"

"Petoskey," he said. "Back to Margo's. Stick with you for a while. Besides, we need to know more than we do now."

"Story of my professional life."

"You going back to town?" Henri said.

"I'll be at the office or AJ's. Where's your car?"

Henri gestured vaguely at the windshield. "Marathon station. I walked down from there."

I drove the two blocks and pulled in next to his SUV.

Henri opened the door and got out.

"Call me," I said.

Henri waved without turning around. He took off down Nicolet like he was trying to beat the light at U.S. 23. He probably did.

I pulled out my phone and punched Lenny Stern's number.

"What'd ya want, Russo? I'm in a hurry."

"Where are you?"

"Almost to Mac City," he said.

"The shooting?"

Lenny was quiet. Golden oldies filled the void. "Mr. Mojo Risin'," I think. *L.A. Woman.*

"What d'ya know, Russo?"

"A dead woman at the overpass, behind the IGA."

"All I got's a shooting," he said. "Getting off 75 now."

"It's Camille North."

"Your client?"

"Yeah."

"Shit."

"Yeah.

"Talk to me."

"Two shots in the chest."

"Cops'll tell me that."

"They won't tell you why she was in Mac City, because they don't know. Oh, and Lenny?"

"Yeah?"

"She wasn't killed at the overpass. She had running clothes on, but she was not running when she got killed."

"Thanks, Russo," he said, and clicked off.

I put the phone back, and headed away from town on Nicolet.

Why did Camille North die in Mackinaw City?

Rather than continuing south at the stoplight, I turned left and turned again on Huron. I cruised by the motels, one after another. A few of the remaining mom-and-pop places were sandwiched between the large chain motels that dominated the waterfront. Big or small, most of them were closed for at least another two weeks. If Camille stayed in town, it should be easy to track her moves. The same was true for restaurants and bars. Only a handful were open all year.

I turned onto Central Avenue and parked. I got out my phone and tapped voice memo. I recorded the names of four places at the intersection and one motel on Huron that were open for business. I put the 335 in gear and drove slowly toward Nicolet. The list was pretty short even after I added Audie's, Holiday Inn Express and Bernie's, a dilapidated excuse for a drinking hole that Camille North would never set foot in. I sent the list to Sandy's phone with the note, "find phone #s. on my way."

Fleener's men would canvass all of them, including gas stations, the IGA and the Welcome Center. I didn't plan to cover the same territory, but some folks don't like talking to the cops. A private investigator, however . . .

29

"I saw the banner," Sandy said, pointing at her desktop screen.

I sat in one of the client chairs in the front window. I'd picked up a Denver Wrap at Roast & Toast on the way to the office. It was late, and I'd only had coffee.

"A shooting in Mackinaw City was all it said." Sandy shook her head. "Turns out to be our client."

I ran it down for her, starting with Fleener's early morning call.

"I still can't believe it," she said.

"Makes two of us. Why she didn't tell me . . ."

"About coming across?"

I nodded.

"Could have been lots of reasons, boss."

"Give me one."

"If she was meeting a friend for the night, and didn't want anyone to know?"

"An affair?"

"Wouldn't be the first time a woman got involved before the ink was dry."

"No, it wouldn't. I've had enough clients on both ends of divorce to know that."

I ate the last of the wrap and folded up the papers.

"You find phone numbers for the list I sent?"

"Just have to print it out."

"You call the motels," I said. "I'll call restaurants. Shouldn't take long."

I looked at my watch. "Of course, if she wasn't alone . . . we'd have ourselves another suspect."

"A better suspect than the husband?"

"There's never a better suspect than the husband."

"Think we'll be ahead of the cops on this?" Sandy said, reaching for the printout.

"I hope so. Our questions might turn something up if the cops haven't made people nervous yet."

"Then let's get started," Sandy said.

"Deal," I said, and stood up. I tossed the crumpled-up sandwich bag in the air, an imaginary free throw to win the game. It bounced off the edge of the basket and landed on the floor.

"Don't give up your day job, boss."

I rolled my eyes. "Can I have a copy of the list, please?"

Less than an hour later, I stretched my arms over my head and went out to Sandy's desk.

Henri sat in a client chair with his feet up, iPad in hand.

"I didn't hear you come in?" I said.

"Didn't want to interrupt," he said, and closed the iPad. "Any luck?"

"No," I said. "Sandy?"

She nodded. "Only one lead, and that was a bit vague. The big motel, over on Huron. Woman told me a couple did stay last night." Sandy looked at her notes. "Checked in late afternoon."

"Description?"

Sandy shook her head. "They weren't teenage lovers, the woman told me that more than once. An older couple. That's it, no details. Nothing."

"She against teenage love?"

Sandy put her arms out, palms up.

I started to ask Henri about Ben Miller when the office phone rang.

"It's Ruth Avila," Sandy said. I pointed at my office.

"Ruth," I said, settling into my chair. I swung around and put my feet on the window ledge. "I was just about to call."

"I was at the courthouse when the news hit."

"How did you find out it was Camille?"

"Don Hendricks' secretary knew I was in the building," she said. Don Hendricks was Emmet County Prosecutor, twice elected by the good citizens of the county. "I was stunned, Michael. I had no idea . . ."

"Neither did I."

". . . she was in danger."

"No reason you would," I said.

"Do you think it was Conrad?"

"My first choice, or his hired gunman."

"Same thing."

"Yes," I said.

"Could it have been Wolfgang or Wilhelm?

"Based on what I've heard they're not ballsy enough to kill her, and if they did do it they're not smart enough to cover their tracks."

"No, they're not very bright."

"Ruth, what about Nicole? Will you call her?"

"I just got off the phone, a few minutes ago. She was devastated, Michael. Honestly, I didn't think it'd hit her that hard."

"It's her mother, Ruth."

"I know," Avila said, stretching out the second word. "There always seemed to be an emotional distance between them. Maybe I'm wrong. It was just an odd feeling I had."

"That might have more to do with Conrad than anything between mother and daughter."

"The man's a prick, Michael."

"No need to convince me," I said. "Is Nicole coming north?"

"Not right now. She wants me to handle the arrangements, but she'll be here for the funeral. I'll call Dodson this afternoon."

"The funeral home in St. Ignace?"

"Uh-huh."

"Burial on Mackinac?"

"Yeah, the family has plots in the Protestant Cemetery."

Mackinac has three cemeteries on Garrison Road near the middle of the island, one each for Protestants, Catholics and the military.

"Does Conrad have a plot?"

"Right next to all the Sandersons."

"You ask Nicole about that?"

"No. She's got enough on her plate right now."

Ruth Avila then said she'd call with the funeral arrangements and Nicole's schedule as soon as it all came together.

"One last thing, Ruth. Let me know if Conrad makes a move on the trust."

"When he makes a move, you mean," she said, and hung up.

Henri was waiting patiently in the same chair. I started to ask him about Ben Miller, when my cell buzzed. I looked at the screen. I put up my hand like a traffic cop and returned to my desk.

"Hi, AJ."

"Why didn't you call me?"

"How'd you hear?"

"Lenny Stern," she said. "Are you all right, Michael?"

"It was all over by the time I arrived."

"That's not what I meant, Michael. I mean, are you okay?"

"Yeah, guess so," I said. "I'm . . . I don't know, I feel like I missed it."

"You mean, if you hadn't missed something, she'd be alive? Is that what you mean?"

"I think so," I said. "Not sure. Can we continue this later? Henri's waiting."

"Sure."

"I'll meet you at home, okay?"

"That's okay," she said. "Before you go . . . Lenny said you called him from Mac City."

AJ's tone of voice seemed to add, "but you did not call me." I passed up the opportunity to respond.

"Is he writing a piece for *PPD Wired*?"

"I just put it up. He'll do a longer one for print tomorrow. He'll probably add a profile of Camille and the Sanderson's family history on the island."

"All right," I said. "Let me talk to Henri."

AJ said good-bye and I put the phone back.

"Glad you're still here," I said, and sat down next to him.

"I have no place to go," Henri said. "Margo's tied up 'till later, and I ought to stick with you. In case Wolfgang or Wilhelm show up."

"Funny man," I said. "I'd rather hear about Miller."

"That I can do." Henri put his iPad on the table and leaned forward, elbows on his knees. "Miller left Mackinac night before last."

"The night before Camille died?"

"Uh-huh."

"She came across yesterday, so Miller was already here."

Henri nodded. "Camille was on the first ferry in the morning. She was spotted on the dock in St. Ignace."

"Think it was a coincidence, him already here?" I said. "Or did he know her plans and come across early?"

Henri shrugged. "Doesn't make any difference. He was here and she was shot dead."

"Any idea where Miller is now?"

Henri shook his head. "Asked around. He's not on the island, I know that."

"So until we know otherwise, he's on he mainland," I said. "Could be anywhere."

Henri sat up. "We assume he's tailing you until we know different."

"No reason to tail me. Camille's dead."

"Then I stick around until we find him."

"Don't argue with him, boss," Sandy said.

"Listen to Sandy, Russo."

"That'd be a first," she said.

"All right. No argument."

I got up and took a bottle of water from the small refrigerator near the door. It'd been a long day, and seemed to be getting longer. I wanted to see AJ. I wanted to sit next to her on the couch in her living room. I feel that way a lot, but there was an urgency to it this time. Death will do that.

"Time to go home," I said.

"Russo?" Henri said.

"Not tonight, Henri, tomorrow. We'll talk tomorrow."

30

"You didn't think twice about it, did you?" AJ asked. We sat on the couch in her living room. The sun had just broken through the late afternoon clouds. It streamed through the front window, tracing long, pencil-thin lines on the floor.

I'd gone home for a fast shower and fresh clothes. By the time I walked to AJ's, she'd traded her work clothes for a beat-up green MSU track suit and an ugly pair of gray wool socks. We each had a glass of Chardonnay. A small glass bowl of unsalted almonds sat on the coffee table.

"Didn't have to," I said.

AJ put her glass on the coffee table. I tossed a couple of almonds in my mouth and put my feet up.

"The thing is, Michael, I knew you'd say that. I knew you would."

"You did?"

AJ nodded. "Once the shock of Camille's murder settled in, I knew what you'd do. We've been together long enough, you're quite predictable."

"I am?"

"In certain circumstances, yes."

"This one of those times?"

She nodded. "I accept it. It's who you are. You're very loyal, Michael. It's one of the things I love about you. But I don't always understand." AJ turned sideways on the couch and put her hand on my arm.

"When you give your word, it's solid as steel. You decide to do something, you do it."

"I've done some dumb things," I said.

"Welcome to the club, but that's not what I'm talking about." AJ drank some wine and put her glass back. "When I said a minute ago, I knew what you'd do?"

"Yeah."

"I knew you'd go after Camille's killer."

"Wouldn't anybody in my position do that?"

"Yes," she said. "But it's more than that for you. Your client's dead, but she hired you to find out about her lease and, by god, you'll do that too."

"Yes."

"For anyone else, no client, no case. A simple decision for most people, but you're not most people. For you, it's . . . different somehow. You're a good man with a good heart."

I folded my arms over my chest and stared at the fireplace on the opposite wall. We were quiet for a moment.

"Remember I grew up in Royal Oak?"

"Sure."

"Something happens. Like this. It all comes back, fast, clear as yesterday." I sat forward and took AJ's hand.

"Tony was two years younger than me."

My brother, Anthony, was a sophomore at Swarthmore College when he killed himself. He sat in his car in the woods a few miles from campus and sucked exhaust.

"It started earlier, but high school was the worst. They picked on him all the time. He was quiet, soft-spoken, a nice kid. Our father . . . our father rode us hard, judgmental, critical. We never did anything right. Easier to, I don't know . . ."

"Try to stay under the radar?"

I nodded. "Yeah. Tony did that a lot when he was a kid. When he was older, too." I took in air and let it out slowly. "It made him a victim. It played right into the hands of every bully in high school."

"How'd you get through it? You weren't a victim?"

"I don't know. I protected Tony, I guess. Didn't think about me. Wanted to keep him safe."

"Did it work?"

"Most of the time," I said. "It did most of the time."

I was quiet. AJ picked up on it.

"Senior year, I was out three days sick. They beat Tony bad. Broke his arm. I knew who did it. When I got back to school I picked out the toughest bully with the biggest mouth."

"Did you beat him up?"

I shook my head slowly. "Didn't have to," I said. "Stood him up against a wall out back of school. Told him if they ever touched Tony again, any of them, I'd kill him. I said that, and walked away. Worked for a while. But it started all over again in college."

"It wasn't your fault, Michael. You were a kid."

"I should have taken Camille's call more seriously. I should have canceled Charlevoix, gone to see her. I let her down."

"Don't second-guess yourself, Michael. It only makes it worse."

"That's not the point."

"I know. I feel bad for you, that's all."

We sat quietly for a few minutes. AJ refilled our glasses. She put a block of Dubliner on a cutting board, added crackers and set it on the coffee table.

I cut a piece of cheese and took a bite.

"What's next, Michael?"

"We find Miller."

"You and Henri?"

I nodded.

"Not Conrad?"

"Conrad's not a killer. He might kill in a jealous rage, but this wasn't rage. This was cold and calculated. He told Miller to kill Camille. He's first."

"What'll you do when you find him?"

I shrugged.

"Don't shrug your shoulders at me, Michael." AJ was edgy.

"Does it matter?"

"Damn right it matters, Michael. It matters to me because you matter to me."

"I take him, the cops take him. However it plays out. Just so it gets done."

"Then, Conrad," AJ said. It wasn't a question.

I nodded. "Then Conrad."

31

"Well, this is a first," Sandy said when she came through the door. "You beat me to the office."

I sat at my desk with coffee and the *New York Times*. I'd stayed at AJ's overnight, and walked home this morning early. I kept alert just to be careful, but the walk was uneventful. I passed on a run despite the bright blue sky, plenty of sunshine and warmer air.

"I'm here earlier than you a lot," I said.

"No, you're not. Take this," she said, handing me a box from Johan's. "Remember, keep your mitts off the cinnamon-sugar."

"Yes, ma'am."

"It's an all-donut-day."

I peered into the box. "Where's the danish?"

"All-donut means, like, no danish."

I forced a smile and chose a plain buttermilk. I tried to look happy and took a bite. It was pretty good, but I'd never admit that.

Sandy put her coat and bag away, poured a mug of coffee and took her usual seat next to my desk. She looked lovingly at the cinnamon-sugar on a napkin in front of her.

"Henri texted a while ago," I said. "He'll be here later."

"Did you ask him about Camille?"

I nodded. "No answer."

"That means he has nothing, or it's too complicated for a message."

We heard someone on the steps.

"Sounds like an elephant," she said.

"Certainly does."

Martin Fleener came through the door, and he looked unhappy.

"We need to talk, Russo," he said from my office doorway. Fleener turned to Sandy. "You, too, Ms. Jefferies."

Never heard him say "Ms. Jefferies" before. He was definitely unhappy.

Fleener hung his coat on the rack and looked at the coffeemaker on the sideboard.

"It'll be done cooking in a few minutes," Sandy said. "Just made a fresh pot."

Fleener came in and sat in a client chair in front of the desk. Then he did something I'd never seen before when he was working. Captain Martin Fleener loosened his tie and opened the collar button. And it was still morning.

"We finished our canvass of Mackinaw City a couple hours ago. Motels, bars."

"That didn't take long," I said.

"It's April, the list is short." Fleener glanced at each of us.

"Our job went faster than we expected because somebody already asked questions. Got in there before my guys could even start working. A man and a woman made phone calls. You know, pretending they're Nick and Nellie Charles, for Christ's sake."

"Who?" I said.

"I think he means Nick and Nora Charles," Sandy said. "*The Thin Man*."

"Shut up, both of you," Fleener said. "The phone calls made our work harder, you know that? Some of the owners didn't mind answering the same questions twice on a slow day, but too many of them did. I don't suppose you know anything about that, Russo? Or you, Ms. Jefferies?"

Despite Fleener's sarcastic monologue, he was serious and annoyed. Calling Sandy "Ms. Jefferies" was only half of it. He didn't get irritated often, but when he did it was best not to push the issue.

"Marty," I said. "We weren't trying to do your job . . ."

"Hard to tell, Russo."

"Look, Marty, some people just don't want to talk with the cops, you know that. I figured we might learn something you couldn't."

"Did you?"

"Did I what?"

"Learn anything?"

I hesitated. Fleener caught it.

"You didn't, did you?" he said. "Both of you?"

I shook my head. Fleener looked at Sandy.

"One motel on Huron had a check-in," she said.

"Yeah," Fleener said. "The woman who's convinced every teenager in town got laid that night. That the one?"

Sandy nodded slowly.

"Thought so," Fleener said. "As luck would have it, I tracked down the couple who checked in, too. It wasn't Camille North."

Fleener leaned back in the chair, almost like he was finished. He wasn't.

"What the hell are you doing, Russo? I told you yesterday to leave it alone. Your client's dead. You got no dog in the hunt."

"Call it curiosity, professional responsibility, call it whatever you want. I want to know who killed her, Marty."

"So do I, damn it. But I'm paid to find the bad guys, Russo, you're not. Right out of the box, you're in the way. And another thing, you're never just curious. At least I've never seen it."

We were quiet. The tension was leaving the room. After a few moments, I said, "Feels like we've lost focus. We still have a killer on the loose." I leaned forward. "Did your canvass turn up anything helpful?"

Fleener took in a lot of air and let it out. He got up, walked to the sideboard and filled a mug with coffee. He slowly went back to the chair.

To his credit, and my relief, Fleener answered the question without further editorial comment. Or sarcasm.

"Nothing," he said. "Lots of pretty bored people up there this late in the winter. Camille's murder was ugly, but it's exciting news. They're ready to gossip, but they didn't know anything."

"You ask about Miller? Anybody see him?"

"We did ask about Miller. No one matching his description."

"Think I'll ask Conrad North," I said.

"I told you to stay out of it, Russo, so stay out. I don't want to have this conversation again. That goes for both of you. I'm meeting North later today. We have plenty to talk to him about."

"You gonna put him in the room?"

Fleener shook his head. "Not this time. Man just lost his wife. I'll talk to him at home."

"Any idea why Camille North was on the mainland?" I said.

Fleener shook his head. "I wish I did."

I sat up and leaned on the desk. "Camille ends up dead, and we don't even know why she was on the mainland. Maddening."

Fleener nodded without much conviction and looked at his watch.

"Time to go," he said. "The autopsy report should be on my desk by the time I'm back in the office."

"It was Dashiell Hammett, by the way," Sandy said.

"What was?" Fleener said.

"Nick and Nora Charles, the husband and wife detectives? *The Thin Man?* Dashiell Hammett wrote the book."

Fleener put on his coat and stopped at the door. "Russo?"

"Yeah?"

"Another reason I want you out of this."

"Yeah?"

"You bust up Conrad North, I'll have to come for you."

32

"Fleener's warned us before," Henri said. "Part of his job."

We sat in the front office. Sandy ate the last of a Bleu Bay Salad from Roast & Toast. I'd long since finished a tuna salad sandwich and drank a bottle of water.

"You're forgetting the obvious problem," Sandy said.

"Who is?" I said.

"Both of you, smart-ass."

"Better call me 'sir' when you say that."

Henri laughed.

"Don't encourage him," Sandy said. "I have to live with what passes for his sense of humor every day."

"My apologies," Henri said, with a wide sweep of his arm. He got up and went to the sideboard. He filled a mug with coffee and sat down.

"What's the obvious problem, Sandy?" I said.

"It doesn't matter if Fleener warned you last month or last year. Beat up Conrad North, let alone shoot him, you are suspects number one. That goes for the sons, too."

"Wolfgang and Wilhelm," Henri said, and shook his head. "They're not worth the effort."

"You're not listening, Henri," Sandy said. "I could care less if you rough up North. He deserves it on principle. But I do care what happens to Sam Spade over here." Sandy jabbed a sharp finger in my direction. "He pays the bills."

"We don't have to work Conrad over," I said. "At least not right now."

"Sure we do," Henri said, and smiled. "Like Sandy said, on principle."

"Hold on," I said, "let's be serious for a moment."

"That's a switch," Sandy said.

I ignored her humor.

"You ever find out why Camille came to the mainland?" I said to Henri. "Where she stayed? Was she alone? Anything?"

Henri shook his head. "Not a thing. You ask Fleener?"

"Same answer. Said he'd keep looking."

I drank some water. "Learn anything about Miller?"

"Not a lot," Henri said. "We already knew he left the island the day before Camille died."

"Uh-huh."

"He's disappeared. Nobody's seen him."

"Back to the island?"

Henri shook his head. "Got it covered."

"Even the airport?"

"He'd be easier to spot up there than down on the dock."

"So he's still on the mainland."

"But is he in our neighborhood?" Sandy said. "That's what you mean, isn't it? Is he here or long gone?"

"He's close," Henri said.

"Because?"

"Because Conrad's too smart not to worry. He has to know Michael's after him."

"Then let's go after him," I said.

Henri smiled. "If we scare him enough, he'll send Ben Miller after you."

I nodded. "Yes, he will. Does that meet your approval, Sandy?"

She faked a smile. "I don't like you being a target, but Fleener can't object if you scare the shit out of the guy."

"Makes life easier for us," Henri said.

"Do you know where Conrad is, Henri?"

Henri drank some coffee and put the mug down. "On the island as of this morning. He moves, I'll know."

"How're we gonna do this?" I said.

"I could march up the front steps and bang on his door," Henri said.

"That'd be fun, but one of the boys might pull a gun."

"All the better."

"Henri." It was Sandy.

"All right, all right."

"We have fewer choices on the island," I said. "Tight quarters. Harder to isolate him."

Henri nodded. "Better on the mainland."

"We catch Conrad out somewhere, a bar, a restaurant. The parking lot on the dock. Someplace like that. Can we do that?"

"I've got people watching," Henri said. "We can do that."

"I'll push him up against a wall, tell him I'll burn his ass for Camille." I smiled.

"That's a good start," Sandy said.

"Then I'll tell him Wolfgang and Wilhelm will never get the cottage."

33

"Miller will come after you, Michael," AJ said, "if you back Conrad into a corner."

We sat at a small two-top table on the sidewall at Julienne Tomatoes, a delightful restaurant with wood floors, high ceilings and brick walls. It was around the corner from AJ's office at the *Post Dispatch*. Many a carry-out lunch has made its way to our office, as Sandy would be quick to point out. AJ ate the quiche of the day, bacon and Swiss, and I munched on a breakfast sandwich.

"That's the general idea."

"I know it is, Michael. But I worry, you know that."

I nodded. "It's on our terms, AJ. We pick the time and place. It's our advantage."

"For Conrad, it's your advantage. What about Ben Miller?"

"That's tougher," I said, and ate the last of my sandwich.

"In fact, you can't predict Miller at all."

"Educated guesses," I said. "We know a lot about the guy, AJ, where he goes, how . . ."

"Like the parking lot that day? In the middle of the afternoon? How'd your educated guesses do on that one?"

I picked up my mug. "Not a good example. Conrad ran that one. He wanted to scare me off. Wide open parking lot was no big deal. But if Miller wants to hurt me, it limits his choices."

"That's reassuring."

"You want more coffee?"

AJ shook her head. I refilled my mug and sat down.

"What I mean is, Miller can only hit me in a few places. He doesn't want to be seen."

"I knew what you meant, Michael. You're good at what you do. I don't always like it."

I reached across the table and put my hand over hers. "Busy day coming?"

AJ shrugged. "Pretty much every day. In the old days, like last year, the print edition of the paper had one deadline."

"Not true anymore?"

"Not a bit," she said. "The online version is twenty-four, seven. The deadline is always right now."

AJ looked at her watch.

"You need to get going?"

"Yeah, it's time. Have you heard about services for Camille?"

I shook my head. "Ruth Avila's making the arrangements. She'll let me know."

"Is it a memorial service or a funeral?"

"Don't know that either."

"All right, my darling, I must be off." AJ stood and took her coat off the back of the chair.

"Come on, I'll walk you," I said when we stopped on the sidewalk.

"No you won't. My office is right over there," she said, pointing down the block as if I didn't know. "Give me a kiss."

We kissed, with a light hug, and said good-bye.

I headed down Howard toward the office. The sun didn't hide behind April clouds this morning. It was warm, and it felt like spring might hang around for a while in northern Michigan. But I'm an optimist.

I made a quick stop at McLean & Eakin for the *Times*, then went up the stairs.

"Morning, Sandy," I said, and hung my coat on the rack.

"Good morning, boss. Two messages." She handed me the slips, and I took a look.

"Did Ruth say what she wanted?"

Sandy shook her head. "Didn't say. She wants you to call. She'll be in all day."

"Except for her lunchtime walk."

"You exercise people are a pretty weird bunch, you know that?"

"So I've been told." I read the second message. "Who's Winifred Hampstead?"

"Beats me. Said she was looking for a good investigator. I tried my best to send her elsewhere, but she insisted on talking to you."

I said nothing. Honestly, I let it go.

"Go to your office and call Ruth Avila."

"Yes, boss lady."

I'd just picked up the office phone when my iPhone screen lit up. Henri was on his way.

"Good morning, Michael," Ruth Avila said. "Thanks for calling back."

"You're welcome. What's up?"

"I've talked with Nicole Sanderson," she said. "I've made all the arrangements on her behalf."

"That's good to hear. Will it be a memorial service?"

"No. Nicole wants a traditional funeral service."

"With a casket?"

"No," Ruth said. "Camille was cremated. The service is set for next Tuesday at Trinity Episcopal on Mackinac. Do you know it?"

"I do. It's a wonderful historic building. Beautiful inside."

I heard the outside door open. Henri nodded as he went by my office door.

"I assume you'll be there, Michael."

"Yes."

"Good. Nicole wants to meet you. I told her I'd set it up."

"Tell me what's good, and I'll make it work."

"Nicole will stay with me for a few days. There're some issues, legal and otherwise, that need her attention."

"Is there any way I can help?"

"No, thanks," Ruth said. "But could you meet us at the dock that morning? The service is at eleven o'clock. We'll ride over together."

We agreed to meet, and talked a bit longer about Camille's death and the investigation. Such as it was.

I hung up and joined Sandy and Henri.

"Morning, Henri. Good news this morning?"

"Depends," he said. "I know where Conrad is."

"Uh-huh."

"We got him."

"Sure?"

Henri nodded. "Might be better if we kept Sandy out of it."

"You mean if you plan to rob a bank, it'd be better I didn't know which branch?"

"My office," I said to Henri.

"Geez, I miss all the fun," Sandy said. Henri and I went into my office and closed the door.

"Where is he?"

"Right where we want him," Henri said.

"That good?"

"Uh-huh," Henri said, and smiled. "He'll be here for two days."

"Here?"

"Petoskey. He reserved two rooms for two nights at the Perry."

"Two rooms?"

"Wolfgang and Wilhelm."

"Overnight gives us an opening," I said.

"It's better than that," Henri said. "The first night, reservations for three at City Park Grill. Unless they hit the bars after dinner . . ."

"That's not Conrad's style."

"He'll be in the open."

"What're you thinking?"

"A straight shot from the Grill to the hotel."

"Through the parking lot next to the County Building?"

Henri nodded. "It's dark, plenty of cars to hide us."

"If the boys head for a bar, all the easier."

"If they don't," Henri said, "I'll keep them busy while you discuss the situation with Mr. North. Unless you just want to kill him and get it over with."

"One step at a time, Henri," I said. "When will they arrive?"

"Later today. The luggage is on the dock, and one of them called a valet for their car. They'll be on the last boat."

I leaned back and put my feet on the corner of the desk. "Good work, Henri."

"Friends in all the right places."

"Any idea how we'll play this?"

Henri put his arms up, palms out, like he was about to offer a prayer. "Of course."

I smiled. "Let's hear it."

34

"You're asking for trouble, Michael," AJ said. "Are you sure this is a good idea?"

We sat at the small table in her kitchen, the window looking out on the ravine behind the house. The trees were just starting to bud. If the temperature didn't dip below freezing, we'd have real leaves, green leaves, out there pretty soon. I put together a quick dinner of spaghetti with an olive oil-garlic sauce. I added a side dish of sliced tomatoes and cucumbers with Balsamic drizzled over the top.

"We don't want Miller to run," I said. "If he has no reason to stay, he goes."

"So you give Miller reason to stay."

I shook my head. "No, Conrad gives Miller an order to stay."

AJ poured more Chardonnay and took a drink. I'd passed on wine tonight – my work day wasn't over yet.

We sat quietly and finished dinner. I cleaned up the dishes and went back to the table.

"Where's Henri?"

"He grabbed a sandwich with Margo."

"What time do you meet him?"

"Eight-thirty," I said. "That gives Conrad a good two hours for dinner. Henri'll text if anything changes."

"Does Henri have somebody working in the restaurant?"

I shook my head. "A pal's keeping an eye on them from a barstool. When they pay the tab, Henri'll know."

"You'd better be off," AJ said.

I nodded. "I'll call you later."

"Do you have your .38, Michael?"

"It's with my coat," I said.

I put on my coat and kissed AJ. She patted my hip and hit the holster.

"I told you I had it."

She smiled. "Just checking. You're naïve about trouble sometimes."

"No trouble tonight."

"Miller'll run for sure if you kill Conrad."

"Do my best not to."

I kissed AJ again and said good-bye.

The night air had cooled but the sky was clear. I could pick out a few thousand stars despite the lights of the city.

I walked three blocks down Bay Street to the Sheriff's Office in the Bodzick wing of the County Building. I turned into the parking lot. Cars were parked at angles on both sides. I continued toward Howard.

Halfway down the row of cars, I heard, "Russo." It was Henri. He leaned against a panel truck parked next to a Chevy Tahoe. Two very large vehicles to hide two men.

"Any word?" I said.

"My guy said they have the tab. They're finishing off a bottle of wine."

"The more alcohol for them, the better for us," I said.

"Just so Conrad's not so shit-faced he can't remember."

"He'll remember, Henri, booze or no booze."

We leaned against the Tahoe and waited. I had little news to contribute to our conversation. Henri had finally rented the last of his apartments for the season. He and Margo planned to visit Europe, Paris and London, after the season wrapped up in November.

"Kind of a rainy month to go to Europe," I said.

Before Henri could answer, his phone buzzed and he read the screen. "They're leaving."

We inched our way down the long body of the Tahoe and looked over the hood toward City Park Grill. The streetlamps gave off just enough light. The door opened and out they came, Conrad leading the way, the boys a step behind. They were laughing, and their voices were loud.

"Nothing like a little wine to liven things up," Henri said.

"Unless it's a lot of wine."

The three men crossed Howard Street, entered the far end of the parking lot, and came right toward us.

"That answers that question," Henri said in a quiet voice.

"Yes, it does," I said. "The boys are all yours."

"We do this just like we said, okay?"

"Okay," I said.

Eight cars away. They moved slowly and unsteadily. Almost as much side-to-side as ahead. They were still laughing, voices louder. They talked about women, not in pleasant ways.

"The broad woulda done me, you assholes weren't here to fuck it up," Wolfgang said.

Five cars away.

"Not a chance," Conrad said. "She wanted me."

Two cars away. "You're an old fart."

Close now. "Old enough to take you," Conrad said, and they all laughed.

Henri and I stepped out. We placed ourselves five feet apart.

"Gentlemen," Henri said. His voice cut the quiet of the night.

They stopped. And stared. Not sure what to do.

Conrad and the boys were clustered together, almost touching. Good for us, bad for them. You can't street fight bunched up, though booze had probably robbed them of that option, to say nothing of age and inexperience.

"Gentlemen," Henri said, and moved his right arm just enough to reveal a Glock 19 in his right hand. All three of them fixed on the handgun. I never saw Henri take it out of the holster. It wasn't there, then it was.

"Wolfgang, Wilhelm," Henri said. "Mr. Russo, here, would like to have a word with your father." Henri reached out with his left arm, took

Conrad by his coat and yanked him toward us, separating him from the boys.

"Check him," Henri said, and I patted Conrad down.

"He's clean."

Henri moved up next to Conrad, still facing the boys, and stuck the 19 into Conrad's rib cage so they'd see it.

"Open your jackets, both of you. Slowly. Put your guns on the ground. Two fingers."

"We don't have guns," Conrad said. "No guns. What do you want?"

Henri ignored him. "Open 'em, now."

The boys opened their jackets, wide. No guns.

Henri said, "In there, nice and easy." The boys moved between the two trucks.

Henri nodded at me.

"Come on, Conrad, let's take a walk."

"What do you want?" Conrad said, trying to speak clearly over the booze.

"Walk."

Five vehicles down, I stopped, grabbed Conrad by the sleeve, and turned him toward me. I shoved him into the side of a large SUV.

"I got a few things to say."

"You can't . . ."

I hit him hard, just below the ribs. He started to buckle, and I slammed him with both arms straight out against the side of the SUV. That hurt. Good.

"I talk, you listen. Got it?"

He didn't move, didn't speak.

"Nod."

Conrad nodded slowly.

"You're going down for Camille, Conrad. Don't give a shit how, but you're going down. Cops fuck up the job, you fuck with the law . . ."

My face, close to his now. "I'll kill you. One shot."

I backed up a step and put my arm across Conrad's chest.

"I know how you did it."

Conrad blinked, not understanding.

"Camille's cottage. I know how you did it."

Conrad blinked, again, eyes wide this time.

"How you switched the names. You'll never get the cottage. The boys'll never live a day in that house."

I leaned in, close. "Not. One. Day."

I stepped back and hit him a hard right in the ribs. Before he landed on the tarmac, I grabbed him with both hands and shoved him toward Henri.

"All right, gentlemen, back to the hotel," Henri said. "Get moving."

We watched them stagger away. At Bay Street, Conrad, arms wrapped around his waist, looked back over his shoulder for a moment. Then he turned and the three men crossed the street.

"Go all right?" Henri said.

"I wanted to shoot him. Be done with it."

"Three dead guys, Russo. It'd be a big mess."

"Yeah."

"Plenty of time," Henri said. "We can kill 'em later."

35

"Did you really say that?" Sandy asked.

I sat in a client chair by the window with a mug of coffee and an almond danish. Henri's treat this morning. He sat next to me with a buttermilk donut.

"Yep."

"Do we?"

"Do we what?"

"Do we know how North changed the lease? How he changed the names?"

"No," I said.

"An educated guess?"

"Nope."

"You made it up?"

"Yep."

Sandy thought for a minute while she ate some cinnamon-sugar donut. She looked up.

"Let me see if I have this straight," she said. "You lied to North about the lease, you lied about taking the house away, you threatened to kill him if the cops didn't get him. You did all that, right?"

I nodded.

Sandy hesitated, thinking. "Conrad'll give Miller the order, you know. You gave him no choice."

"No choice."

"Miller'll come after you. But you know that."

I nodded again.

"That's what you want, isn't it? You want a professional killer to come after you."

"Yes," I said. "On my terms."

"On your terms? What the fuck does that mean, 'your terms?' It's a goddamn rationalization and you know it. You want to kill him, don't you? It's as simple as that."

"Yes."

"You set him up. Why? To make your conscience feel better 'cuz he comes after you? That's bullshit."

I shrugged.

"If Miller's dead it evens the score, doesn't it? Did you think about that?"

"Well . . ."

"Yeah, you thought about it. I bet you didn't think about his brother, what's the name, Nils? Why, he'll come gunning for you fast, you kill his brother."

I hesitated, and Sandy caught it.

"Look at you. You didn't think about the brother at all."

"I did," Henri said. "One gunslinger's just like another gunslinger. I'll take care of Nils."

"You guys," Sandy said. "You really think this is *High Noon*, don't you? Nils could be with his brother and Conrad right now, for all you know."

"Nils Lundberg's in Pittsburgh," Henri said. "Allegheny County Jail. He's not going anywhere for a while."

"So you think that lets you off the hook?"

Henri shook his head. "Changes the odds."

Sandy shook her head, but some of the anger, the fear, had eased. She rubbed her eyes.

"Did you talk to AJ about this?"

"Last night," I said. "Called her when I got home."

"Is she okay with it?"

I took a deep breath and let it out slowly. "AJ accepts it. She'd never be okay with it."

"Is she as scared as I am?"

I nodded. "Probably. She doesn't swear as much as you do when she's scared."

"God, I hope not," Henri said.

Sandy laughed, a little, and the tension in the office was broken. She had tears in the corners of her eyes.

"I have to use the bathroom," she said, pointing toward the gender-neutral restroom at the top of our stairs.

We heard the door close and the automatic fan start.

"Is Nils Lundberg really in jail?" I said.

Henri nodded. "Gun charge. Tried to rob a store. He's stuck unless he has a sharp lawyer on retainer."

"Or his employers do."

"Or his employers do. Arraignment's next week. I'll know more then."

"Any update on Ben Miller?"

"Nope," Henri said. "Not a word. But Conrad'll call him. I don't care how arrogant the prick is, he knows he can't fight you. His sons are no help. He knows that, too."

"Maybe Conrad'll call it off as too dangerous."

Henri shook his head. "Miller's coming for you, Russo. It's only a matter of time."

36

"Fleener called. Stop at Hendricks' office before you leave the courthouse." The voicemail came from Sandy. I'd just spent too much time in chambers with a judge who didn't like me as a lawyer, even less as an investigator. But I had a few clients who still needed my legal services.

I made my way to the office of Donald Hendricks, well into his second term as Emmet County Prosecutor. He was behind his desk when I got there. Hendricks was in his late fifties, six-two with brown hair and too many soft pounds around the middle. He always looked rumpled, sleeves rolled up, tie loose, collar unbuttoned. He didn't suffer bullshit easily. But he didn't give it either. Two words always came to mind when I entered his office: "quietly institutional." The colors were muted, gray or green. I think.

"Come on in, Russo," he said. "Sit down."

On the sidewall sat Martin Fleener, in a double-breasted suit, black with a faint red stripe, a red and black striped tie over a white spread-collar shirt.

"Been waiting long?" I said, and sat down.

Both men ignored me.

"You wanted to see me," I said to Hendricks.

"Marty," Hendricks said, and looked over at Fleener.

"Thought I'd update you on Camille North," he said.

"Okay, but why here?" These two officers of the court weren't usually so polite. "You could've just called me, Marty."

"We'll get to that in a minute," Hendricks said.

Uh-huh. Figured something was up.

Fleener pulled a reporter's notebook out of his pocket and flipped it open.

"First, the autopsy. Camille was dead about four hours when a man on his way to work found the body. She was shot twice with a .22 using centerfire ammunition. The shots were spaced close together. No powder burns. No shell casings were found anywhere near the body."

"Shooter knew what he was doing," I said. "That's Gunnar Lundberg, not Conrad North. Speaking of North, he got an alibi?"

Fleener nodded. "Never left the island. People saw him on and off all day downtown. Post office, City Council meeting, dinner at Seabiscuit. Didn't get on a ferry. Didn't get on a plane, scheduled or otherwise."

"I'm not surprised," I said. "Miller's the shooter, not North."

Fleener turned back a page in his notebook. "Lot of inconsistencies, Camille's body and the wet, muddy ground."

"I told you she wasn't shot at the overpass."

Fleener looked up but didn't respond.

"We tracked her movements. We put her on the ferry to Mackinaw City the day she was killed. We have two people who can place her at the Star Line dock that afternoon. She picked up her car from valet and drove off."

"That's all," I said.

Fleener shrugged. "We couldn't trace her to a restaurant or motel around town."

"But you already knew that," Hendricks said, with an edge in his voice.

"We pulled her cell records," Fleener said. "Checked all her calls for forty-eight hours. We got her call to you."

"That was the day before she left the island."

"It was, yes," Fleener said. "That was the last call she made. On her phone, anyway."

"That's not much help."

"Think you can do better, Russo?" Hendricks said.

Now we get to why I'm here. Maybe I can head this off.

"My client was shot, Don. She was a nice woman who had a problem and got killed for it."

He was not deterred.

"Solving murders is our business," Hendricks said. "Finding out who did it is what the taxpayers of Emmet County pay us for, Russo, Marty and me."

"You do your job with distinction." I said that with a perfectly straight face and without sarcasm.

"I'd glad to hear you think so," Hendricks said. "So you don't plan to interfere, right?"

I shook my head.

"No plans to mess with Conrad North? Nothing like that?"

I looked over at Fleener, who had his head turned to one side, scratching an ear, like he wasn't listening. I saw no reason to irritate Hendricks anymore than he already was. For now, at least.

I shook my head again. "Nothing like that." I didn't lie. I had no plans to mess with Conrad now. Better to wait for him to react to last night's little 'rousting.'

"Make sure you keep it that way, Russo," Hendricks said. "We'd take a dim view, you sticking your nose where it doesn't belong, making our job tougher."

"I understand," I said. "Anything else?"

Hendricks looked at Fleener. "Marty?"

"I'm done," he said.

"You can go, Russo," Hendricks said.

I stood up. "Don, Marty." I turned and left the prosecutor's office.

That seemed like a waste of good time. It's as if Hendricks had to make certain I knew the obvious.

I left the building on the Lake Street side. Northern Michigan was aimlessly drifting through another cloudy day, a few degrees warmer than yesterday. I put down my brief bag and tapped AJ a text, "can you leave yet?"

"palette bistro bar 15 min."

I sent off a thumbs up and started down Lake Street for the restaurant.

37

I turned at Symons General Store and went down Howard to Bay Street. Palette Bistro sits above Little Traverse Bay, on the other side of the parking lot from the office. The restaurant had a modern, contemporary feel, with two floors and tall windows overlooking the bay.

It was a quiet evening. Only a few tables were busy, but it was early. I sat at the bar, close to the street-side windows. We leave the scenic window seats for visitors.

"Hello, Michael," I heard the bartender say as he came my way. Tall and lanky, with a thin face, Chad was in his early thirties. Most people assumed he was a runner. In Chad's case they were right.

"Hey, Chad," I said. "You run this morning?"

"Almost eight, give or take," he said. "Come out with me some morning. I usually run the tarmac toward Charlevoix."

"Five's better for me," I said. "Might push it to six."

"Do you guys ever talk anything but running?" AJ said as she sat down.

"No," we said, almost together.

"I didn't think so."

"Good evening, Ms. Lester," Chad said as he put down a menu.

We ordered a Chardonnay for AJ and an Oban for me.

We leaned in and kissed. I took AJ's hand and held it.

"You look deliciously sexy this evening," I said.

AJ smiled. "You're very sweet, darling, but you always say that."

"I think I said 'wonderfully sexy' last time."

"I probably had a sweatshirt on."

"You did," I said. "The green one with all the bleach stains."

"Here we are," Chad said, putting down napkins and our drinks. We ordered a small Margherita pizza to split.

AJ picked up her glass. "Just in the nick of time to end that silly conversation."

I touched her glass with mine. "Here, here," I said. "How was your day?"

We talked work as we often do at the end of the day. AJ spent most of her time as an editor, but she was born curious, born to be a reporter. It didn't take long for her to ask.

"Do you think Hendricks knows you rousted Conrad?"

"Doubt it," I said. "If North had complained or someone'd seen us, we'd have heard from those guys a lot sooner."

"Hendricks was what? Warning you to stay away?"

"Yeah. Fleener, too. No surprise. They're convinced I'm going after Conrad or Miller."

"Or course, they're right."

I shrugged.

Chad put down the pizza, with two small plates. "Enjoy," he said.

We sat quietly for a few minutes and ate some pizza.

"Got to love the mozzarella and basil," I said.

"Thumbs up to that," she said, and drank some wine.

"Michael, does it bother you that you set up Miller to come after you?"

I touched AJ's arm. "I know you worry when someone's after me."

"I do worry," she said. "I love you, Michael, so I have a license to worry when you're in danger, but that's not what I'm talking about."

"Okay." I sipped some Oban and waited. I didn't need to ask.

"You suckered Miller. You want him to come after you, Michael. When he does, you'll kill him."

"Not necessarily."

"Not necessarily, my ass," AJ said, louder, but there was no one close enough to hear except Chad. Like the good bartender he was, Chad paid no attention.

"Fleener could arrest him, AJ."

"You won't give him the chance."

"Conrad tells Miller what to do, AJ, not me."

"That's a bullshit distinction, and you know it." She picked up her glass, but set it back down without taking a drink. "You set this in motion, you and Henri. You'll find a way to put Conrad in prison, but that's not what you want for Miller, and you know it."

I was quiet and sipped some Oban. AJ understood, she always did.

"I went after those two shooters from LA a couple of years ago. You didn't seem to mind."

"Bad analogy, Michael. Those gunmen tried to assassinate a friend of yours. Then you went after them."

"Now who's making a bullshit distinction?"

AJ shook her head. "No, it's not, Michael. You tracked the LA men. You didn't know how it would turn out. That's not the case this time. You set up Miller for only one reason."

I took a deep breath to give me a few extra seconds. "It doesn't bother me, AJ." I shrugged. "It just doesn't. Maybe it should, but it doesn't. It's what I need to do."

"Yes, it's what you need to do."

"I might not be as nice as you think I am, AJ."

She smiled and took my hand. "You are a nice man, Michael, and I love you. It's just you have some, ah, interesting ideas about friendship, about loyalty."

We finished the pizza, and Chad brought the tab.

We stopped on the sidewalk outside the restaurant. "It feels like spring might be here, after all," AJ said.

"Don't get your hopes up," I said. "It's still April."

"Where's your car?"

"At home."

"My car's right here," she said, and pointed at her SUV across the street. "Come home with me." AJ put her arm through mine. "I might be persuaded to put on that sexy sweatshirt you like so much. The one with the bleach stains."

"I'd rather persuade you to take it off."

"Persuasion will not be necessary, darling."

I pulled AJ in close and kissed her, hard. She kissed back. We crossed the street and AJ beeped the door locks.

"I'll have to be out early tomorrow," I said.

"Camille's funeral?"

"Uh-huh."

"What ferry you taking?"

"First one. I'm meeting Nicole Sanderson on the dock. We'll talk on the ride over."

"A funeral's an important ritual. It might bring all the players in this ugly drama together."

"Not all of them," I said. "Ben Miller won't show up."

"You sure about that?"

38

I sat at the table in my kitchen, drank coffee and checked email. The walk from AJ's was uneventful, even though I kept one eye on the street. I took a fast shower and dressed in charcoal slacks and a navy blazer, a white shirt with a red and black striped tie. And I put on real lace-up shoes. Black wing-tips.

I pulled the car out of the lot, worked my way over to Mitchell, Division, and U.S. 31 North. The eastern sky showed its colors this morning, orange, yellow, red all mixed with a cloudless blue.

The ride up 31 to Mackinaw City was fast and smooth. No cops, and few cars. I slowed up on the approach to the bridge. The south tower, still over a mile away, stood very tall in the blue sky. Maintenance work on the bridge had yet to resume, so the run across the five-mile span was easier and quicker than it would be later in the day.

I made my way up North State Street and found a parking space nowhere near the dock. I took the boardwalk along the water. The air was warm, the sky was a bright blue and a few tree branches were budding. It was the kind of early spring morning that people who live in northern Michigan appreciate differently than anyone else.

It was a nice day to bury a friend.

I spotted Ruth Avila and a woman I assumed to be her client standing near the ramp. Ruth saw me and waved.

"Good morning, Ruth," I said.

"Michael," she said. "Meet Nicole Sanderson."

Nicole was five-six, in her mid-thirties, maybe one-twenty with an angular face like her father's. She had brown eyes and brown hair, cut to the shoulders. She wore a two-piece black suit trimmed with small, shiny brass buttons. The skirt fell just above the knee.

"Mr. Russo," Nicole said.

"No formality," Ruth said. "It's Michael and Nicole. Okay?"

I reached out and we shook hands. We both said "okay" at the same time.

"Let's go," Ruth said, and we boarded the *Huron*. The ferry was crowded with workers, managers and business owners. I suppose a few tourists were mixed in, but it was hard to tell. We found bench seats in the rear cabin.

"Thank you for coming to my mother's funeral," Nicole said.

"I wanted to be here," I said. "I'm sorry for your loss."

Nicole smiled. "Thank you."

The *Huron* sounded its horn, pulled back from the dock and swung around to leave the harbor.

"Ruth told me you'll be staying with her for a few days."

"Yes," Nicole said. "A few issues that need attention."

"Do any of them involve the cottage and the lease?"

"Well," Nicole said, and hesitated.

"I don't mean to pry . . . to break into private matters," I said.

"Don't worry," Ruth said, "either of you. I'll make sure privacy is respected."

"I only meant to ask about the house," I said. "Since that's why your mother hired me."

"Did you ever learn anything?" Nicole said. "Find out what happened?" Something about her voice . . . I wasn't sure if she was edgy or simply impatient.

"No. I wish I had another answer for you, but I don't."

"That's too bad," she said. "I'd hoped for more."

"Me, too," I said. "But I haven't found it yet."

"Yet?" Nicole said. "I don't understand. Are you still working on the lease?"

"I am."

"I didn't hire you to pursue the matter," Nicole said. "I'm damn sure Conrad didn't hire you." She was edgy. No doubt about it now.

"I'm on my own," I said. "Just thought I'd keep at it, see what shows up."

Nicole nodded and but remained silent.

The *Huron* motored along slowly. We passed the west end of the island and in front of the school and Grand Hotel.

"Will you stand with the rest of the family at the gravesite?" I said.

"I am the family," Nicole said. "The others, I don't care. I will sit where I want in the church and stand where I want at the cemetery."

We'd almost reached the west breakwater when Nicole turned to me and said, "I'm sorry, Michael. I didn't mean . . . I snapped at you."

She looked out the glass, started to talk again, but the words weren't there yet. Finally, "I'm burying my mother today," she said. "A lot going on. Conrad, damn him. He started all this. He'll take the house . . . the Sanderson house. Our house. I don't understand. It's not fair."

"No," I said. "It's not fair."

Tears appeared in the corners of her eyes. Nicole nodded, but said nothing more.

The *Huron* rounded the breakwater and sounded its horn. The usual migration to the lower deck had already begun.

Ruth Avila and Nicole Sanderson left the rear cabin and got in line near the stairway. I waited for the *Huron* to tie up. When passengers began moving up the ramp, I left the cabin. The two women were halfway up the dock by the time I was off the ferry.

At Main Street, I went east, turned at Doud's, and walked up Fort Street.

Trinity Episcopal Church, and the Parish Hall next door, sit half-way up the hill across the street from the visitor's entrance to Fort Mackinac. A slender white building, the church was constructed in 1882 after the congregation spent years meeting inside the fort.

A few people milled about near the front steps of the church and the Parish Hall. One of them, Henri LaCroix, stood on the other side of Fort

Street where he had a good view of Marquette Park, the front and side doors of the church and the road up the hill to the governor's house.

"Morning, Henri."

"Russo," he said. Henri had traded his tan Carhartt jacket, again, for a black blazer, unbuttoned, a black turtleneck and black pants.

This was a Mackinac funeral, some people dressed up, ties, coats, dresses. Some came in work uniforms, kitchen pants, DPW shirts and jackets. Others were casually dressed in the attire of resorts, even one guy in tan cords with little green ducks all over them.

"See anybody interesting?"

"No sign of Ben Miller, if that's who you mean."

"Wouldn't be the smart move," I said.

"No. North and his sons went in a few minutes ago. I saw Ruth Avila and a woman I presume to be Nicole Sanderson. Some folks from the island, of course. Talked with Althea Baldwin."

"You know Althea?"

Henri nodded. "We've been friends for quite a while. I like her."

I noticed a familiar figure coming up the hill. His single-breasted black suit with narrow lapels, skinny tie and white cotton shirt (not ironed) gave him away.

Lenny Stern.

"Morning, Lenny," I said. "Are you a friend of Camille North, or is a funeral on Mackinac Island big news in Petoskey?"

Stern smiled. "A murder below the bridge is big news, Russo."

We shook hands. "LaCroix," Stern said. "What's your interest in the departed?"

"This on the record?"

"Oh, don't be so touchy, LaCroix. I know why Russo's here. Just asking."

Henri stuck his hands in his pockets. "We're neighbors. Been casual friends for years."

Stern smiled. "See, that wasn't so hard."

Henri was not amused.

Stern looked around. "The husband here yet?"

"Inside," I said.

"What about her sons?"

"They're not her sons, Lenny."

Stern shook his head. "Are they here, or not?"

"Inside."

"You're a couple of hard-asses, you know that?" Lenny said. "You going up to the cemetery?"

"Yeah," I said.

Lenny nodded. "Later."

The church bell rang, and Henri said, "You go ahead. I'll be along in a minute." His eyes scanned the road up the hill, the park. Henri was always cautious.

I heard organ music as I went up the front steps of the church. Inside, Trinity was all dark wood, a massive altar and beautifully-detailed stained glass windows. One hundred people, maybe, filled the pews. They chatted as they waited for the service to start.

I took a seat in the back and looked around. Conrad and his sons sat in the front row on one side of the center aisle, Nicole on the other. Between them, a few feet way was a small raised table holding a dark wood box with brass trim. Camille North's ashes.

A door opened at the rear of the church and the organist wrapped it up with a flourish. The priest came forward and welcomed everyone to the service.

She opened a prayer book. "I am the resurrection and I am the life . . ."

The man who rang the bell closed the outside door, and no one walked in during the service except Henri, who eased his way in and sat close to the door.

"In the assurance of eternal life . . ."

The tension in the room was thick. Conrad, the sons and Nicole. Everyone knew it, everyone felt it. I didn't expect an outburst, but I couldn't be sure. We had assembled to honor the late Camille North, but she was hardly the center of attention.

"Comfort us in our sorrows at the death of our sister . . ."

When it was time for communion, Conrad and the boys moved quickly out of the pew for the altar railing, ignoring Nicole. No empathy, and certainly no class.

Nicole held back until a few others had gone by. When Conrad was seated, she took her turn at the altar and returned to the pew without looking Conrad's way.

"Let us go forth," the priest said, and the service was over.

39

Mourners filed out slowly. Nicole waited until Conrad walked out and moved away from the church. I stood at the door until Nicole and Ruth Avila went by. They were the last ones outside.

Henri was across the street again, talking with Althea Baldwin.

Several large tour carriages were lined up to take people to the Protestant cemetery in the middle of the island. A taxi waited at the head of the line.

A small, private carriage, dark blue with gold pinstripes, sat down the street. Conrad and the boys climbed aboard and the driver pulled out of line and went toward Market Street.

The priest, Nicole, and the container of ashes took the taxi. Henri and I sat with Ruth on the first tour carriage. Lenny Stern sat three rows behind us.

I said to Ruth, "Do you know Lenny Stern?"

She nodded. "The man's a pain in the ass."

"Makes him a good reporter, Ruth."

"I can tell he's never written a story on you."

As the line of carriages methodically wound its way up to the cemetery, Henri leaned over. "Althea wants to talk to you," he said. "After the service."

"Okay."

No lunch had been scheduled. Few restaurants were up and running and Conrad did not offer an alternative, not that Nicole would have gone anyway.

As we neared the cemeteries, I noticed a lone carriage, small, black and fully enclosed, parked around the corner on Fort Holmes Road. I nudged Henri as the door opened and two men stepped out. Carmine DeMio and bodyguard, Gino Rosato.

"Lot of firepower for a funeral," Henri said.

The carriages stopped in a line at the side of Garrison Road, near the front entrance. People walked to the gravesite at the back of the cemetery. Conrad and Nicole stood opposite one another during the service, but did not speak.

In contrast to their father, Wolfgang and Wilhelm wore neither a suit nor a tie. They acted thoroughly bored with the proceedings. They shifted from foot to foot, stared off into the trees. Conrad, at least, pretended to show some respect for his wife of more than forty years.

I was ten feet from Nicole. Henri stood thirty feet away from us, with a better view of the site.

"May . . . the souls of all the departed . . . rest in peace," the priest read from the prayer book, and the service was finished.

People wandered slowly back to the street and the waiting carriages. With no after-service lunch scheduled, they were in no hurry. Small groups formed and talked, others stopped at different graves and read the headstones. Still others meandered into the Catholic cemetery or down the street to the one reserved for veterans of the military.

As the carriages filled up, I walked over and stood with Henri.

"Anything?"

"Quiet," he said, "although I thought about needling Rosato. Just for fun."

Nicole and Ruth came over. I introduced Henri.

"Could I have a minute, Michael?" Nicole said.

"Sure."

"Catch up when you're done, Michael," Henri said.

"I wonder if you would have some time for us to talk," Nicole said after Henri walked away. "Not right now. I'm just . . . well, not right now."

"I understand."

"Michael," Ruth said, "how about tomorrow morning? My office."

"Yes," I said. "That'll be fine."

We made the arrangements, and the two women climbed aboard the taxi with the priest for the ride downtown.

Henri chatted with Althea Baldwin near the front gate of the cemetery. I'd forgotten that she had something to say.

"Hello," I said. "It's nice to see you again, even if it's here."

Althea shook her head. "It was quite a shock. When I heard the news . . . I couldn't believe it."

"When did you see Camille?" I said. "The last time."

"It was that morning. Not the morning she died, I don't mean that. I mean the morning she left the island. Before she died."

"What did she talk about?" I said.

"Nothing in particular. We had coffee. We always do that first thing." Althea hesitated. "I mean that's what we did, have coffee. Most mornings."

"Did Camille tell you she was going across?"

Althea shook her head. "I had no idea. She was at the house when I left. She was gone when I got home."

"You were on the island?"

Althea nodded. "In the Mission. We discuss books every week, five of us. It was Jane Smiley that day. *A Thousand Acres*. Do you know it?"

I nodded. "Did you take a taxi back and forth?"

"I took one home, yes," she said. "But I usually walk down. It's very good exercise."

"You didn't see Camille?"

"No, I didn't see her at all."

"Did you see Conrad?"

Althea had a disgusted look on her face. "That man's . . ." She crossed her arms over her chest. "Let's just say I have no use for that man."

"Did you see him that day?"

"No," she said. "Our paths don't cross very often. Until he showed up at my door, I . . ."

"Conrad was at your house?" Henri said.

"Yes," she said.

"When was this?" I said.

"Two days after Camille died. He banged on my door. I told him to go away, but he didn't listen."

"What did he want?" Henri said.

"Camille's things. Clothes mostly. A few personal things, books, a laptop. That's all. He just barged through the door with those awful boys of his. They hardly said two words. I couldn't stop him. They picked up as much as they could carry and walked out."

"Did you call the police?"

Althea shook her head. "It was her husband. What would I say?"

Most of the carriages had pulled away for the ride back down. The last of the mourners made their way to the street.

"We'll have to get going pretty soon," I said.

"Althea," Henri said. "We've been asking all the questions, but you wanted to talk with Michael."

"Yes," she said. "I don't know if it means anything."

"What does?"

"What Camille said to me. It wasn't like a long talk or anything. She said a name: Helen Simons."

"Helen Simons?"

Althea nodded. "Helen Simons."

"Not a familiar name?" Henri said.

"Not at all."

"What else did she say?"

"Nothing. Just the name."

"A woman from the island?" I said. "Or Mackinaw City?"

"I have no idea," Althea said. "But the name meant something to Camille."

"How did you know?" I said. "Sorry about the question. Don't misunderstand, I believe you, but how could you tell?"

Althea smiled. "I understand you, Mr. Russo. It's why I wanted you to know. Camille knew the woman. I could just tell, that's all."

I started to ask another question, but the driver of the last carriage got our attention. He was about to leave for downtown.

"We'll be right there," I said, and waved.

Helen Simons . . . Helen Simons. I kept saying the name over and over again in my head, like it would help me recognize Helen Simons. It didn't help.

"It was good to see you again, Mr. Russo," Althea said.

"You're not coming with us?"

"It's an easy walk home," she said. "Good-bye."

Henri and I climbed aboard for the slow ride downtown.

"You taking the last boat?" Henri said.

"Yeah, I need to get back." I told him about Ruth and my appointment with Nicole in the morning.

"Did she say why?"

"No. It didn't seem like the time to push the issue. I'll find out tomorrow."

The carriage dropped us at Doud's corner. We walked down Main Street toward the boat dock. Most of the work crews had called it a day so the men could take the last ferry. Scaffolding remained in place at the Chippewa Hotel. Two drays sat at the curb. Both were filled with trash, smashed drywall, cut two-by-fours, a door.

"Going to the post office," Henri said, and started up the walkway next to the Tourism Bureau. "Call me tomorrow."

"Will do," I said, and crossed the street to the dock.

The *Huron* was already crowded by the time I got there. I found a seat in the front cabin, near the door, and pulled out my phone. I tapped AJ, "back in the office by 6. dinner?"

Sure be nice to figure out what's going on. Helen Simons? Who are you, Helen Simons? Why were you important to Camille North?

40

"I'm with you this time, boss," Sandy said. "I don't believe it's a coincidence any more than you do."

We sat in client chairs in the front window. Since the office was officially closed for the day, Sandy had kicked off her shoes. I poured two fingers of Oban in shot glasses and handed one to her.

"Boy," she said. "That's good. Give me a raise, I'd drink this stuff more often."

"I'll keep that in mind during your annual performance review."

"We don't have an annual review."

"Never mind then," I said. "So, you never heard the name before?"

"Never."

"Haven't read it anyplace?"

"Not that I remember. But there has to be a reason Althea Baldwin told you. She thought it was important."

We heard someone on the stairs.

"Aren't we closed for the day?" I said, holding my glass in the air.

"Yep."

"Tell whoever it is to go away."

"You tell 'em," she said. "It might be a new client, you know, with money."

We looked over at the door.

AJ walked in and stopped when she saw us staring.

"What?"

"Ma'am," I said. "Are you a paying client, looking for a hotshot investigator?"

"How many of those have you had?" AJ said, and pointed at our glasses.

"On our way to *numero dos*," I said. "Care to join us?"

"I'll get it," she said. AJ hung her coat on the rack and opened the cabinet door on the sideboard. She took a glass and wheeled Sandy's desk chair over.

"Salute." We raised our glasses.

"What'd I miss?" AJ said, and sipped some scotch.

"You first, boss," Sandy said.

I filled in the blanks for AJ, finishing up with the mysterious name 'Helen Simons.'

"I agree with Sandy," she said.

"Thank you," Sandy said, and smiled.

"Camille mentioned the woman's name to Althea Baldwin because it was on her mind. That wasn't the end of it. Althea picked that up. Now what?"

"You're the reporter," I said, "what would you do?"

"Assign a first-rate researcher to find Simons."

AJ and I turned and stared at Sandy.

"Is that all I am around here, a researcher?"

"A first-rate researcher," AJ said, and raised an index finger in the air.

"BFD."

"It will be if you find Simons," I said. "Treat you to a fifth of Oban."

Sandy finished off her scotch and held up the empty glass.

"Allow me," AJ said.

"You guys are too much."

AJ refilled our glasses.

"All right," Sandy said. "A serious question, AJ?"

"Ask away."

"Where would you start? If you were still a reporter, I mean."

AJ smiled and said, "Same place as you."

Sandy hesitated. "I'd start with *Google*."

AJ shrugged. "Me, too."

"What about a veteran like Lenny Stern? A *Google* search?"

"As much as he'd hate to admit it, yes." AJ leaned forward, the professional journalist taking over the conversation. "These days, it's where everything starts. We've got other sources, sure. Sometimes they're even real people who've been doing their job for a long time."

"Like Lenny Stern."

"Yeah, like Lenny."

"Gee," I said. "How about *Wikipedia*?"

"Russo, you'd make a lousy reporter," AJ said. "You'd believe some fourteen-year-old in Butte, Montana, making shit up."

"Sorry I asked."

"You should be. We have a woman here," AJ gestured at Sandy, "in desperate need of our help, and the best you've got is *Wikipedia*?"

"I wouldn't call me desperate," Sandy said. "Helpless, naïve, maybe, but certainly not desperate."

AJ laughed and looked at her empty glass. "I'm hungry. Anybody up for food?"

"Think Lenny'd help if I asked?"

"Of course he would," AJ said. "But this one's in the weeds, Sandy."

"I'll say it's in the weeds. We don't even recognize the name." Sandy drank the last of her scotch and stood up. "Time to go home. I have beef stew waiting for me."

"Start first thing in the morning, Sandy," I said.

She gathered up her coat and briefcase and left for the day.

"I'm hungry, too."

"Where you want to eat, Mr. Detective?"

"How about I fix penne pasta with an olive oil sauce?"

AJ smiled. "With lots of garlic?"

"Is there any other way?"

"A salad and bread, too?"

I nodded. "Thought we could stream an old Alfred Hitchcock film."

"*North by Northwest*?"

I shook my head. "*The Lady Vanishes*. It's about a missing woman."

"I know what it's about, wise-ass," AJ said, and slapped me on the shoulder.

"*Gone Girl*?"

"Enough, already. You make the dinner. I'll pick the movie. Deal?"

"Deal," I said. "Before we go . . ."

"What?"

"You really think Althea Baldwin had a reason?"

"I don't know for sure she had a reason, Michael, but she clearly thought the name was important enough to tell you."

"Okay," I said. "Come on, let's go home."

41

"I can't decide which I liked better," AJ said, "your terrific pasta or the movie." We sat on the couch in my living room, relaxed and no longer hungry.

"Well," I said, "*North by Northwest* is one of your favorite films."

"An innocent man, wrongly accused," AJ said. "That's not your problem with this case."

"It certainly is not."

AJ stretched out with her feet on the coffee table, hands behind her head.

"Anything new on Miller?"

I shook my head. "Henri'll find him sooner or later."

"Let's hope it's sooner. Do you think Conrad's given the order?"

"To come after me?"

"Yes."

I hesitated, and AJ picked it up. "Michael? Are you holding out on me?"

"No."

"What is it then?"

"I think Conrad gave the order the night we rousted him in the parking lot."

AJ nodded slowly. "What's he waiting for, the right moment?"

I shrugged. "Or the right opportunity."

"But you give him plenty of opportunities, Michael."

"Like when?" I said, a little annoyed.

"Like when you run alone. And don't get touchy, Michael. It's your ass I'm worried about."

"I run with lots of people around, AJ. Ever see all the construction people in Bay View this time of year? They're everywhere. It's a built-in audience. Miller knows that."

"You told me Miller likes to do the unexpected."

"Joey DeMio said that, not me."

"Well, he ought to know. He's a mobster for Christ's sake."

"Now who's getting touchy?"

AJ put her hand on my hand and squeezed gently.

"Maybe Miller's trying to rattle you by not hitting right away."

"I'm not the one who's rattled," I said, wishing I hadn't said it.

"Don't remind me." She pulled her hand away. "Don't get lippy with me, either."

I reached over and took her hand back. "I'm sorry, AJ. I really am."

"Then why don't you take the threat seriously?"

"I do take the threat seriously. We've had this discussion before, but I can't let it consume my life. I can't hide in my apartment."

"I know, I know."

"Besides, Miller'd lob a Molotov cocktail through the living room window, I tried that."

AJ put her hands in the air like she was under arrest. "Truce?"

I nodded. "Of course," I said. "I love you."

"I know you do, sweetheart, and I love you. It's a good thing, too."

AJ looked up, around the room.

"What?" I said.

"Darling, how about we go to the bedroom?"

"Sounds like a wonderful idea. What'd you have in mind?"

"Well . . ."

"Yeah?"

"I was just thinking, more like brainstorming, but if Miller's going to blow up the living room, I'd rather be in another room."

"What?"

AJ broke out in a loud, deep laugh. “You said I shouldn’t be so rattled.”

“You are a pain sometimes, you know that?”

“Is this . . .?”

“Yes. Are you staying the night or not?”

“I am indeed,” AJ said. “But I want a bath first.”

She leaned over and kissed me on the lips, hard. Then, easier on the cheek as she got up.

“That thing in the movie, you know, on the train?”

“Cary Grant and Eva Marie Saint?”

“Uh-huh. Hiding from the bad guys.”

“When they stuffed themselves into an upper berth?”

“Uh-huh.”

“That was a train car, AJ. We don’t have a train car.”

“Well, we have a bathtub, for Pete’s sake. Use your imagination.”

42

"I have to go, darling," AJ said. We were a tangle of legs and arms, pillows and sheets. The early sun came through the window and lit the room with a dull haze.

"Stay another hour or so," I said, tightening my arms around her.

"I'll put the coffee on." She untangled herself and sat on the side of the bed.

"You don't have any clothes on," I said.

AJ turned around. The light from the window outlined her breasts. I reached out, but she took my hand and kissed it. "You had enough fun last night, buster."

"Can you stay for coffee?"

"I'll be late for work if I don't get out of here."

She got off the bed and turned around to face me.

"Take a good last look, darling."

And I did as she slipped on panties and a bra and stepped into her skirt.

"I'll be gone a couple of days," she said.

"Where to?"

"Michigan State. Maury and I'll leave after work."

Maury Weston was publisher of the *Petoskey Post Dispatch*. The resort season affected the news business, too. More coverage of more activities for more readers. Weston hired a dozen interns for all departments of the paper each summer. Most were journalism or advertising majors at MSU.

AJ finished dressing, sat back down and leaned over to kiss me.

"Are you running today?"

"Yeah," I said, stretching out the word. "Before I go to the office. Why?"

AJ put her hand on mine. "Just be careful. Okay?"

"Still worried about Miller?"

"Yes," she said. "And you should be too, Michael."

AJ sometimes worried too much. But, there was a fine line between reassuring her and being dismissive of her feelings.

"I'll pay attention," I said. "Promise."

"You'll stay in Bay View?" That was her way of asking that I not go to isolated areas this morning.

"Yep. Plenty of construction workers around."

She nodded. "Have to go." She kissed me again and left the bedroom.

I went over to a small chest that held my running gear, found a pair of wind pants and a long sleeve T-shirt.

Ninety-five minutes later, I sat at the kitchen table with a plate of eggs, scrambled, wheat toast and a large glass of orange juice. And hot coffee. The run, all forty-five minutes of it, went smoothly and safely. Even without AJ's urging, I paid more attention to my surroundings: driveways, big trucks, a long hedge row. Any place Miller could hide.

I grabbed my brief bag, put on a light cotton jacket and walked to the office. The spring sun warmed the air as it climbed higher in the sky. I cut through the parking lot and into McLean & Eakin to get the *Times*. I needed to come back later and pick out a new novel. Maybe not another mystery this time.

"Good morning, boss," Sandy said when I came through the door.

I hung up my jacket and she handed me three messages. "Nothing urgent."

"Good to hear."

"But," she said.

"Yes?"

"You have two appointments."

"Nicole Sanderson," I said, and looked at my watch. "In half an hour."

"Yes, at Ruth Avila's office. After that, on your way to Cheboygan."

"Lunch at Mulligan's. The banker, what's his name?"

"Don't remember, but the file's on your desk."

Sandy turned back to her screen and tapped the keyboard.

"Any luck?"

She shook her head. "Just started. I've tried different ways to search 'Helen Simons' but only two hits so far."

"Uh-huh."

"Don't get too excited, boss. The first was a cat groomer in Sausalito, California. Never heard of Petoskey or Mackinac. I'm not sure she even knows what Michigan is."

"The other one?"

"A nineteen-year-old sophomore at Mississippi State. That's in Starkville.

Apparently, Mississippi is a hotbed of catfish."

"I need to know this?"

"Indeed, you do," Sandy said. "Sarah Jane, that's the kid's name, Sarah Jane, goes to class and works in the catfish fields, or tanks, or whatever they're called. Her family has the largest catfish farm in the Old Confederacy."

"Do tell."

"Could I make that up?"

"I assume you didn't," I said. "I'll be in my office."

I worked through the client file for my Cheboygan appointment and made a few notes.

"Okay, on my way to Avila's office," I said on my way out the door. "Be back after Cheboygan."

Sandy waved, but never looked up from the screen.

43

Another few days like today and either I wouldn't need a jacket or I'd need my winter coat again. Northern Michigan in the spring.

I walked up Lake, crossed against the light – it was still April, after all – and headed up Howard. Near the bank on the corner of Mitchell and Howard stood a three-story building. The top two floors housed the legal offices of Jagger-Stovall.

I searched for the stairs because I like to climb stairs. They were tucked into a far corner of the main floor. One floor up I found the lobby of Jagger-Stovall, a firm that preferred leather, muted colors and oil paintings to chrome, glass and tile.

"Ruth Avila is expecting me," I said to the man at the reception counter next to the elevator I hadn't used. He was in his twenties, conservatively dressed in a three-piece gray suit and a white shirt.

"A moment, please," he said, and picked up a desk phone. As he put the phone back, he said, "Through the door behind me. Ms. Avila's on her way up."

I nodded and went through the door. Ruth Avila was coming down the hall.

"Michael, good morning. Welcome to the hallowed halls of Jagger-Stovall."

We shook hands, and I followed her to the end of the hallway. Ruth's corner office was a clone of the lobby in tone and feel. The paintings, some oil, some water-color, big and small, all depicted Petoskey or Harbor Springs. The other wall was all shelves filled with books about the law. I recognized many of them. The sidewall was all glass, and offered a terrific view of the bay five blocks away.

Nicole Sanderson stood at the window, but turned her attention away from the view as Ruth and I came through the door. She was dressed more casually than she'd been at the funeral. Black jeans that fit tight and well, black oxford shoes and a lightweight rose turtleneck.

We shook hands.

"Hello, Michael," she said. "Thank you for coming."

We all sat down, Nicole and I in client chairs, Ruth behind her desk.

"Michael," Ruth said, "we have two items on the agenda this morning. Both were Nicole's idea, and I concur with her decisions. Nicole?"

"First," Nicole said. "yesterday, the funeral, you understand, wasn't the best time to talk."

I nodded. "Of course."

"Would you please summarize what you know about my mother's death and her lease."

I recapped what I knew, finishing with the only new wrinkle, Helen Simons.

"I've never heard of her," Nicole said. "Ruth?"

Ruth shook her head. "No."

I said to Nicole, "Never heard your mother or father say the name?"

"I don't speak for Conrad," she said. "It's not a name my mother ever mentioned."

"Well, that's it, I'm afraid. As I said yesterday, I wish I had more to offer you."

"Are you still planning to pursue the matter? On your own, I mean?"

"I am."

"What if I object?"

I paused. "I'd take that into consideration."

"Does that translate into you'll do it anyway?" Nicole's voice was clear and edgy.

Before I could concoct an evasive answer, Nicole said, "It's because my mother was your client and she was murdered on your watch. That's it, isn't it? You're doing this for her. Your loyalty is to her, isn't it?"

Nicole was very sharp. No point being evasive.

"Yes," I said.

I looked over at Ruth. She shrugged. "I told her you'd say that."

"As long as you're being so stubborn," Nicole said. She was angry now, rather than edgy. It wasn't aimed at me. "I want to hire you, on the record and in front of my attorney. Stay on the case, will you? Find out who killed my mother and figure out what the hell happened to that lease."

"I encouraged her," Ruth said. "When we talked about this."

"The cops are more likely to solve the murder than I am."

"You and Ruth know more about that than I do," Nicole said. "Work on the lease then. If it helps on the other end, good. Now, tell me how much you charge for your services."

"Twenty bucks."

"No, seriously, how much?" she said, and pulled out her checkbook.

"I am serious. Twenty bucks. Give it to Ruth. I learn what happened, I collect the twenty. If not, buy yourselves a couple of drinks."

Nicole smiled and put away her checkbook. She handed a twenty-dollar bill to Ruth Avila. "You have a deal."

"Good," I said. "Two questions."

"All right."

"Do you think your . . . do you think Conrad killed your mother?"

Nicole took a deep breath.

"I'm convinced Conrad's responsible. But he paid to have it done. He doesn't have the balls to do something like that himself." Equal measures of anger and disdain fueled her comment.

"Can you find evidence Conrad had my mother killed, Michael?"

"If the police don't, you mean?"

"Yes."

"I don't know."

"At least you're honest about it."

"Thank you," I said.

"Did you have more for me?" Nicole said.

"One more thing," I said. "Do you want your cottage back?"

Nicole leaned forward and looked first at Ruth, then at me. Tears appeared at the corners of her eyes.

"It's not my house," she said. "I mean, I haven't thought of it as mine since my mother married Conrad and those . . . those children of his moved in." The word "children" hung unpleasantly in the air.

"With Camille gone, the cottage will go to you."

"Not legally," Ruth said. "Not unless we can successfully challenge the validity of the lease with Conrad's name on it."

"Is there any way to prove it's not my mother's original lease?"

Ruth shook her head. "First thing, I checked the Register of Deeds in St. Ignace. No member of the Sanderson family ever registered the lease."

The office was quiet until Nicole broke the silence.

"I want the cottage. There, I've said it. I grew up in that house, Michael. I'm a Sanderson, and the cottage is Sanderson history. I want the cottage."

"We have to find out how the names were changed," Ruth said.

"I can do something about that," I said.

"Then do it," Nicole said. The edge was back, but again it wasn't directed at me.

"All right," Ruth said, and stood up. The meeting was over.

"I leave day after tomorrow," Nicole said. "I want to know if something changes."

"You will."

44

I left the car at home as usual, so I walked back down Howard. There wasn't much to be done until I returned from Cheboygan.

My mind wandered as I enjoyed the warm, sunny day. It was an occupational hazard of runners who live in the upper Great Lakes. People who live in states without a change in seasons never quite appreciate the arrival of spring the way we do, especially the way runners do.

I crossed Lake Street, with the light this time, and continued on my way. A spring day like today always puts a smile on my face and energy in my legs. Runners are always . . .

I would look back on this moment, this second in time. I wasn't paying attention.

I couldn't get my breath . . . I choked . . . he grabbed my collar and yanked back . . . a hard punch to the kidney . . . he spun me around.

Miller hit me high, under the ribs. I lost my air. Second hit, same place. He slammed me against the brick wall. In the small alley, ten feet off the sidewalk. I tried to put up my hands. The searing pain of the blade cut me through the jacket. Blood ran down my arm. His blade cut my left side, waist high. I threw a Karate punch with my good arm. Caught him with a glancing blow to the throat. I slid down the wall to the tarmac. Miller stumbled back a step. It was just enough. I pulled out my .38. Bam . . . bam . . . bam. Grouped, chest high. Miller was dead before he hit the ground.

45

"What's the last thing you remember?"

I tried to focus, tried to see.

"Mr. Russo? Here, Mr. Russo. Look at me, please."

I moved my head. A woman's face. A white coat.

"That's better. What's the last thing you remember?"

"Um . . . I . . . where am I?"

"The hospital, sir. They brought you in yesterday."

"I, ah, the alley."

"Focus, Mr. Russo. Look here, please."

"The alley. I was . . . the other man?"

"I don't know about anyone else, sir. Sorry."

"Michael?"

I turned my head. It hurt to do that, but I recognized the voice. "AJ?"

AJ picked up my hand, the one that didn't hurt, and squeezed it.

"Yes, darling."

"I'm fuzzy."

"We sedated you, yesterday, to help you sleep. It wears off fast. Your head'll clear up pretty quickly now."

"Do I . . .you look familiar."

"I'm Dr. Rochelle Silverstein," she said, and smiled. "I was in the ER two years ago. You'd been beaten up."

"Yeah, right. Thanks."

"You're welcome," she said.

I was in a small room with light blue walls, a big window and one bed.

"Have I been out since yesterday?"

"Yes," AJ said.

"You been here since yesterday?"

"Yes. I went home for a few hours last night. When I knew you'd be all right."

I started to move my left arm, but the pain stopped me.

"They put a lot of stitches in that arm of yours," Dr. Silverstein said. "Bad cut."

I moved my good arm to my side.

"More stitches," she said.

"It's sore."

"You were lucky, Mr. Russo," the doctor said. "A knife like that's meant to kill. It didn't hit anything. All you got was a cut, and not a particularly bad one at that. You'll still hurt for a while."

"You fix me up?"

She shook her head. "Docs in the ER did that."

"Thank them for me."

"I will," she said. "Mr. Russo, be more careful, will you? I'd rather not see you a third time." She smiled. "I'll be back later."

"I thought you were in Lansing?"

"I never left," AJ said. "They called me."

"What about Miller? Is he dead?"

AJ moved closer to the bed. "Is your head clear?"

"Pretty good," I said.

"Clear enough you're piecing things together?"

"Yeah. I think so."

AJ leaned in. "You almost got yourself killed. You know that? What the fuck were you doing?"

"You're yelling."

"Damn right, I'm yelling," she said. "You got jumped in broad daylight. The only hiding spot on the whole fucking block and you didn't see it?"

AJ straightened up and turned around. We were quiet.

"Feel better?" I said.

"No."

"What about Miller?"

"He's dead."

"You sure?"

"The cops that caught the 911, one of them's in my class." AJ taught evening classes in writing at North Central Michigan College. "He called me from the ER."

"Petoskey Police have the case?"

"Not anymore," she said. "Martin Fleener's got it now."

"Is he here?"

"On the floor someplace," she said. "He had a call."

So Fleener had the case. A shooting downtown would not make anyone happy. Not the police, the Chamber, City Council. With tourist season fast approaching, there'd be pressure to clear it quickly. Just like Mackinaw City after Camille North was gunned down.

"Well, well," Martin Fleener said. "Is Petoskey's favorite private eye finally awake?"

Fleener did not often try sarcasm.

"Marty," I said.

"I read the report," he said. "There's a few holes in the story."

"Yeah?"

"They tried to piece it together, crime scene people, what you told them, what they found."

"Yeah?"

"Got some questions," Fleener said. "I told you to stay away from this. Stay away from Miller, North, all of it. Let us handle it. But no. Now Miller's dead. You ought to be handcuffed to the bed."

"Is there a question in there?"

"Shut up, Russo. You couldn't just walk away?"

"I was hired to do a job."

"You didn't have a job, Russo. Camille North is dead."

"I was hired by another client."

Fleener did a classic double take. "What client?"

"You didn't tell me you had a client," AJ said.

"Didn't have a chance. It was yesterday morning."

"Who's the client?" Fleener said.

"I'd rather not say."

"Bullshit. I'll find out sooner or later. Do us both a favor."

"All right, it's Nicole Sanderson."

"Camille's daughter?"

"Yeah. Satisfied?"

"You want to tell me what happened?"

I did, starting from the time I left Ruth Avila's office. In the middle of my saga, Dr. Silverstein returned to the room.

"I heard that," she said. "That saved your life, that Karate punch."

"Because it slowed him up?"

"No," she said. "That punch. You rotated your torso. It was muscle memory. That knife was meant for your stomach, Mr. Russo. If you'd tried to hit him with a left hook, well, it's a good thing you didn't." Her voice trailed off.

She put a small bottle on the table. "For the pain. Don't take them unless you have to. Take it easy for a while. Don't overdue it, okay?"

"A question?" I said.

"I know what you're going to say," AJ said. "I should have guessed."

I ignored her. "When can I run?"

"Bingo," AJ said. "You can take time off, you know. You won't crumble."

"Runners," Dr. Silverstein said, and shook her head. "You're a stubborn bunch."

"Obsessive is more like it."

"AJ, let the doctor talk."

"Describe an average week of running."

I did, and she gave me a couple of suggestions to stay in shape.

"Thank you, again," I said, and she left the room.

"I feel better already," I said, trying very hard to be sarcastic. "Marty?"

"What?"

"You have ballistics yet?"

"Yeah," Fleener said. "You shot Miller with your .38."

I wasn't in the mood for Fleener's sarcasm, but I let it go.

"Miller's gun," I said.

"He had a Beretta on his belt. A 9mm Nano."

"Any luck finding a .22?"

"As matter of fact, yes," Fleener said. "It was hidden in a bag in the trunk of his car."

"In his car?"

Fleener nodded.

"Maybe Miller wasn't as smart as we thought."

"Smart enough to sucker you in the alley," Fleener said. He put his hands out front, like a traffic cop would. "Before you ask, it's the weapon that killed Camille North."

"Good to know," I said. "We assumed it was Miller from the start."

"You still have to prove North ordered it," AJ said.

"You anywhere on that?" I said.

Fleener shrugged. "Nothing I can take to the prosecutor."

AJ moved closer to the bed.

"You're not going to yell at me again, are you?"

"No, but I should." Instead, she took my hand and held it quietly.

"Where do we go from here, Marty?" I said.

"We don't go anywhere," he said. "I have a case to solve. Would it do me any good . . ."

The door opened and into the room came Henri LaCroix. He walked straight over to the bed.

"Michael?"

"I'll be fine, Henri. In a few days."

"It's going to take more than a few days," AJ said. "He's had a rough ride, Henri." She looked at Fleener first, then me. "Just so you know, both of you, I called Henri, told him to get over here."

"Pointless of me to ask if you're carrying," Fleener said to Henri.

"Ask all you want," Henri said. "Permit, too, but you already know that."

"The gunplay is over. Do I make myself clear? We had one dead until Wyatt Earp over here," Fleener pointed at me, "made it two. I sure as hell won't miss Miller, but North can hire another gunman. We'll watch for anyone new. He wouldn't be on the island five minutes, we'd pick him up."

"It's not Conrad I'm worried about," AJ said.

"Nils Lundberg?"

"Yes," AJ said.

"He's still in jail," Henri said, "as of two hours ago."

"Not likely to get out soon either," Fleener said. "We can reach out to the Allegheny County sheriff. If and when Lundberg walks away, we'll know about it."

"That's not very reassuring, Marty," AJ said. "The man's a pro. He finds out who killed his brother, first place he'll come is here."

"It's the best I can do, AJ."

"That's why I called Henri."

"I've said my piece. I'll have an officer in the hallway, twenty-four-seven until he goes home, AJ."

"Am I under arrest, or is the officer protection?"

"It's still a shooting, Russo. It's a good shoot, but Hendricks'll want to see you."

"Doc says two days."

"Don't make me come and get you."

"Call as soon as I'm out."

Fleener nodded and left the room. A succession of nurses came and went, changing IVs, offering food or a sponge bath. One nurse was adamant that the flow of people into the room was not helpful to my recovery. Nothing I said convinced her otherwise, so AJ took her for a lap around the floor.

Henri took out his cell, looked at the screen. "Sandy for you."

I took his phone with my good arm. "Hey. Yeah, yeah. Much better.

Nothing new since you talked to AJ. Except I'll be out tomorrow sometime. Anything I need to know?"

Sandy caught me up on two cases, especially the banker in Cheboygan who ended up having lunch alone. I clicked off and gave Henri his phone.

AJ returned and said, "The nurse'll be fine. She understands the situation now."

Henri stood by the window and AJ sat down.

"We need a plan," she said. "The three of us."

"For what?" I said.

"To keep you in one piece."

"Miller's gone," I said. "We'll know if his brother gets out of jail. I'll be careful anyway."

"You said that the other day, but here you are. You let your guard down, Michael. Doesn't matter why, you did. It can happen again."

"I'm on AJ's side this time, Michael," Henri said. "I'll stick a little closer 'till this is done."

"Don't argue, Michael, please," AJ said.

"Okay," I said.

AJ leaned over and kissed me. "Thank you."

46

The next morning, the hospital kicked me out of my room. I'm here to tell you sooner was definitely better than later. The nurse put me in a wheelchair and pushed it to the front door. AJ provided escort through the hallways, and Henri met us outside with his SUV. The sun had warmed the air quickly. It would be a nice spring day in northern Michigan, especially since I was still around to enjoy it.

"Where to?" he said.

"My apartment. I want a shower, and fresh clothes that don't feel like a tent. You good with that, AJ?"

"Stay close, Henri. I'll be at work if you want me."

Henri nodded. "Under control, AJ."

Henri pulled out on U.S. 31, to Mitchell, then left on Howard and home.

By the time I finished a hot shower, dressed in clean khakis, a blue shirt and navy crewneck, I felt human again, but I'd used up a lot of energy. For some reason, my arm hurt more than my side.

I was also hungry for real food. "How about we stop at Roast & Toast on the way to the office?" I said. "You hungry?"

"I can always eat," he said. "Feel good enough to go to work?"

"You want to sit around here all day?"

Henri shook his head.

"Then let's go."

"Truck's out back, next to your car."

We went down the stairs and Henri stopped at the rear door. "Let me check."

"Check for what? You think Wolfgang's out there?"

"I certainly do not," he said. "Just being careful."

Henri went first, walking a slow lap around the small parking lot. He waved, and I went out to his SUV. Henri drove straight up Howard and parked behind the office.

"Do you want to go on upstairs, and I'll order the food?"

I shook my head. "No, Henri. Careful is one thing, but I can't cut myself off."

"All right," he said. "But I'll stand in line to order."

We went up the back stairs, but it took me longer than it did Henri. The morning crowd had disappeared, leaving only a few tables busy. I kept away from the order line until our food was ready for pick-up. We took the bags and headed to the office.

"Morning, Sandy," I said. "Any messages?"

"A carload of them," she said. "Most of them can wait."

Sandy came around her desk and put her arms around me. We hugged.

"Careful," I said. "I don't want to bust any stitches."

"Don't worry," she said. "Fresh coffee, and there's water in the fridge."

"Got you a veggie wrap," Henri said.

"Always a good choice, my man. Thank you."

My desk became our breakfast table. We got coffee and water and opened the wraps.

Sitting around my desk with Sandy and Henri, it was almost as if nothing had happened. But I was aware that carelessness had almost cost me my life. That wouldn't happen again. With Miller dead the immediate threat had faded, but until we knew Conrad's next move it was necessary to tread carefully, stay alert.

We ate and talked and caught up. You'd think I'd been out of the country for a month.

"I'll call Don Hendricks and set up an appointment," Sandy said. "Let's not piss him off if we don't have to."

"Make it for tomorrow, even if he wants me over there today." I finished the Denver wrap, scrunched the paper up and tossed it, free throw style, in the basket. Swish. All net.

"You have other plans?" Sandy said.

"Maybe I'll take it easy for a day or two."

Sandy nodded. "Good decision for a change," she said. "One thing, Ruth Avila. She's called twice since she heard about you and Miller."

"You got her number?"

"Top message."

"Stick around, both of you," I said. "We need to talk."

Sandy got up. "Holler for me when you're done, boss."

"Me too, boss," Henri said, and they both laughed on their way out.

I sifted through the messages. I made a note to call the Cheboygan banker I'd stiffed at lunch while I was busy being stabbed. I used the desk phone for Ruth Avila.

"Michael," she said, "I appreciate you calling back. Such a terrible thing. How are you?"

I gave her only basic details, and she offered her client's best wishes.

"I feel partly responsible, Michael. My client, I mean, my clients, got you into this. I got you into this."

"Ruth," I said. "You had nothing to do with it. I can't control some crazy guy with a knife, and neither can you. It's part of the job. Better it doesn't happen, but it's still part of the job."

When the call was over, Sandy and Henri resumed their positions around the desk.

"You meet Don Hendricks tomorrow at ten, his office."

"Did he care that it wasn't today?"

"Not after I explained that you were a mere shadow of your former self."

"You really say that?" Henri said.

I laughed. "She'd never talk to Hendricks like that. You talked to his assistant, didn't you?"

Sandy changed the subject. "You said we needed to talk, boss?"

"As a matter of fact," I said. "Conrad North."

"What about him?" she said.

"Because the only link between Camille's murder and Conrad," Henri said, "is lying on a slab in the morgue with three slugs in him."

"The only link we know of," I said.

"Do you think there's another way to connect Conrad to the murder?" Sandy said.

I shrugged. "For the sake of argument, let's assume there is another link. We just have to find it."

We ran it all around the block, again. More than an hour later, two things became clear. First, as much as I hated to admit it, the knife wounds had taken their toll. Second, I was eager to go home.

"It's the State Park lease," Sandy said. "The lease connects Conrad and Camille."

"But with Camille dead," I said, "the divorce is dead. The cottage passes to the surviving spouse, even if half the island thinks Conrad's a murderer. He can sit on the front porch of Camille's cottage and flip me off every time I run by."

"What Sandy's trying to say," Henri said, but he looked at her first.

"Go for it," she said.

"What Sandy's trying to say is that the lease is still phony. The fact that nobody's going to see it in court is beside the point. The lease was bogus when Camille walked into this office to hire you, and it's bogus now. How'd I do?"

"You nailed it," Sandy said. "Nicole Sanderson hired us to discover what happened, didn't she?"

I nodded.

"Then we're back to square one, pardon the cliché."

"Not exactly square one," I said. "There's Helen Simons."

"Not much of a lead," Henri said.

"Not yet," I said. "Sandy?"

She shook her head. "I was sidetracked, you know, with everything."

"Find out who she is and find her," I said. "As soon as you can." I sat back in my chair. "I'm done for today."

"Another good decision, boss. Get him out of here, Henri."

"My pleasure."

We went down the stairs, cutting through Roast & Toast to the parking lot.

We stood next to Henri's SUV. "I'd rather walk home."

"Give yourself another day," he said. "Walk to work in the morning."

Henri beeped the door locks and got in. "Besides that, Russo, you're a smaller target in the truck."

47

"I have to go in a minute," AJ said. She stood at the kitchen sink and drank coffee. "Early meeting." She wore her old favorite Spartan green running suit and beat-up Brooks shoes.

"I always enjoy being with you, darling, but you didn't have to stay with me last night."

"I did if Henri wanted to go see Margo. We agreed we'd be extra careful, at least for a while."

"We?"

AJ smiled. "Henri and me."

"You didn't think I'd be safe here for the night?"

"Depends on your perspective," she said. "My perspective says you don't have the Michigan National Guard outside the building, you're not safe."

"Camp Grayling's a long way from here."

AJ ignored my humor and looked at her watch. "I'm late," she said. "Henri'll be here in plenty of time for your meeting with Hendricks."

"Think I'll be safe inside the County Building?"

"That doesn't dignify an answer," she said as she grabbed her jacket. "Bye. Let me know how it goes."

I took a hot shower, dressed in khakis, a blue shirt and, for added professionalism, a navy blazer. I still wore scruffy deck shoes. I had just finished scrambled eggs and an English muffin when my phone buzzed. Henri's message read, "buzz me in."

I opened my door slowly, checked the hallway, and hit the release button. I went to the top of the stairs, stood to one side, and pulled out my .38.

Halfway up the first short flight of stairs, Henri called out, "It's me."

He came up the second flight and saw the .38 at my side.

"I thought you were the guy who didn't need to be cautious?"

"Just don't tell AJ."

"Ready to go? You don't want to be late for the show."

I put on a light jacket, more to cover the holster on my hip than for the spring weather, which grew warmer each day. We cut through the parking lot to Bay Street, across the old tracks, and into the Bodzick entrance of the building.

"You joining me?"

"Not a chance. The cops want me, let 'em arrest me."

"Seems like a prudent philosophy."

"Come out the Lake Street door when you're done. I'll be across the street."

I peeled off for the prosecutor's office, and Henri waved as he kept going down the hall.

When I arrived at his office, Don Hendricks was behind his desk, sleeves rolled up, tie loose, collar button open. A stack of manila folders a foot high sat on the left side of the desk, an ancient monitor on the other side. No surprise, his office had not received a fresh coat of paint since my last visit.

Martin Fleener sat in a straight back chair to the right of the desk, under a huge map of Emmet County. His suit, all three pieces, was a fine worsted wool in charcoal.

"Come on in, Russo," Hendricks said, and pointed to a scarred and dented wooden ladder back in front of his desk. Perhaps the old metal chair was out for repairs, or the crusher. "Take a seat."

"Morning, Don. Marty." I pointed at the large map. "That wasn't here a few days ago."

"Wire broke," Hendricks said. "Now it's fixed."

Hmm. I guess small talk isn't on today's agenda. I won't chat about the weather. Bet he won't ask if I want coffee either.

"Am I under arrest?"

"If I wanted you in jail, you wouldn't have slept at home last night."

I tried again, politely. "Will I be arrested for Miller?"

Fleener spoke first this time. "No, we have no plans to do that. I've read the reports, all of them. It was a clean shoot."

"Yes, it was," I said.

"What'd you think, Don?" Fleener said.

"It was clean. It's just . . ."

"Just what?" I said.

"It was nice of Lundberg to give you the opportunity."

"The opportunity to do what?"

"Kill him," Hendricks said. "That's what you wanted, wasn't it? Revenge for Camille?"

A comment best left alone.

"It was a clean shoot, you just said so."

Hendricks nodded without another word.

"Okay," I said, "what's next?"

Hendricks took another deep breath, glanced at Fleener and said, "Conrad North."

"Agreed. We know he ordered Lundberg to shoot his wife."

"But we can't prove that, or North'd be in the room right now with Marty all over him." Fleener's reputation for interrogating suspects was legendary. Prosecutors, attorneys, even cops hoped for a chance to watch him work. He was the consummate professional, cool under pressure, articulate and – most of all – prepared.

"Where are you with Conrad?"

"Let's get something straight, Russo," Hendricks said. "I know you're officially on the case again, thanks to Nicole Sanderson. If I tell you to stay out of it, you won't pay any attention, right?"

I nodded. "Right."

"Okay, a few ground rules," Hendricks said, "simple and clear. We share information for starters. Only Marty or the sheriff take people into custody, not you. We clear so far?"

"Clear."

Hendricks used the pen in his right hand for emphasis, jabbing it my way. "Most of all, no more dead bodies."

"Lundberg didn't give me much choice."

"Well, don't put yourself in that position again."

Hendricks sat back in his chair. He dropped his pen on the desk. "Want coffee?"

The prosecutor obviously had cleared the air. He'd had his say, and was okay with me remaining on the case. Hendricks seldom wasted time or words when it came to doing his job, or helping Fleener do his. But he wouldn't have offered coffee unless he was ready to move on.

"I'm fine, thanks. Back to Conrad North."

I felt my iPhone vibrate in my jacket pocket. A message.

We spent the next hour hashing out the same territory that Sandy, Henri and I already covered yesterday. With the same result.

"I'm done," Hendricks said. "Anything to add, Marty?"

Fleener shook his head. "Wish I did."

"Russo?"

"Maybe," I said.

"Maybe? Maybe what?"

"It's a small thing. Might be nothing. Sandy's working on it."

"What is it?" Fleener said.

"Just a name. That's all we got."

"Who is it?" Fleener said.

I hesitated. "Don't want to toss a name at you for the hell of it."

"How 'bout you toss it, and let us decide."

I shook my head. "Give me a couple of days. If it's anything, anything at all, I'll tell you about it. Two days."

"Marty?" Hendricks said.

Fleener shrugged. “Why not?”

“All right,” Hendricks said. “Two days. But we get the name, you learn anything or not. You tell us the name. That’s the deal.”

“Deal,” I said, and left the office.

“Two days,” I heard Hendricks say again on my way out the door.

48

On my way down the hall, I pulled out my phone. The message was from Sandy: "come back asap." Henri got it, too.

I went out the Lake Street entrance. Henri saw me and started across the street.

"You read the message?" I kept walking as Henri caught up.

"Yeah."

"Why didn't you go ahead?"

"You know goddamn well why."

We moved quickly, easily dodging people who lingered on the street, peering in store windows.

We took the stairs two-at-a-time and charged into the office.

Sandy was at her desk. The smile on her face was a combination of kid-at-Christmas and Cheshire cat. She stood up, put her hands in the air like a ref signaling a three-point basket and said, "I want a raise."

We stopped and stared.

"You all right?" I said.

"Helen Simons. I found her. You won't fucking believe it."

She caught us. No doubt about it. We were surprised; stunned, really.

"You serious?" Henri said.

Sandy nodded. "You're damn right I am. Have a seat, gentlemen," she said, with a wave of the arm.

Henri and I went over and sat by the windows.

"One question first," I said. "I have to ask, is Simons a part of this case?"

Sandy smiled. "Oh, yes."

"Then let's have it."

"I won't bore you with all the details unless you want them."

"I'll ask if I want more," I said.

"All right," Sandy said, leafing through a few pages on a yellow pad. "It really started to come together last night."

"You were here last night?"

Sandy shook her head. "Home. I couldn't sleep. Didn't feel like reading, so I started with *Google* again. I checked some other sites, *Facebook, Intelius,* stuff like that. Even tried *YouTube.* I searched 'Helen Simons' and got nothing except a few females who were not our Helen, like the one in Mississippi I already told you about."

Sandy got up and refilled her coffee mug.

"I tried all sorts of combinations, spellings, states, cities, you name it. *Nada.* I went to the Social Security Death Index. That's when things got interesting."

"Helen on the list?" Henri said.

Sandy shook her head.

"Not showing up on the dead list made things interesting?" Henri said.

She ignored him.

"I tried some obscure websites nobody's heard of, and got nowhere. But I kept thinking about the Death Index, so I pulled it up again. I filtered by states, but that didn't help. For the hell of it, I tried 'Simons' but not Helen. I mean, no first name, just 'Simons.'"

"Why?"

"Why?" she said, annoyed. "How do I know why? I couldn't sleep, I ran out of Maker's Mark. Hell, I was willing to try anything." Sandy ran her fingers through her hair. "Sorry, boss. I didn't get much sleep."

"Forget it," I said. "Did the last name lead you anywhere?"

"Yes, indeed. A ton of hits. I filtered for Michigan to cut the list down. Don't remember if I'd tried that before. I went through every 'Simons.' I didn't recognize any of them, of course. Why would I? But get this.

One of them died in Mackinaw City, a 'Harold Simons.' So I searched the cemetery index . . ."

"You can search cemeteries?" Henri said.

"Yep, and he's buried in Lakeview Cemetery. On Central Avenue, just west of town."

Sandy laughed. "I figured it had to be a big coincidence." She looked right at me when she said that. "Did you like that one, boss?"

I shook my head.

"Anyway, I checked other records over again, this time looking for Harold. Turns out he got married along the way, on Mackinac Island no less."

"Could just be a coincidence," I said, with a touch of sarcasm.

"If you think that's a coincidence," Sandy said, "you'll love this one. The woman he married? Her name was Helen."

"No shit."

"Could I make that up?"

I shook my head. "You could not," I said. "But why didn't you find a 'Helen Simons?'"

"I didn't find 'Helen Simons' because when Helen married good 'ole Harold, she was 'Helen Weaver' and . . ." Sandy rolled this out slowly, "'Helen Weaver' never took her husband's name."

Sandy held her mug in the air, then drank some coffee.

"By that time, even I wasn't joking about coincidences anymore. I ran the names through as many indices as I could find. It turns out Harold spent his career working for Mackinac State Historic Parks. Early on in Mackinaw City, Fort Michilimackinac, but most of it was on the island at Fort Mackinac. General maintenance, painting. Stuff like that."

"Anything on Helen? What's her name again?"

"Weaver," Sandy said, glancing at the yellow pad. "Listen to this: Helen Weaver also worked for the state. A few years in Lansing, at the old library on Michigan Avenue. But most of her years, she worked for Mackinac State Historic Parks, too. Retired in 2017."

"Probably where she met Harold," Henri said.

"Probably," Sandy said. "Want to know what she did?"

"What?" I said.

"Her title was chief assistant, executive assistant, something like that, to the State Park Commission. Remember them?"

"They're the folks who write leases for the bluff houses. Like Sanderson's on the East Bluff."

"The very same. She worked at the Commission's island office in the summer, Mac City in the winter."

I went to the refrigerator and took out a bottle of water. I walked to the window. A few more tourists than last week wandered up and down the sidewalks. The warm sun and blue sky was luring them up north earlier than usual. I drank some water and leaned against the window casing.

"Well," I said. "That's interesting stuff. Helen Simons is, or was, a real person."

"I didn't find a death record for Helen Weaver either."

"Okay, so we assume Helen's alive."

"At least we have Helen linked to the Commission," Henri said. "That's a lot more than we had yesterday."

"Yeah, but it's a big leap, working in the Commission office to writing a bogus lease."

"I ain't done yet," Sandy said.

"There's more?" Henri said, and we waited.

"The big finish, gentlemen," she said, and smiled again. "Do either of you speak German?"

"German?"

"You heard me."

"You know I don't speak German," I said.

"French," Henri said. "Not German."

"Good," she said. "It's more fun this way."

"You're enjoying this, aren't you?" I said.

"You bet your ass I am," she said. "Remember, I searched everything I could think of? Well, I played with the names some more." She stopped and smiled again. "Do either of you gentlemen know what 'weaver' means in German?"

Of course we didn't. Sandy held back, but only for a moment.

"Okay, 'weaver' translates to 'weber' in German. They mean the same thing."

"Like a person who weaves yarn?"

Sandy nodded. "Exactly. So, you're German, you live in the U.S. and you want to change your name, make it look more American. So you change 'Weber' to 'Weaver.' It's an easy choice, because they mean the same thing."

"Your point is?" I said.

"Does the name 'Helene Weber' sound familiar?"

"It does," I said. "Can't remember why."

"Remember the Hoffmann family? Conrad's family before they changed their name?"

"Yeah."

"Do you remember that the Hoffmann family rented cottages at Wawatam Beach in Mackinaw City?"

"Go on."

"They visited good friends who owned a place there. Those friends were Emil and Lena Weber. Is it coming back now? The Weber family?"

I stood up slowly. "They had three children."

Sandy nodded. "One of them, Helene."

"The son's in Florida, right? What about the other daughter?"

"Lara," Sandy said. "Nothing yet."

"They were kids together," I said. "Helene grew up with Conrad Hoffmann."

"And years later they became adults together on Mackinac Island."

"You just put Conrad North in Helen Weaver's office on Mackinac Island."

"Yes, I did."

49

Henri made fresh coffee while Sandy ran downstairs for a salad. I tried to digest what I'd just heard. A few puzzle pieces locked together. Our picture grew a little clearer.

"How did you catch that Helen didn't change her name?" Henri said.

"Luck and time served," Sandy said as she ate her salad. "Her driver's license, that's how I caught it. She tried to renew her Michigan license."

Sandy filled her mug when the coffee was ready.

"There have been a lot of security changes over the years because of nine-eleven. You know, the name on a plane ticket, the name on a passport or driver's license . . . the names have to match, right? Try to renew your license if the names don't match."

"Helen's name didn't match?"

"Nope. Her license didn't match her birth certificate or her Social Security records. She'd been Weaver ever since her father Americanized the family name. Back then nobody cared. She tried to renew her license and it red-flagged."

"Jesus, what a story," I said. "Hope you get that lucky on Lara. I wonder where Helen Weaver is now . . . could you find her?"

Sandy nodded. "But she's Helene Weber again, not Helen Weaver. The driver's license dust-up was such a pain, she reverted to Weber. That was easier than changing Social Security records."

"How'd you find all that out?" I said.

"She told me."

"You talked to her?"

"Uh-huh," Sandy said. "On the phone, before I texted you."

"Where is she?"

"California," Sandy said. "Palms Springs. Moved out there when she retired."

"You find her on *Google*?" Henri said.

"And *Facebook* and *Whitepages*. It was a lot easier when I had the correct name."

"She deserves a raise, Russo," Henri said, pointing at Sandy. "A big one after figuring that out."

"I'm curious about something," I said.

"I know what you're going to say, boss. Why did I call her?"

"Yeah. Usually we'd talk about it first. Glad you did it. I was just curious."

Sandy sat back and folded her arms across her chest.

"I tried to put myself in her position. At some level, she's tied to Conrad, a phony lease, a messy divorce, maybe murder. We don't know. We know what it looks like from here, in Petoskey."

Sandy tapped her desk several times. "But if I were her, in Palm Springs, and a man, a private detective from northern Michigan called, well, I might clam up, or hang up."

She shrugged. "But if a woman from Petoskey called, explaining that she needed help with one of the firm's cases, you know, she used to work on Mackinac a while back . . . see where I'm going with this?"

"Yeah," I said. "Did it work?"

"Well, she didn't hang up on me. Once I explained who I was and told her a little of what I wanted, she talked to me."

"Think she'd talk to me?"

"She said she would. She'll be home all day." Sandy held up a sticky note. "Want me to call her?"

"Yes."

"One thing, boss," Sandy said. "Something in her voice. Maybe I'm reading too much into it."

"What's your gut tell you?"

"I'm not sure. It could be she's frightened. She doesn't know me, but I put her past on center stage. She's being cautious, perfectly reasonable."

"What do you think it is?"

"She might be a hard-ass," Sandy said. "No. That's too harsh. Defensive. She was defensive, I could hear it when I asked about the Commission."

"Might be a natural reaction," I said. "She worked with those people a long time. You ask her about the leases?"

Sandy shook her head.

"Conrad?"

Sandy shook her head again. "I backed off. I didn't want to screw it up. I established a connection, figured that was a good start."

"It was a good start."

"Want me to call her?" she said again.

"Yeah. Use the landline. I'll take it in my office."

I stood up and looked out the window. The world of Lake Street hadn't changed much since Henri and I arrived at the office. Big surprise. I stretched my hamstrings. My runner's legs were clamoring for a workout.

We joke a lot about coincidences. Truth is, my friends make fun of me. But I have a hard time writing off anything as coincidence. Take all the new information Sandy'd just tossed at Henri and me. Could be the next pieces of the puzzle, the ones that make the big picture clearer.

"Line one, boss." Sandy said. She put a sheet of paper in front of me with a biographical sketch of Helene Weber she'd worked up earlier.

"Hello, Ms. Weber. How are you?" I tried to pronounce it "vey-ber" and not "web-er," hoping to score a few points. She didn't seem to care.

"Yes, Mr. Russo," Weber said. "What is it that you want?" Not exactly warm and fuzzy, but I'd give her the benefit of the doubt.

I scanned the bio. Helene Weber's voice was clear and resonant for a woman in her mid-sixties.

"Ms. Weber, as Ms. Jefferies explained, I represent a client who asked me to look into matters regarding her house on Mackinac Island."

"Yes."

"More specifically, it concerns one of the cottages on the East Bluff."

"Why do you believe I can help you?"

She already knew the answer to that one, since Sandy had mentioned the Park Commission during her initial call. Might as well push a bit, see what happens.

"Well, Ms. Weber, the cottage in question is on State Park land. You used to work for the State Park Commission, correct?"

"Yes."

"The Commission approves the leases, correct?"

"Yes."

This is a little like talking to myself.

"You also worked directly with the leases and the leaseholders, also correct?"

"I think you have overestimated my importance, Mr. Russo. I was merely paid clerical staff."

The conversation went on like this for far too long. I tried different ways to ask the same necessary questions, but it didn't help. It was time for a different approach.

"Ms. Weber, I'll be in the area on business at the end of the week. Rancho Mirage, to be exact. Could I make an appointment to see you?"

The line was quiet for a moment. Then, "If you would like to do that. Yes, it would be all right."

We ended the conversation. It wasn't exactly on a high note, but I had bought myself time to brainstorm. She was a good lead.

I went back to the outer office. Henri remained in the chair by the window, Sandy at her desk.

"Rancho Mirage?" Sandy said. "What possessed you to dream that one up? You checking into the *Betty Ford Center*? Too much scotch these days?"

"It's the first thing that came to mind," I said.

"Not the best thing," she said. "Maybe an Oban would have helped."

"I don't need your editorial comments."

"What are you looking at?" I said to Henri, who stared at us.

"You two're married, right?"

"Smack him around for me, would you," Sandy said.

"Remember, I carry a gun."

"Enough," I said. "Can we cancel the vaudeville routine for a few minutes? This is the best lead we've had."

"You think Weber is that solid?" Henri said.

"Yes, I do. Where she worked, who she knew, old family connections. Even if she turns out to be a bad lead, we have to find out for sure."

"Yeah, you have to check her out." Henri got out of the chair and walked towards the door. "Meeting Margo. I'll be back later, when you're finished for the day."

"Hey, you don't have to escort me to Chandler's. It's only two blocks."

"I'll check back," Henri said, and left the office.

"What do you think about Weber? Is she for real?"

Sandy nodded. "I think so. You're right, boss. Helene Weber's a lead we have to follow. What's next?"

"A plane ticket to Palm Springs," I said. "A place to stay for a couple of days."

"You want to go out of Traverse or Pellston?"

"Your decision, I've only flown into LAX. Do you know where in Palm Springs she lives?"

"Yep. I have the address, and I printed a map."

"Find me a place as close to her house as possible."

"Palm Springs isn't that big. Bigger than here, but not that big."

"Maybe a place close to her and the airport?"

"Quit worrying, I'll take care of it," she said. "A car, too."

"Thanks."

"Boss, for what it's worth?"

"I'm listening."

"I might have been too hard on Weber. She received a phone call out of the blue asking questions about her past. That'd unnerve anybody."

"Your point is?"

“Weber’s cautious, defensive even. She could have told you to go to hell.”

“But?”

“She agreed to see you anyway.” Sandy paused. “Why?”

50

"When do you leave?" AJ said. We'd met after work at Chandler's. We sat at the bar with two Chardonnays and a plate of sautéed shrimp, the one with mushrooms and Brussels sprouts.

"Day after tomorrow. One-twenty flight to Detroit."

"Pellston or Traverse City?"

"Pellston."

"Do you think Weber will cooperate?"

I shrugged. "She could've told me to mind my own business, but she didn't."

"Do you really think she knows anything about Camille's lease?"

I shook my head and speared another shrimp. "I have no idea, but given where she worked, it's worth asking."

I ate the shrimp and followed it with wine.

"Food to your liking?" the bartender said. Jack had been mixing drinks here as long as I could remember. Short, wiry, with salt-and-pepper hair, he offered a bright smile and welcomed conversation.

"Always is, Jack," I said. "Thanks."

"Have you thought how you'll approach her," AJ said, "what you'll ask first?"

"AJ, I haven't even decided if I want another shrimp or a Brussels sprout next."

"A little touchy, are we, Michael?"

I put my hand on AJ's hand. "Sorry," I said. "Sometimes I feel like it's slipping away. I couldn't get the cottage for Camille. Now I'm trying to get it for Nicole. Conrad killed his wife, but I can't prove it." I took a deep breath. "I'm nowhere on any of this."

"Don't be so hard on yourself," she said. "Besides, you now have an opportunity with Helene Weber. Don't forget, you got Gunnar Lundberg."

"Yes, I did."

AJ picked up my hand and kissed it. "I almost forgot to ask. How're you feeling?"

"After Lundberg roughed me up?"

"Yeah."

"I'm better. My arm hurts more than my ribs. The stitches are sore. I keep hitting things, a doorjamb, the steering wheel, lots of things." I picked up my glass. "Wine helps."

AJ picked up her glass and tapped mine.

"Hope I'm not interrupting," Henri said as he sat next to AJ.

"Mr. LaCroix," Jack said, and put a napkin down. "What can I get you?"

"Blue Moon, no glass."

Jack nodded and went down the bar.

"You didn't need to come by, Henri. I found Chandler's all by myself," I said, pointing vaguely toward the bay.

The bartender put a beer down, and Henri took a drink.

"My treat," I said. "Go back to Margo."

"Wait a minute," AJ said.

"Are we going to argue about this?" I said.

"I sure hope not," Henri said. "It's been a pleasant evening so far."

AJ said, "Jack." She held her glass up, and a refill was on the way.

"You changing the subject?" Henri said.

"Well if she doesn't, I will," I said.

"Sounds like you need a refill, too," Jack said, and laughed as he put AJ's glass down.

"Please," I said, handing him my glass. "Remember I told Hendricks I might have a lead? He wanted to hear back."

Henri drank some beer, AJ shrugged.

"You guys are a big help."

"We remember," AJ said. "Get on with it."

I sipped my newly filled glass of wine. "That was before Sandy found Weber."

"So?" Henri said.

"Do I tell Hendricks about Weber, or wait 'till after I talk to her?"

"I vote for now," AJ said.

"I don't care," Henri said.

I ignored Henri, although I almost laughed.

"Why, AJ?"

"Try this," she said. "You tell him and nothing comes of it, Don says thanks and moves on. If you don't tell him and nothing comes of it, he's pissed for a half-minute and moves on."

"But if Weber's the real thing?"

"If Weber's the real thing," AJ said, "he'll go off like a rocket if he thinks you held out on him."

"Wouldn't be the first time," I said.

"The point is," AJ said, "if she's the real deal, you'll need Hendricks. You'll need a prosecutor here to help you with a witness in California."

"Is that what she is, a witness?" Henri said.

"More like a co-conspirator, if she and North doctored Camille's lease," I said. "Worse than that if she helped kill Camille."

"All the more reason that Hendricks needs to know before you leave for Palm Springs. You're not betraying a source. The woman may have information about a crime."

"The crime was committed in Mackinac County, AJ," I said.

"But Camille North died in Emmet County," Henri said.

"Another reason you need to tell him, Michael," AJ said. "Whatever label describes Weber, it's up to the professionals to sort out jurisdiction."

"I changed my mind," Henri said, and drank some Blue Moon. AJ and I turned his way.

"The label doesn't matter. If Helene Weber needs to be in Petoskey or

St. Ignace, we can't do that. Not legally, anyway. We fuck up, Hendricks'll have a legitimate reason to be pissed."

There was a slow but steady stream of people coming through the door. Most were locals meeting after work for a drink or dinner. The tables had filled up while we talked. A couple in their twenties sat at the opposite end of the bar with two strange, colorful drinks in front of them.

I had the last of the Chardonnay.

"All right," I said. "I'll call over there in the morning, see Hendricks before I go."

"I'm glad that's settled," AJ said, and pushed her empty glass away. "I'm still hungry. You two want more appetizers, or dinner?"

"You don't have to stay, Henri," I said. "AJ can drop me off on her way home."

"That okay with you, AJ?" Henri said. "Feel safe enough?"

She nodded. "Two blocks, it's okay."

"I'm off to Margo's," Henri said. He kissed AJ and said good-bye.

"Jack," AJ said. "A menu please."

"You want to stay with me tonight?"

"Of course I do, darling. But first," she said, setting the menu down between us, "dinner. I'll nibble on you later."

51

"You have two choices," AJ said. We sat in my kitchen with coffee. AJ had dressed in her clothes from last night, I wore an old running suit. We'd slept in later than usual. It was after seven.

"Do I have time to finish my coffee?"

"Depends on you," she said. "I suppose you're running this morning."

I smiled. "Always knew you were a pretty smart broad."

"Is that a yes or no?"

"It's a yes," I said. "Forty-five minutes, maybe fifty."

"Then I'll pick you up in ninety minutes and drop you at work."

"I'm tired of the babysitting, AJ. How come you're okay with a run but not a walk to the office?"

"You'll run in Bay View?"

I nodded.

"All those construction workers you tell me about are still there, I assume."

"How about the people on the sidewalk between here and work?"

AJ sighed. She put her mug in the sink.

"Gotcha there, didn't I?"

"One condition?" she said. "A message when you arrive at the office. Deal?"

"Deal."

We kissed, AJ left and I dressed for a pleasantly warm April morning run. I loosened up easily and moved smoothly, dodging moving vehicles and stacks of construction materials. A quick shower and fresh clothes, and I left for the office. I admit I was more cautious than usual. Such is life these days.

I went through McLean & Eakin to pick up the *Times*. It was after ten when I walked through the door.

"Morning, Sandy. No smart-ass remarks about the time," I said before she had time to respond.

"Would I do that?"

"Yes."

She handed me three messages, and said, "You have an appointment after lunch. It's the top message."

"Donald Harper? We know this guy?"

"I never heard of him," Sandy said. "He wants only fifteen minutes on behalf of his client." She laughed. "I played the dumb secretary and asked who the client was."

"He didn't answer."

"Nope, but it was worth a try."

"Call Don Hendricks' office. I want to see him before I fly west. Today if possible. I'd like to do a long run tomorrow morning before I stuff my legs in cattle class seats for five hours."

I tapped a message to AJ, "safe and sound." I took care of the messages and tried to reschedule a meeting with the banker in Cheboygan.

"I'm going downstairs for food, boss. Want anything?"

"Sure. A chicken club on sourdough."

"Okay. You're in with Don Hendricks late this afternoon, by the way. After four."

I ate the sandwich at my desk with the *New York Times*. Sandy nibbled on a Lake Street Salad and tried to finish *The Sun Also Rises*.

"I read it in high school," she said. "I was too young to appreciate Hemingway. Same for Fitzgerald. I just read *This Side of Paradise*. I thought it was better than *Gatsby*, which is saying something."

-A little after one-thirty, the outer door opened and in walked my appointment. Donald Harper was six-one and a trim one-seventy. He had green, narrow eyes and a tapered nose. His black hair was jelled into a careful messiness on top.

I met him in the outer office and we shook hands. "Come in, Mr. Harper."

He unbuttoned the jacket of his tailored three-piece black suit and sat in a client chair. He handed me a business card. "Attorney-at-law" it read, with a Traverse City Post Office box and a phone number.

"Your office in Traverse?" I said.

"Yes, but the cell is the easiest way to find me."

"Sandy told me you're here on behalf of a client."

Harper glanced over his shoulder. "Mind if we close the door?"

"Not at all," I said, and went around my desk and shut the door. Makes no difference to Sandy. She'll hear it all anyway.

"Are you with a firm, Mr. Harper?"

He shook his head. "I represent one client, Mr. Russo."

If I wait long enough, I probably won't have to ask.

"I believe you know Joseph DeMio?"

"Joey? I thought the family had a Chicago firm keeping them out of jail."

"That would be Sterns-Blatnic. It represents the business interests of Mr. DeMio."

"Then what do you do?"

Harper looked uncomfortable. He rearranged himself in the chair. Not sure he liked my question.

"I take care of insignificant assignments like this one, Mr. Russo."

Now I was positive he didn't like my question.

"You Harvard Law? Joey's partial to Harvard."

"Yale."

"Heard that's a good school, too," I said.

"Mr. DeMio alerted me that you have a smart mouth, Mr. Russo."

"And I didn't even go to Yale."

He rearranged himself, again.

"What can I do for you, Mr. Harper?"

"Mr. DeMio would like you to be aware that a certain, how should I put this, indiscretion on your part interfered with Mr. DeMio's interests. It would be to your benefit to rethink the intersection of your interests and those of Mr. DeMio."

"Somewhere in the middle of that recitation, Mr. Harper, I drifted off to MSU basketball. The Big Ten, March Madness . . ."

Harper stared straight ahead.

"You want to cut the bullshit and tell me why you're here?"

"Mr. DeMio would appreciate it if you'd . . ."

"I don't care what Joey would appreciate," I said. "Plain English, then get out."

Harper stood up, picked up his briefcase, and said, "Gunner Lundberg? You called him Ben Miller, I believe."

"What about him?"

"Mr. Lundberg worked for us. He stepped across a line. He was our responsibility to deal with, not yours. Don't interfere again. Is that clear enough?"

I smiled. "That your job, too?"

Harper actually smiled. "No, Mr. Russo, we have professionals for that."

Harper turned, opened the door and walked out. I followed him.

"You hear any of that?"

"Enough," Sandy said. "Do you think he's DeMio's new front man?"

"I guess Santino Cicci and Gino Rosato are too old country for the sophisticated work Harper does."

"Like threatening to kill people?"

"Exactly like that."

52

"I'm on my way to AJ's after I'm done with Hendricks."

"I'm leaving early anyway, boss. I have a few errands on the way home."

"Okay."

"You have the map for Palm Springs?"

"Right here," I said, and held up my brief bag.

"Did you print your boarding pass yet?

"Put it on my phone."

"Will you stop here before you go to the airport?"

"Not sure. I'll let you know."

"About Helene Weber."

"What about her?"

"Why's she so willing to talk? Why didn't she tell you to leave her alone? There has to be a reason."

"I don't have an answer for you."

"Well, keep it in mind, that's all," she said. "Have a good flight if I don't see you in the morning."

I locked the office and headed up Lake Street. I'd be foolish to ignore Sandy's instincts. She's probably on to something. I'll pay attention when I meet Weber, see how I react.

Even the grass in Pennsylvania Park looked greener in the warm April air. A few more tourists, a few more cars stopped at the light at Howard. The season builds slowly, and then it explodes. Somewhere between Memorial Day weekend and mid-June when school vacations start, the tourist season goes into full swing.

"Afternoon, Don," I said when I arrived at his office.

"Russo," he said, and closed the door. I put my brief bag on one chair and sat in the other.

"I have a meeting," Hendricks said as he looked at his watch. "You've got twenty minutes. Is this about your lead?"

"It is," I said. I explained what I knew about Helene Weber.

Hendricks tugged at the collar of his shirt. It was unbuttoned, of course, and the tie was pulled away.

"Sandra Jefferies," he said, and smiled. He didn't do that very often. "I could use a smart woman like that around here. Whip this place into shape. So she just played with different combinations until it all came together?"

I nodded. "Not the first time she's done that," I said. "She's good."

"All right," Hendricks said. "How much does Weber know?"

I shrugged. "I have no idea. That's why I'm spending half the day in airplanes. What's your best-case scenario? What would you like to hear? As prosecutor, I mean."

Hendricks leaned forward and rested his elbows on the desk. There was barely enough room to do that amidst the clutter.

"Camille North was shot dead in Mackinaw City," he said. "I'd like to know about that."

"We have the killer."

"Correction. We know Lundberg pulled the trigger." He shook his head. "But we don't have him to ask, thanks to you."

I ignored the comment. "You'd like to know if Weber can put North and Lundberg together."

Hendricks nodded. "Be nice, wouldn't it?"

"Chances are better Weber knows something about Camille Sanderson's lease. How she lost her house on the island."

"What if she does?" Hendricks said.

"Suppose Conrad North blackmailed her, paid her, whatever, to make a new lease? Could you use that?"

"To get to Conrad? On the murder?"

I nodded.

Hendricks scratched his nose and rubbed his eyes. "It'd be a stretch."

I sat up straight and leaned toward the desk. "Okay," I said, "but if Weber ties Conrad to a phony lease, is that enough to arrest him?"

Hendricks rubbed his chin this time. "Might be."

"Enough to put him in the room with Fleener?"

Hendricks nodded slowly. "I think I could make that work."

"Do you think Mackinac County would object?"

"I know the folks up there," Hendricks said. "They'd help out. Besides, murder pulls rank."

We spent a few more minutes on details, on North, Lundberg and Weber. Hendricks looked at his watch.

"My meeting," he said, and stood up. We walked out of the office together and went in separate directions.

"Russo." I stopped and turned around. "Keep in touch."

I wound my way through the building, went out the Bay Street door and headed for AJ's house. I'd just crossed Williams when a horn beeped twice. Being the savvy detective that I am, I deduced no assassin would announce his arrival with a car horn, so I looked over and saw a familiar SUV.

"Hey there, big fella, want a ride?"

I laughed. "Is that all I am to you, a hunk of meat?"

"Among other things," AJ said. "You want a ride or not?"

I waved her on. "I'd rather walk. But, if you had a Porsche. . ."

She flipped me a distinctive middle finger and gunned her SUV.

"Well, that wasn't very nice," I said to no one.

By the time I arrived at AJ's, she was on the front porch.

I joined her on the steps and watched spring arrive. A few buds on the trees, two gray squirrels chasing each other around the yard, the guy across the street raking his flower beds.

"Well, it sounds like you have a plan," AJ said.

"Calling it a plan is a little optimistic."

AJ moved a bit closer and put her arm through mine. "You're determined to get the cottage for Nicole, aren't you?"

"Yes."

"Because you couldn't get it for Camille?"

"Something like that."

"Michael, I'll say it again, you didn't let Camille down."

"It still feels like that. Not always, but often."

"She was murdered, Michael, she was taken out by a hired killer. You had no control over that. Nicole isn't Camille. No matter how hard you try, Nicole isn't Camille."

"Nicole said the same thing, that I was doing this for her mother."

"Michael, you work for Nicole now. She wants her mother's house. She's a Sanderson and it's her house now."

"Maybe."

AJ put her hand out and touched my face. "Look at me."

I turned and put my arm around her shoulder.

"I love you," she said.

"I'm happy about that," I said. "I love you, too."

53

"Good pace, Russo," Henri said. "Eight miles and a good pace." I left AJ's house early, went home and changed into shorts and a long-sleeved T. Henri met me in the parking lot for a run through Bay View. He wore a baggy single-layer jacket over a small holster on his left hip. Running long and alone was not an option, not this morning. I didn't even bother to argue when Henri backed AJ's insistence that he tag along.

"Longest run since all this started," I said. "Felt good."

We stretched our hamstrings, leaning against trees behind my building. That felt good, too.

"By the time you're back from California, we should have more to work with."

"Couldn't have any less," I said.

We walked four easy laps around the Perry Hotel.

"You want a lift to the airport?"

"I'm just going to Pellston," I said. "Think I can handle it. Besides, I'll be back in two days."

I took a hot shower, put on fresh khakis, a faded gray polo shirt and a dark red V-neck. I packed a small bag with enough for a short trip. But it was Palm Springs, after all, so I added a navy blazer.

Small rural airports can be annoying. Flights are canceled for no reason (well, too few passengers is a reason, but they call it mechanical), regional flights to hub cities sell out quickly (especially at peak times). On the other hand, security moves quickly and smoothly, parking is much closer to the terminal than in cities and, in Pellston's case, free.

The Delta flight to Detroit left on time and arrived twenty minutes early. That gave me enough extra time to pick up a sandwich from Plum Market when I changed terminals. The Palm Springs flight took off only fifteen minutes late. I pulled out my sandwich, a copy of Steve Hamilton's *The Second Life of Nick Mason*, and settled in for five hours at thirty-eight thousand feet.

I closed the cover as we began our descent into Palm Springs. Local time, the attendant informed us, was five-thirty-five. I walked off the plane into a very warm, sunny afternoon. I learned this because half the terminal was outdoors. You know, in the open air. Literally. We don't try that trick in Michigan.

I signed for the rental car, a rather drab Buick sedan. I drove out of the airport on Tahquitz Canyon Way, fifteen minutes later stopping in front of The Willows Historic Inn. Originally built as private home in 1924, the house had gone through several owners and some hard years. By the late 20th Century, it had been rescued and turned into a quiet eight room inn, an easy four blocks off the business district. Sandy earned a nice bonus for choosing The Willows.

I checked in, dropped my bag and went downtown for food. I wandered up and down Palm Canyon Drive looking at menus, finally stopping at Sherman's Deli. I ate a corned beef on rye and thought about Helene Weber. I had made a few notes on the plane, but two things topped my list: why was she so willing to talk with me, and what did she know about Camille's lease? Maybe she'd answer direct questions, maybe not. I couldn't shake Sandy's nervousness about her, but I'd have to wait until tomorrow morning to find out anything.

I polished off my sandwich in record time and went for a walk. When I got to the Art Museum, I sat on the steps and watched the world of Palm Springs stroll by. Tourists and retirees, families and couples and plenty of well-preserved vintage automobiles. I could get used to a spot like this. Especially in April.

54

The next morning, the sun was California strong. I took a cup of coffee to the porch above the swimming pool and found a comfortable lounge chair. I looked over my notes, but new insights hadn't made the cross-country flight or arrived in dreams overnight. I'd have to let the conversation take its course.

I put on a crisp blue button-down and added the blazer to my khakis. Even a pair of old-fashioned penny loafers, nicely polished. Michiganders are a sophisticated bunch when you get right down to it.

After a late breakfast in the dining room, I showed the map to the staff. They knew right where I wanted to go, and sent me on my way past the Art Museum to Belardo Road. I worked my way around the O'Donnell Golf Club, which was busy with players decked out in brightly colored shorts and strange hats. I zigzagged through the neighborhood streets and ended up at N. Rose Avenue, which ran along the base of the mountains.

Most of the houses on the street were one-story bungalows. Only two of the houses were not surrounded by tall fences or walls. Half-way down the block I found Helene Weber's house, separated from the outside world by an eight-foot high wrought iron fence. I peered through the gate at the driveway. Her bungalow was tan, with white trim and a two-car garage. The front yard was devoid of green except for a stray cactus or two and a skinny palm tree growing too close to the house.

I punched the buzzer and waited. The front door opened and out came a small woman, maybe five-one and one-thirty. She looked sixty-five-ish, with an oval face and wide-set eyes. Her gray hair was pulled back tight into a bun. She wore straight leg pants, navy, a white cotton blouse (not tucked in) and navy flats.

"Mr. Russo?" she said before opening the gate.

"Yes," I said. "Ms. Weber?"

"No, dear," she said. "I'm Nan Burdette. Please come in." She punched a button and the heavy gate slid silently out of the way. I followed her up the walk as the gate closed behind us.

"Helene and I have been friends a long time," Burdette said. "She asked me to come by this afternoon. I'm also Helene's attorney."

Attorney? Does Helene Weber need an attorney? To talk with a guy from Michigan? I'd give her the benefit of the doubt, but I could hear Sandy's voice rattling around in my head.

"Is your practice in town?" I asked.

"More or less, Mr. Russo," she said. "I retired to Palm Springs after many years in LA. I worked for a large firm in those days. I have a few clients here, mostly friends like Helene who need help from time to time."

I followed Burdette through the front door, and we entered the living room. It was a square room painted mauve with white trim. A wide archway in the rear wall led to an equally square dining room. A hallway straight ahead probably led to the kitchen. The floors were a highly polished hardwood. A charcoal sisal rug covered the center of the living room floor.

Standing in front of a long couch was a woman only slightly taller than Nan Burdette, weighing about one-ten. Her dark hair was parted on one side and pushed behind her ears. She wore a dark brown skirt that fell below the knees and a light green sweater over a tan man-tailored shirt.

She put out her hand. "Mr. Russo, I'm Helene Weber." She pronounced it "web-ber." We shook hands.

"Please sit down."

I chose one end of the couch so I wouldn't be isolated in one of the chairs on the other side of the room. Weber took the other end of the couch. *Good.* Nan Burdette was relegated to a chair.

"Would you care for iced tea?"

"That would be nice, yes."

Weber left the room. Burdette and I sat silently until she returned carrying a round wooden tray with three glasses and a small bowl of lemon slices. She put the tray on the coffee table in front of the couch and handed me a glass.

"Thank you," I said, "and thank you for making time to see me."

"You're welcome." She gave Burdette a glass, and sat down.

"I asked Nan," she gestured at her friend, "to stop by this afternoon. I'm more comfortable this way. I hope you don't mind."

"Not at all."

Helene Weber struck me as a pleasant, soft-spoken woman. She could use Burdette as a club to keep me in line, but there was no indication that she would do that.

"Now, Mr. Russo," she said. "How can I help you?"

I drank some tea and put down the glass. "I was hired to look into a matter that involves the leases issued by Mackinac State Historic Parks. You worked for the Commission for a number of years."

"Fifteen years," she said, and smiled. "Until I retired and moved here. But why ask me? I'm sure people in the Park office could explain the leases."

"Yes, they've been quite helpful," I said, "but you also know one of the lessees, Conrad North."

She wasn't surprised by the question, she still smiled pleasantly.

"You've known him for a long time?"

"Since we were children, yes. My brother and sister, too."

"He was a Hoffmann in those days, before his father changed the family name to North."

Weber sipped some tea. "My father changed our family name, too."

"To Weaver," I said.

"Yes. How did you know that, Mr. Russo?"

"But you never took Harold Simons' name, your husband's name."

She wasn't surprised, but her eyes narrowed and her head tilted up, ever so slightly. I saw it in her face. It was an unpleasant reminder.

"I preferred my own name," she said. "How did you find that out?"

"Sandra Jefferies," I said, "from my office. She called you." I gave her the condensed version of Sandy's internet adventure.

Weber laughed, and her eyes almost sparkled. "My driver's license. I remember that fiasco. It was so frustrating." She paused. "But I'm happy to have my family name back. I'm the last of the Webers, you know. No children." She took a deep breath. "I'm the last Weber."

"Did you see Conrad often?" I said. "After you were grown, I mean. When he was on Mackinac in the summer."

She shrugged. "I'd see him in the summer, on the island, but I wouldn't call it often. We'd have lunch two or three times. He'd take me to the Jockey Club. He'd always say hello when he came by the office, on business."

"Did business at the office have anything to do with his Park lease?"

Weber shot a quick look at Burdette.

Weber shook her head. "He never told me his business."

"Did you like Conrad?" I said. "Was he a decent man?"

She reached over and moved the tray an inch or two on the coffee table. She picked up her glass, but put it back without taking a drink.

"We were children, Mr. Russo. We grew up together. Our families, in Chicago, up north. We just grew up together, you know."

Which didn't answer my question, of course.

"Some people aren't very fond of Conrad," I said. "Did you like him?"

"Conrad could be . . . distant. He's not an easy man to like. Some people, I'm sure, thought him imperious."

Not to mention rude, arrogant, and belligerent.

"Did you regard him that way?"

"That's who the man is. I ignored it. No, I overlooked it. As I said, we grew up together."

"Did your husband share your opinion?"

"In a manner of speaking," she said.

I waited, since I had no idea what she meant.

"Perhaps it's because Conrad and I go back so many years."

That wasn't much of an answer either. *Well, let's try this.* "Your husband didn't know him very well, then?"

Weber sat up straight, shoulders back. "Harold was a gambler and a drunk, Mr. Russo. An ugly drunk. We weren't exactly Martha and George . . ."

"Edward Albee? *Virginia Woolf*?"

She nodded. "Uh-huh, but Harold was darn close. Nobody wanted to be around an ugly drinker. We didn't have many friends because of Harold." She shook her head. "He spent his money on cheap gin and blackjack."

"I'm sorry," I said.

"Thank you," she said. "Would you like more tea?"

"Please."

She walked back through the dining room.

"She's had a difficult time, Mr. Russo," Nan Burdette said. "Her husband was, well, he ruined her life, not to mention his own. He lost all their money at the casino. She put up with him for far too long."

I sat in the living room of an expensive house, in an expensive town. Particularly if you were a woman short on cash.

"How long are you in town, Mr. Russo?"

"My plane leaves noon tomorrow."

Weber entered the room, smiled politely, and handed me a refilled glass.

She sat down and said, "It's Conrad's lease you're asking about."

It wasn't a question. Her late husband, Harold, must have vanished in the kitchen.

I nodded. "Camille Sanderson's lease, actually. Her family cottage."

"On the East Bluff," she said. "I know the house. Why are you asking?"

"I was originally hired by Camille Sanderson," I said, "to look into a discrepancy with the lease."

Helene looked at Burdette again, but it was slow and obvious this time. "What do you mean by discrepancy?"

"Camille's attorney examined the paperwork in the divorce filings . . ."

"Divorce? Who?" Weber sat forward.

"Camille and Conrad," I said. "That's how this all started. I was trying to find out what happened with the lease. After Camille died . . ."

"Died? Camille's dead?" Weber was startled.

"I'm sorry," I said. "I thought you knew. I wouldn't have just said it like that. I'm very sorry."

Weber sat motionless and stared across the room at nothing. After a moment she glanced at Burdette, then back at me. Her eyes were wet.

"What happened? Was it a heart attack?"

"Well." I wanted to be tactful, for Helene's sake. "It's worse than that."

Weber was silent.

"I'm afraid Camille was killed."

"How?"

"She was shot to death."

"Murdered?"

"Yes."

Both hands came off her lap and covered her mouth. Tears ran down her face.

"Excuse me," she said, and walked quickly out through the dining room.

Burdette's friendly face and eyes were expressionless. She probably wasn't stunned like her friend, but she'd learned after years in a courtroom how not to react.

Without a word, Burdette got up and followed Weber's path out of the living room.

I sipped my tea. The low hum of the air conditioning seemed louder.

I felt for Helene Weber. Getting hit with the news of death delivered by a stranger is hard enough. But murder? That's harder, more disturbing. I got up and walked to the front window. I didn't understand all the walls, the fences. I could barely see the houses across the street, or a lawn maintenance crew two doors down. Why do they need fences? Are people afraid? Afraid of what?

"Mr. Russo," Weber said as she entered the living room, followed by Nan Burdette. She held tissues in her left hand. "Mr. Russo, I'm sorry for . . . I didn't mean to walk out on you like that."

She and Burdette returned to their seats.

I reached out and took Weber's hand. "I shouldn't have assumed you knew about Camille. I'm sorry. I should've asked."

Weber smiled. "It's all right, Mr. Russo. It's not your fault, it's no one's fault. Things just happen."

I nodded. "Sometimes, yes."

Weber was quiet, but Nan Burdette said, "Mr. Russo, Helene and I talked a little. She'd like to tell you a story, if that's all right."

"Yes, of course."

"This time, however," Burdette said, "I'm also Helene's attorney. I'll act in her best interests should I need to. Is that understood?"

"Yes," I said. Like I had any other choice if I wanted to stick around.

"If I don't want Helene to answer a question, I'll stop her and you. Also understood?"

"Yes."

Burdette looked at her friend and said, "Helene? Are you sure?"

Weber nodded.

"If it's too uncomfortable, Helene, you can stop."

Or if it's too uncomfortable, Helene, just get it off your chest.

"Thank you, Nan," Weber said, and took a drink of tea. She sat back on the couch.

"I knew you'd knock on my door, Mr. Russo. Oh, not you exactly, but someone would knock on my door one day and ask." She folded her arms across her chest. "And here you are."

I kept quiet. Weber had the floor.

"Murdered. Do the police know who did it?"

"Yes."

"Has he been arrested?"

I shook my head. "He's dead."

"Somebody killed him, too?"

"Yes," I said. "I shot the man who killed Camille."

They sat motionless without response, listened willingly when I resumed speaking. I told them only what they needed to know of Ben Miller.

"You didn't exactly say it, Mr. Russo," Burdette said, "but you implied this Miller fellow did not act on his own. Am I correct?"

I paused, not long, but long enough.

"It was Conrad, wasn't it?" Weber said. "He told the man to kill Camille."

"We have no evidence," I said, "but yes. The police think so, and so do I."

"Helene?" Burdette said.

"I'm all right, Nan," Weber said. She fell silent again.

I waited, then said, "A minute ago, Ms. Weber, you said someone would knock on your door. Someone would ask. You didn't know about the divorce or Camille, so . . . I don't understand. What did you expect to be asked about?"

Weber paused, as if remembering.

"Harold," she said, shaking her head. "Harold was worse than a bad drunk, Mr. Russo. Honestly, it was worse than George and Martha. His liver blew up one morning. I called 911, but it was too late. He was dead by the time they put him in the ambulance."

Weber took a deep breath. "It was a relief, really, until I found out the money was gone. Everything. Savings. Mutual funds. He cashed in his retirement. I had a small retirement account with the State, of course, but it wasn't enough. He borrowed on our house to gamble. I couldn't pay it back."

"What about your brother or sister? Wouldn't they help?"

"My sister passed five years ago," Weber said, and looked away. "I haven't talked to Rolf in years. I was sixty-one years old and I had nothing."

Dim, fuzzy puzzle pieces started to take shape.

Weber looked at Burdette and said, "Nan?"

"Your decision, Helene," she said. "I'll stop you if I need to."

Helene Weber took in a lot of air and let it out slowly.

"I fixed the lease, Mr. Russo. There, I said it. I knew it'd come to this, that someone would ask. I changed the lease."

"How?" I said. "How did it happen?" I glanced at Burdette. She was quiet. "Was it Conrad?"

"It was Conrad," Weber said. "After Harold was buried, word got around, I guess, about me and money. I don't know. Conrad takes me to the Jockey Club for lunch and tells me he can help. Of course, I listened. Who wouldn't? We grew up together, he had money. Who wouldn't listen?"

"Did he ask you to take Camille's name off the lease?"

She shook her head. "Conrad doesn't ask, Mr. Russo," she said with disdain in her voice. "He told me to remove her name from the lease, take her name off, put his name on instead. It was Conrad's idea, but I was the one who did it, made the change."

"You had access, correct?"

"Correct."

"Did he offer you money?"

"No. He said there would be no money. He had that all worked out. He told me to retire. He'd buy me a house anywhere, as long as it wasn't in Michigan. He'd set up a fund so I'd have income."

She stopped.

"Look around, Mr. Russo. This house isn't extravagant, but it's paid for. Living's a lot cheaper, even in Palm Springs, when you don't have a mortgage."

"Did Conrad pay off the debts, too?"

"All of them. I walked away free of debt, with a new home in a new community and money to live on. All I had to do was create a new lease."

She picked up her glass and drank some tea. "And I've lived with a guilty conscience ever since. Now Camille's dead."

"If it was that uncomfortable," I said, "why didn't you go to the authorities?"

"Too scared, Mr. Russo. I didn't want to go to jail."

"If something could be worked out . . ."

"No, Mr. Russo," Burdette said. "Let's not go there."

I looked at Burdette, then Weber. "Suppose your information about the lease might help get Conrad for Camille's death? What then?"

Burdette said, "We won't discuss this. Period."

"I understand your fear, Ms. Weber . . ."

"No, you don't, Mr. Russo," Weber said, "you don't."

"No, I don't. That's true, I'm sorry. But Camille's death's inevitably linked to the lease and the divorce."

"Nan?"

"Mr. Russo, that's enough." Burdette stood up. "We should end this conversation."

"If you don't mind . . ."

"I do mind, Mr. Russo," Burdette said. "You're a decent man with a job to do. However, I must insist."

Helene Weber stood and said, "Good day, Mr. Russo."

The two women were thoughtful and decent people. I liked them. I'd pushed a little, but was unwilling to push harder.

"Thank you for seeing me," I said. "Nice to meet you both."

I walked out of the house into the hot sun. The puzzle I'd struggled with had just gotten a lot clearer. Clearer than any day since Camille hired me. I walked slowly back to The Willows. No need to hurry.

I turned off Belardo onto Museum Drive. I found a shady spot on the Art Museum steps and sat down. I wanted Helene Weber to talk to the police, of course. If she didn't want to talk to the cops or Hendricks, there wasn't much I could do about it. Didn't mean I shouldn't try. I needed some time to think about the implications of what Weber had told me. Implications for Nicole, for Camille, for justice. Maybe I'd become creative if I sat here long enough. Perhaps the wisdom of the museum itself would rub off on me if I wandered around inside for a while.

55

"It's noisy," AJ said. "Where are you?"

"On a bench on Palm Canyon Drive in the heart of beautiful downtown Palm Springs, California."

"It's ten o'clock at night and you're sitting on a bench?"

As comfortable as my bench was, it was no match for the museum steps. Not to mention my time in the museum's hallways.

"First of all, darling, it's only seven out here and I'm hungry. There happens to be a little Italian place right across from my bench."

"Why am I not surprised?"

"Already looked at the menu."

"Of course you have," AJ said. "Michael, I have to ask, has there been any trouble?"

"You mean is Nils Lundberg tailing me? How about two guys with automatic weapons at the sushi bar next door?"

"All right, all right, sorry I asked. Do you want to tell me about Helene Weber?"

"How about tomorrow?" I said. "I should be home by ten, ten-thirty."

"Just tell me if the trip was worth it."

"If you mean was seeing Weber worth the trip, I think so, but I'll know better after I'm home."

"What else would I mean?"

"Palm Springs. If you meant Palm Springs, the answer's yes, the trip's worth it. If you meant The Willows Inn, definitely yes."

We chatted for a while, and I clicked off. I went across the street to Kalura Trattoria for pasta Bolognese, then went back to my room to pack.

I did not have a restful sleep. I couldn't shake Weber, or her tale of Conrad and the lease. By seven the next morning, I had returned to my bench on Palm Canyon Drive, this time holding a French Roast from Starbucks. I needed a break from murder, leases and Conrad North. That would have to wait until my flight was airborne and I could focus on finishing Steve Hamilton's *Nick Mason*. Fiction sounded more appealing than truth. Not stranger, but more appealing.

I gave myself plenty of time for the trip to the airport. I returned the Buick and checked in. I bought a granola bar, water and a *New York Times*. I found some empty seats near a window and opened to the op-ed page. Up first, Frank Bruni.

"Mr. Russo?"

"Ms. Burdette. What a surprise." She wore jeans, a tan cotton sweater and carried a briefcase. Her face was serious, but she smiled easily.

"May I sit down?"

"Of course," I said, and folded up my newspaper. "Where're you off to?"

She shook her head. "I'm not flying, Mr. Russo."

"But you're inside the security perimeter."

"I do some work for the Airport Authority," she said. "I have credentials, but I came to see you."

That was a bigger surprise.

"We don't have much time, Mr. Russo," she said. "I need to talk. This is the best way I could think of. I didn't want you to change your flight, so here I am."

"All right."

"I thought yesterday went well, with Helene. She was comfortable meeting you, talking to you."

"She had some difficult moments, Ms. Burdette."

"That's true," she said. "Her nice safe world was tossed around a bit yesterday, but she didn't blame you for that."

"I'm also an attorney, Ms. Burdette. Does your client know you're here?"

She put her hand on my arm.

"I know that, Mr. Russo. I checked you out before you ever set foot in Helene's house. To answer your question, Helene encouraged me to see you. Before you left town, I mean."

"Thanks for clearing that up."

Burdette sat back and opened her briefcase. She took out a large manila envelope and put it in her lap.

"I've known Helene a long time. We first met here," Burdette said, remembering, "in Palm Springs. She was on vacation . . ."

"With her husband? On vacation?"

Burdette shook her head. "No, no. With women friends. They toured the Art Museum, and I was a docent. It started just that way, we just met."

"When did you become her attorney?"

"When she moved out here. After Harold died."

"Did you know about Conrad and the lease?"

Burdette nodded. "Helene asked for my help. Buying the house, finding a financial adviser, that kind of thing. I helped her set it all up. So, yes, I knew the whole story." She glanced at her watch.

"She was never happy with . . . no, that's not right. She was never comfortable with the arrangements. She's always felt guilty. She told you that."

"Guilty because?"

"It's obvious, isn't it, Mr. Russo? Taking Conrad's money for swapping leases. Every time she pays a bill, she feels guilty. That's what she meant when she said someone would knock on the door."

"She lives a nice life because of it."

Burdette nodded. "Yes, she does."

"She could have told the police, she wanted to clear her conscience that badly."

"It's not as simple as that," she said.

"You sure?"

Burdette stiffened. "Don't go judgmental on me, Mr. Russo. I'm also Helene's friend."

"Sorry," I said. "But you're asking me to understand her. From the outside, she took money for creating a phony document."

"Helene had a chance, she took it. It's as simple as that."

"A chance for?"

"A decent life, Mr. Russo. All those years with a drunk, only to discover you have no future."

"Along comes old friend Conrad with a cash deal."

Burdette nodded. "And a future."

"If she had it to do all over again?"

"You'd have to ask Helene," she said. "But we're running out of time, Mr. Russo. You're boarding pretty soon."

Burdette handed me the manila envelope. "Save it for the plane, or after you're home. Whatever you like."

She gave me a business card. "Have your people call me," she said. "Just remember the time difference, will you?"

I held the envelope up. "What is it?"

"Helene Weber's future."

I stared at the envelope, not sure what to say.

"They're calling your flight, Mr. Russo. Safe travels."

I stood, and we shook hands. Nan Burdette then disappeared into the crowd of people who, like me, were just waiting. I stuck the envelope inside the *New York Times* and got in line.

56

I'm never surprised when flights are delayed during the winter in the upper Great Lakes. But here we sat, on the tarmac at the gate, for thirty-five minutes. I was leaving sunny California, and it was seventy-eight degrees. I checked Detroit. Rain and forty-four, certainly no problem for an Airbus 320. Still we sat.

By the time we hit cruising altitude, I'd taken a hot coffee from the attendant and was munching on a granola bar. Steve Hamilton would have to wait.

I opened the envelope.

I didn't know what I expected, but I assumed it was good enough for Nan Burdette to come all the way to the airport just to hand me an envelope.

I removed three documents.

The first one was a little more than three double-spaced, 12-point pages. It began . . .

Mr. Russo,

Subject to the conditions drawn up by Nan Burdette, you may use this as you wish. Read the last page before you continue.

I flipped to the last page. It was notarized with today's date. I continued reading. It covered all the territory Helene covered yesterday: Conrad, the lease, financial support for the move to Palm Springs. There was nothing new, but nothing was left out either.

The second document was titled *Ground Lease: Mackinac Island State Park Commission, Lessor and Camille Sanderson, Lessee.* It was a copy and it, too, was notarized. I didn't understand why until I read the third document, written by Nan Burdette.

The original Sanderson lease was in a safety deposit box, Burdette wrote. She'd had my copy notarized to prove the existence of the original. Conrad had ordered Helene to destroy it. She had not.

How about that? The original lease. Some days it's better to be lucky than good.

The rest of Burdette's two pages outlined under what circumstances Weber would cooperate with the authorities. Burdette would handle all negotiations on Weber's behalf, but the details of any agreement would need to be approved by Weber and Burdette both.

I finally had something to work with, and Helene Weber had given it to me.

I played out several scenarios. First, the obvious one. Two of the documents would likely be enough to get the East Bluff cottage away from Conrad. Hendricks or the prosecutors in Mackinac County could work that out; furthermore, Conrad would have to answer some tough questions when confronted with Weber's information.

But I wanted to use the documents, use Weber, use anything else we could dig up to prove that Conrad North had ordered Gunnar Lundberg to kill his wife. I would've liked nothing more than to give Don Hendricks another file that did just that. But I didn't have another file.

I could only read the documents so many times before I began staring out the window. The lease reminded me why I grew tired of all the sentences that used "wherefore" and "whereas" over and over again. I had virtually memorized two of the documents by the time we were over Nebraska, or Kansas, or some other flat state. I put them in my brief bag, and pulled out Steve Hamilton. It was time to find out how *Nick Mason* fared with his problems.

I was vaguely aware of the attendant moving in the aisle. I must have dozed off after *Nick Mason* arrived precariously at the end of Hamilton's story. The attendant picked up trash as we slowly descended for landing at Detroit Metro.

I made my way off the plane and walked toward the middle of the mile-long terminal. Above my head, on tracks down the center of the building, ran a bright red tram. After five hours in an uncomfortable seat, I preferred the long walk. I entered the Westin Hotel and walked through the lobby. No matter how loud the clatter in the terminal, the hotel's restaurant-bar was dependably quiet. The atrium had plenty of room for people to roam around or sit quietly. Today, the place was almost empty – three women in their thirties, dressed as if they'd just come from a long business day, sat at one end of the bar. I picked a small table in the corner.

I had two hours before my flight to Pellston, so I ordered a burger, fries and a glass of Chardonnay. I took out my phone and punched AJ's number.

"Where are you?" she said.

"Metro."

I nodded a 'thank you' as the waitress left my wine.

"Is everything okay?" AJ said.

"I'll be glad to get home, that's all. But I did have an unexpected surprise at the Palm Springs airport."

"Aren't they all?"

"Aren't what all?"

"Aren't all surprises unexpected?"

One of the things I like about our easy, comfortable relationship: I had no inclination to snap back. Instead, I drank some wine.

"Would you like to know why I was surprised at the airport?"

"So you're telling me my humor isn't really that funny?"

"Compared to the drone of jet engines, your humor is refreshing."

AJ laughed. "I love you, too, darling. What's the surprise?"

"Helene Weber's lawyer gave me an envelope just before I boarded my flight."

I described the documents. "If this were your story, AJ?"

"First off, she must have felt guilty from the moment she wrote the new lease. Why else would she keep the original when Conrad told her to get rid of it?"

"Exactly."

"Unless," AJ said, "she planned to keep it all along."

"She didn't plan any of it. Her attorney was right. Weber was desperate after her husband died and took a flyer when it came her way."

"She's been living with the guilt a long time."

"Do you think they'll get Conrad on the phony lease?"

"If I were writing the story," AJ said, "I'd run it by our lawyers before a word of it went public. Just in case."

"I'll call Hendricks first thing in the morning," I said. "Give him the papers."

"Michael?" she said, and hesitated.

"I'm one step ahead of you, AJ. I'll give Lenny a heads up."

"He'll write a good story."

"Anything to help the press, darling," I said.

"Very funny."

"My food's here, AJ. Call you later."

We said good-bye, and I settled in with my burger and fries.

The short hop back to Pellston left Metro on time. The city lights sparkled below. I picked out Woodward Avenue as it ran north from the Detroit River, through the northwest suburbs, the land of my childhood. I gave my head a rest from all things Conrad and the lease. I went back to the *Times* and finished all I was interested in by the time we touched down in northern Michigan.

I came out of the gate into the small waiting room that doubled as baggage claim. Over in one corner of the room sat Henri LaCroix. He waved, and I walked over.

"Dare I ask why you're at the airport at eleven at night?"

"I could be on my way out of town."

"The next plane out of here is six tomorrow morning," I said, "but you already knew that."

The luggage carousel rumbled to life. "Let's get your bag," Henri said.

We left the terminal and went to the parking lot. The sky was dark and clear, a few stars visible even with all the lights.

"My car's over there," I said.

"I know where it is," Henri said.

I popped the door locks and put my bag in the back seat.

"You want to tell me?"

"Why I'm here?"

"Uh-huh."

"Nils Lundberg."

"He out of jail?"

Henri shook his head. "He'll be sentenced tomorrow, know more then."

"Okay."

"You headed home or AJ's?"

"My place," I said.

"I'll follow."

We took U.S. 31 south through Pellston and Alanson. Very little traffic moved in either direction until we arrived at the outskirts of Petoskey. I stayed on 31 by the bay, turned off on Rose and went around the Perry Hotel. I parked the car and Henri pulled in behind me. I walked up to his driver's window.

"Give me the short version," he said.

I did, starting with Helene Weber and the documents.

"We should be able to turn that into something."

"Yeah, but is it enough to put Conrad away for Camille?"

"Sounds like a job for Hendricks," Henri said. "Of course, I could stick a Glock in his ear, see what he has to say."

"If you figure out a way to have that admitted as testimony, I'll back you."

"See you tomorrow," he said.

"Feel better you got me home safe and sound?"

"Yes."

57

"Don Hendricks can see you in an hour," Sandy said. I sat at my desk with coffee and a J-bun from Johan's. The walk to the office that morning had been as pleasantly warm as April could be around here. The bright sun reflected off the water in Little Traverse Bay just the way it did in the *Pure Michigan* ads.

"Good," I said. "I want to push this along."

I tore off a chunk of cinnamon roll.

"Did you hear back from Lenny Stern yet?"

I shook my head. "He'll call as soon as he sees my message."

"I copied the documents," Sandy said. "One copy for us, one for Lenny. The envelope's ready to go to Hendricks when you do."

My phone buzzed on the desk. "It's Lenny," I said, and Sandy went back to her desk.

"Morning, Lenny."

"So you got a story for me, Russo?"

"The one you've been waiting for," I said, and told him the highlights.

"Sounds promising," Stern said.

"One condition."

"I don't do conditions, Russo."

We'd played this game before. I waited him out. Stern can be quite reasonable when a good story's at stake.

"What do you want?"

"A trade, Lenny."

"Let's hear it."

"Wait two days. I meet Don Hendricks in a few minutes. Give him two days to put something together. You do that, I give you an envelope with copies of the documents. You'll still have time to write the piece."

Stern went silent, but he always does.

"I say no to the deal, I don't get copies?"

"Nope."

"I could write the story anyway, Russo."

"Lenny," I said, "Sandy has the envelope. Pick it up anytime."

"Deal," he said, and clicked off.

"You're gonna be late, boss," Sandy said from the other room.

I went to the outer office and picked up my jacket and the envelope for Hendricks.

"Lenny Stern will . . ."

"Pick up his copies. I know," Sandy said.

"You listening in again?"

"I won't dignify that with an answer. Get a move on."

The morning was warmer than any resident of northern Michigan might reasonably hope for, but there it was. I enjoyed every step up Lake Street to the County Building.

Hendricks was at his desk when I went in, sleeves rolled up, tie loose. Martin Fleener was there, too, in a dark blue suit pressed and ready for another day.

"Don," I said, and handed over the envelope. "Marty, didn't expect to see you this morning."

"Crime took the day off," Fleener said.

Hendricks pulled the contents out of the envelope.

"I only made one copy," I said. "Didn't know Marty'd be here."

"I'll take care of that," Hendricks said, and left the office. He returned momentarily, handing Fleener his own set of papers.

"Amuse yourself, Russo," Hendricks said, "while we read." The two officers of the court started in on the documents.

Fleener finished first, Hendricks a minute later.

"Well," I said. "What do you think?"

Hendricks glanced at Fleener. Fleener nodded, but the prosecutor was leadoff hitter.

"Good work, Russo."

"Well, you don't have to sound so unhappy about it."

"Sorry," Hendricks said. "I didn't mean it that way."

"Apology accepted."

"Tell me about . . ." Hendricks looked at the papers. "Helene Weber. Now that you've met her, I mean."

I gave both men my opinion of the woman and her predicament.

"Have to admit it, Russo, you made a good call doing it yourself," Hendricks said. "If we'd sent the Palm Springs people in, she might have clammed up."

"A woman afraid doesn't become more comfortable talking to us," Fleener said.

"Think it's enough to pick up North?"

"It's enough," Hendricks said.

"What about Chippewa County?" I said.

"They're good. Already talked to them. If we can roll the lease into a murder charge, all the better."

"Think you can, Marty?"

"I have no idea," Fleener said. "Based on what we have right now, I doubt it."

"He killed two wives, Marty."

"We don't know he killed wife number one," Fleener said.

"Annie," I said, "her name was Annie."

Fleener nodded. "Officially, Annie's still missing. That's all we know."

"Get him for Camille," I said.

Fleener shrugged. "Try my best."

"I know."

"Anything else?" Hendricks said.

"That's it," I said, and stood up. "You'll call?"

Hendricks nodded. "Yeah."

I left by the Lake Street exit. On my walk back to the office I called Lenny Stern, told him the prosecutor was on track and that I'd get back.

Henri was in a client chair talking with Sandy when I walked into the office.

"Hi, boss," Henri said.

"Don't steal my lines," Sandy said, "or no more Johan's for you."

Henri put his hands in the air in mock surrender.

I sat down next to Henri. "Any word from Ohio?"

"Eighteen months," Henri said. "Could be out in eleven if he plays it straight."

"Is this Nils Lundberg?" Sandy said.

"Uh-huh," Henri said.

"Does your guy think he'll behave?" I said.

Henri shrugged. "I asked. Lundberg's unpredictable."

"That's not very reassuring," Sandy said.

"Best I can do," Henri said. "What'd Hendricks have to say?"

I recapped my meeting with Don Hendricks and Martin Fleener.

"Hendricks say when they'll pick Conrad up?" Sandy said.

"No."

"He won't wait," Henri said. "They want to clear Camille's murder."

"Assuming they can pin it on him," I said.

"What are the chances?" Sandy said. "Did Hendricks say?"

"With what they have now, not likely. But you never know what will come pouring out once Fleener gets at him."

58

I sat quietly at a two-top at Julienne Tomatoes with coffee and my iPad. I'd gone for a long run this morning. It felt good to leg one out. I didn't need to be in the office early, since everything was now on the prosecutor's desk.

I refilled my mug and drank some coffee. I'd just started a piece by Joan Walsh in *The Nation* when my screen lit up. It was Martin Fleener.

"Morning, Marty."

"You in town, Russo?"

"Julienne Tomatoes," I said. "I'll buy you coffee."

"I'll take a rain check. Get yourself to the Bodzick Building. Ten minutes."

"You don't mind me asking, why would I want to do that?"

"They're bringing in Conrad North."

"Who is?"

"Sheriff deputies picked him up at the boat a half hour ago."

"Under arrest?"

"Yeah. Mackinac Island police did it last night."

"Conrad North spent the night in jail?"

"Not exactly," Fleener said.

"The hell's 'not exactly' mean?"

"Let's say the officers made it clear his ass'd better be on the dock for the first boat. Island cops handed him off to Emmet County in St. Ignace."

"What'd they arrest him for?"

"Enough to put the cuffs on," Fleener said.

"Couldn't happen to a nicer guy."

"North's lawyer met the boat, too."

"Who's the lawyer?"

"Don't know. Enough questions, Russo. Move," Fleener said, and clicked off.

I looked at my watch. I tapped contacts and punched Lenny Stern's number. It rang. And rang.

"Come on, answer." It went to voicemail instead. "Lenny, get your ass to the Bodzick Building." I told him why. "Bring a photographer."

One last gulp of coffee, and I took my mug to the counter. I hurried out the door and down Howard. I crossed Mitchell in the middle of the block and went through Pennsylvania Park to Lake Street across from the jail.

I stopped on the sidewalk and watched for a minute. There was no activity near the door, but a lone figure with a briefcase leaned against a patrol car. He was under six feet, stocky, with a dark complexion and round face. His black hair was thin on top and combed forward. He wore a dark, two-piece suit. *It's not rocket science. The man's a lawyer.*

I crossed the street. A horn sounded behind me, and I moved out of the way. A white SUV with Sheriff's Department markings drove up and stopped near the door. The man with the briefcase moved closer.

Two uniformed officers got out of the car and opened a rear door. Out climbed Conrad North, wearing jeans, handcuffs and an angry look on his face. The man with the briefcase said something to the officers. Had to be Conrad's lawyer.

"Russo," I heard from behind me. I turned just as Lenny Stern came quickly toward me. Trying to keep up was a skinny little man, who looked hardly old enough to vote. He had a camera, a real one.

"Get the shots, Max," Stern said. "Go."

Max did as he was told and began snapping pictures before Conrad or his lawyer realized what he was doing. The officers ignored Max.

"Get out of here," the lawyer said, almost shouting. Conrad turned his face away from the camera.

Max obviously had done this before. Every time Conrad moved, Max moved; every time the lawyer moved closer, Max moved again. The officers continued to ignore Max as he snapped more photos.

"Thanks for the heads-up, Russo," Stern said.

"You're welcome."

"Get away," the lawyer said to Max, who did no such thing.

"Inside, Mr. North," the lawyer said. "Officers, take him inside."

The officers escorted Conrad through the door, and the lawyer followed.

"Good job, Max," Stern said when the photographer walked up. Stern introduced us.

"That had to be North's lawyer," I said.

"Hold on," Stern said, and flipped over several pages in a reporter's notebook. "North's lawyer is a man named Oliver Kilgore from Chicago."

"How'd you find that out?"

"He registered at the desk," Stern said, and pointed at the jail. "I called on the way over. Apparently he's a big shot and *tres* expensive."

"I'd expect no less from Mr. Conrad North of Lake Forest and Mackinac Island."

"I'll have plenty of time to check him out this afternoon."

"When're you writing the story?"

"It's done," Stern said, "the outline of the piece anyway. The documents were a big help, Russo. Thanks."

"My pleasure."

"I'll add a bit about the arrest and it'll be ready to go."

"I look forward to reading it."

"Russo," Stern said as he put his notebook away, "think they'll get North for his wife's murder?"

"Seems to be the question of the moment, Lenny."

59

"Sit down, Russo," Don Hendricks said. AJ and I had been at McLean & Eakin deciding which Scott Fitzgerald classic to reread, *This Side of Paradise* or *The Beautiful and the Damned*, when his office called. I left the literary decision to her and made my way up Lake Street to the County Building.

"Don," I said, and sat down. Martin Fleener nodded a greeting from his usual chair beneath the county map. He didn't look happy.

"What's going on?" I said.

"Hold on," Hendricks said, "we're waiting."

He started to say something else when Ruth Avila came through the door.

"Sorry I'm late," she said, and took the chair next to me.

"Haven't they disbarred you yet, you crazy broad?" Hendricks said with an outsized wave of his arm.

"Such a way to talk," Avila said, "from a corrupt public servant who buys votes."

The two of them broke into loud, obnoxious laughter.

"From the look on your face," Fleener said, "you've never sat through the 'Don and Ruth' show before."

Avila quieted down long enough to put her hand on my arm. "We go back a long way," she said, nodding at Hendricks. "It's been a few years, hasn't it, Don?"

"We were fresh out of law school," Hendricks said, "didn't know our asses from third base. We worked in the public defender's office."

"Hell," Ruth said. "We were the PD's office."

"That we were, Ruth, that we were."

Hendricks leaned forward and put his elbows on the desk. "All right," he said, "let's get this over with. Did you talk to your client, Ruth?"

"An hour ago, yes."

"You talking about Nicole Sanderson?" I said.

"Yes, Michael," Avila said. "I was about to call you when Don said he wanted us here."

"It all came together fast," Hendricks said. "Last night, again this morning."

I sat back and looked at Fleener, then Hendricks. "You cut a deal with North, didn't you?"

"Yeah," Hendricks said.

"You knew about this?" I said to Avila.

"This morning," she said.

"It was done by then," Hendricks said.

Silence. It hung in the air.

"You didn't get him for Camille, did you?"

Hendricks shook his head.

"Tell me," I said.

"I thought we had a good shot at him," Hendricks said. "Not perfect, but good enough."

"The Weber documents?" I said. "You couldn't use them?"

"Of course we used them," Hendricks said, shaking his head slowly. "But they only took us so far."

I looked over at Fleener. "You had North in the room, Marty?"

Fleener nodded.

"You couldn't make it work? Even with Weber's papers?" I wondered what had happened to the State Police Captain with the legendary reputation for interrogating suspects.

"It was good stuff, Michael," Fleener said. "But it . . . no, I couldn't make it work."

"It wasn't Marty's fault, Russo," Hendricks said. "Kilgore . . ."

"North's lawyer?"

Hendricks nodded. "Oliver Kilgore, yeah. He wouldn't let North say a word. No answers, no statements. Nothing."

"I had nowhere to go," Fleener said. "Kilgore's one smart dude."

"You've had less to go on," I said.

"Kilgore set it up," Hendricks said. "He knew Marty's only hope was to sucker North into saying something stupid."

"So North didn't talk at all?" I said.

"He certainly did not," Fleener said.

"Then what did Kilgore set up?"

"The house," Hendricks said.

"You mean the family cottage?"

Hendricks nodded.

"What kind of deal we talking?"

"North admitted he forced Helene Weber to create a new lease and swap it for the real one."

"That's no deal," I said. "You had him on that anyway."

"We probably had him on that, Russo," Hendricks said, "only probably. We couldn't get him for murder."

"So it's a slap on the wrist instead of prison."

"It's what we could get," Hendricks said.

"I don't imagine Nicole liked the deal very much," I said, and turned to Ruth Avila, who'd remained silent for too long.

"Nicole didn't like it at all, Michael," Avila said.

"But she agreed?"

"Let's say she accepted reality."

"It's bullshit, is what it is," I said.

"Sometimes it is," Hendricks said. "Sometimes it is."

60

"Did you talk to Nicole yet?" AJ said after I'd filled her in on the meeting. We sat on the front steps of her house enjoying the warm, humid spring weather. Tomorrow was the first day of May, not that it mattered. But when we trade the living room couch for the porch steps, summer is closer than we think.

"I called her after we finished."

"Did Hendricks and Avila tell it straight?"

I nodded. "Pretty much. She wasn't surprised they didn't get Conrad for murder. Annoyed, frustrated, yeah, but not surprised he got away with it."

"Did she say why?"

"That she wasn't surprised?"

AJ nodded.

"She always knew Conrad was smarter and more devious than the people he dealt with."

"And he has plenty of money for good lawyers."

"That, too."

"She say anything about the cottage?"

"It's bittersweet. She's happy to have it back in the family. She's especially happy to have Conrad gone. That's what her mother wanted."

"Good," AJ said. "At least the cottage gave her some satisfaction."

"Most important, she wanted it over with."

"Then I'm happy for her it's over."

"Some kind of day this has been," I said, and shook my head. "I'm not happy with it. I fucked up."

"No, you didn't."

"Conrad deserves jail, but I didn't put him there."

"Don't forget the 'moral arc,' Michael. It 'bends toward justice.'"

"You're quoting Dr. King on me? I don't think this is the kind of mess he had in mind."

"Of course not, but you tried to get justice for Camille, for Nicole. You did your best."

"It wasn't good enough, AJ. He got away with murder."

"It's a trade-off, Michael," she said. "Hendricks accepted it. Fleener, too. Even Nicole, and it was her mother who died."

"But . . ."

"Let it go. This isn't the past. Somebody . . . I don't know who . . . somebody told you it was your fault. Probably that bully father of yours after your brother died. This isn't your brother. This isn't Camille before she was killed. Things just happen."

The sun knifed its way through the trees, painting streaks of light on the house across the street.

AJ put her arm around my shoulder.

"Some days are like that, Michael. They just are."

COMING SOON

The Final Act of Conrad North

A Michael Russo Mystery

Turn the page to read the first chapter

The Final Act of Conrad North

I could have said no when Sandy answered the office phone. I heard her say, "Yes, I remember you." I looked up from the file I was reading and Sandy silently mouthed "Patricia Geary," then gave me a look that asked "yea or nay?"

I nodded and took the call.

Three hours later, I was angry and annoyed as I pulled off U.S. 31 in Traverse City and slowed for traffic on Front Street. Geary was Senior Vice President of Boardman Bank & Trust, but I knew she didn't want to talk interest rates or mortgage defaults. She wanted to hire me, she said, about a "personal matter."

Geary wanted to talk about Annie North, her lover who had disappeared nine years ago. But that meant, eventually, we'd have to deal with Annie's ex-husband, Conrad North.

The Bank building, on Front Street in the center of town, didn't look any more appealing on this crisp October afternoon than it did the last time I was there two years ago. It was short on style and long on glass and chrome. It was as if 1970s suburbia had invaded northern Michigan a half-century late.

Patricia Geary met me outside her third floor office after the receptionist told her I'd arrived for my appointment.

I walked over and we shook hands. Geary was stocky, about five-seven, with long salt-and-pepper hair pulled into a ponytail and clear blue eyes. She wore a conservative two-piece business suit, black, over an ecru silk shirt.

"Good to see you again," she said, but it didn't sound that way. Geary pointed down the hallway.

Her office was a large, square room with wooden floors, Oriental rugs and a huge mahogany desk that sat in front of a wall of windows overlooking West Bay. It was a pleasant contrast to the sharp angles in the rest of the building.

"Have a seat," she said.

"Thank you," I said, and sat down.

Geary fingered a manila folder on the desk, then handed it over.

"What is it?" I said.

"Everything I know about Annie."

"About her disappearance, you mean?"

"About her murder, Mr. Russo," she said with a sharp edge to her voice. "I didn't get you down here . . ." Geary pulled back her next words. She folded her hands, like a church steeple, in front of her mouth. Tears dotted the corners of her blue eyes.

"I'm sorry, Mr. Russo," she said.

"It's all right. We've been here before."

"Yes, we have, but Annie was murdered. I loved her, you know that."

I nodded. "You talk to the cops lately?"

Geary gestured at the file in my lap. "It's all there. The police said she disappeared. That's still what they say."

I glanced at the folder. "Police reports?"

She nodded.

"They're usually not that accommodating."

Geary smiled. "It was their way to shut me up."

"Uh-huh," I said.

"No new leads, or witnesses, or information. Nothing. The cops have given up."

"But you haven't."

"No," Geary said as she shook her head.

"If you think Annie's dead, Ms. Geary, how can I help you?"

"I have to know what happened to her. You know all the players, Mr. Russo. I need closure, resolution. Call it what you like, but I have to know."

"One thing," I said. "What if Annie's not dead . . ."

"She's dead, Mr. Russo. Conrad killed her. You prove that, the cops'll reopen the case."

"The police couldn't prove it," I said. "What makes you think I can?"

"You can do things," she said. "I called because you have ways to get things done." I saw a small grin, barely noticeable. "The police are, what's the word, more constrained?"

I thought about that, but let it go.

"You know where Conrad is now?"

She shook her head. "I kept track of him after he left Mackinac Island, but I had to stop. I was obsessing about the man."

I leaned forward and considered Patricia Geary for a moment. She was thoughtful and sincere. But she'd fallen in love with a woman caught in an ugly play directed by a very bad man.

"What if Annie really went missing," I said, "really wanted to disappear? Are you ready for that?"

Geary straightened her shoulders and stared at me for a moment.

"I need closure, Mr. Russo, whatever that means."

"It won't be enough."

I started to say something else, but she interrupted, "I need closure."

"All right," I said. We shook hands. "I'll call soon."

I took the file and went for the door.

"Mr. Russo."

I turned around. Tears slowly streamed down Geary's face.

"You're right," she said, angry now. "Closure is not enough. Conrad North murdered Annie, goddamn it. Get him for it."

ACKNOWLEGEMENTS

I've said this before about Russo and his adventures and I'm happy to say it again, I made it all up . . . the characters, the plot, the scenes, all of it. I love to read private eye stories, so I invented Russo, AJ Lester, Henri LaCroix and an assortment of killers, detectives, prosecutors and crazies to give the stories life.

A group of delightful people willingly helped make this yarn better, more accurate and more interesting. They include Frances Barger, Aaron Stander, Marietta Hamady, Leanne Broder-Bunker, Bill Borst, Shawn Cordes-Osborne, Steve Hoffius, Wesley Maurer, Marta Olson, Joan Slater, Phil Porter, Cathy Cryderman, Stuart Fenton and the writers around the table at the Mystery Writing Workshop at the Interlochen Center for the Arts. Three of the four scenes written and critiqued at the workshop made it into this novel. How about that?

Heather Shaw and Scott Couturier edited the manuscript. Their critique was helpful and incisive. Whatever I wrote, they worked over pretty good, I must say. They made the writing more readable and the mystery more exciting. I have tried to learn the lessons they've taught me and use them when I write.

PETER MARABELL

Peter Marabell grew up in metro Detroit, spending as much time as he could street racing on Woodward Avenue in the 1950s and visiting the Straits of Mackinac. With a Ph.D. in History and Politics, Peter spent most of his professional career on the faculty at Michigan State University. He is the author of the historic monograph, *Frederick Libby and the American Peace Movement,* soon to be published by Kendall Sheepman Company. His first novel, *More Than a Body*, was published in 2013. The first three Michael Russo mysteries, *Murder at Cherokee Point, Murder on Lake Street* and *Devils Are Here* were published in 2014, 2015 and 2016, respectively. As a freelance writer, he worked in several professional fields including healthcare, politics, and the arts. In 2002, Peter moved permanently to northern Michigan with his spouse and business partner, Frances Barger, to live, write and work at their Mackinac Island business. All things considered, he would rather obsess about American politics, or Spartan basketball, after a good five-mile run on the hills of Mackinac Island.

OTHER BOOKS BY PETER MARABELL

MICHAEL RUSSO MYSTERIES

Murder at Cherokee Point

Murder on Lake Street

Devils Are Here

also

Frederick Libby and the American Peace Movement

More Than a Body

Made in the USA
Lexington, KY
24 April 2018